The Brits are going to be pissed. *Royally pissed.*

Like drop everything, it's-now-a-national-freaking-imperative-to-figure-out-what-happened pissed. But, hey, Puo wanted to drop on way more sites than we are, underwater carpet bomb the Sea of London. But I argued for a more focused approach and won out. Now the authorities will think it was Greek activists or a Greek crew that was involved.

So, if you think about it, I single-handedly saved countless iconic English sites from being destroyed from Puo's underwater carpet bombing. I'm practically a patron of English culture. Maybe I should join their preservation society.

The Elgin Deceptions

THE ELGIN DECEPTIONS

SUNKEN CITY CAPERS BOOK 2

by
Jeffrey A. Ballard

NEW ROCHESTER PUSBLISHING

Chapter One

L ET'S GET THIS SHIT STARTED," I say with a spike of adrenaline. I love this part. I bounce a little on the balls of my feet as I walk over in the black, skin-tight anti-gravity suit to the bottom-loading doors in the back of our rental air-delivery vehicle.

"Approaching drop zone," Puo says in his deep Samoan voice. "I would like to, just once again, lodge my official opposition to this immense stupidity."

"Opposition noted," I say with a grin. I can't help it. *Damn, it's been too long since I've been in my anti-gravity suit.* "It wouldn't be any fun if you weren't bitching about something."

Puo *harrumphs* and hits the button to open the loading doors.

We need this job. We weren't able to make a full payment to the Citizen Maker last month, so now we have a late fee—*isn't that sweet?* Just three and a half more payments plus a late fee and we'll have these indispensable, insanely expensive modified citizen chips with hacked CitIDs paid off.

Cold air roars up into the cabin, enveloping me. The helmet of the closed-system anti-gravity suit cuts off any scents, but I imagine I can smell the salt of the North Sea ten thousand feet below me. I cherish the feel of cold sweat in my gloves and boots.

The North Sea is dark under the cloudless sky, the surface visible only from the barest hints of silver ripples from the October half moon hanging over the horizon. Distant green and red lights of merchant vessels speckle the landscape like will-o'-the-wisps in the night.

I shift the straps of my backpack on my shoulders, and mentally check off its contents—none of which is a parachute.

"Pipe it," I order Puo.

Puo doesn't respond.

"Pipe it!"

"You need help, Isa! This has got to stop!"

"Pipe it!"

German techno music erupts in my helmet. Beating. Thumping. Moving. It's so loud there's no room for thought. No room for fear.

It leaves only the raw energy of adrenaline and the beating, thrumming, ministrations of the German Puppet Master and a parachuteless ten-thousand-foot free-fall.

Puo shouts over the music through the comm-link in my ear, "Now!"

I jump out through the loading doors into the void below and scream at Puo, "Turn that shit up!"

* * *

I'm laughing, although I can't hear myself. All I can hear is the kick-ass music pumping in through my helmet. The only way I know I'm laughing is a great bellyful of energy and the tightness on my cheeks from smiling.

The thick, cold nighttime air rushes over my body in great big gobs. I hold my hand out and flutter my fingers slowly, feeling the air rushing up between them.

Then I tuck my head down and streamline my body into a headfirst vertical human bullet.

The black, silver-tipped ocean rushes up to greet me.

I use the retina-tracking controls to turn on the heads-up display in the helmet. Green pixelated information projects downward, snapped to the ocean's surface as if it were a giant chalkboard with rapidly changing altitude and speed information written on it.

"One hundred and sixty miles per hour!" I shout over the music to Puo.

I can't hear Puo respond.

The drop zone spreads out below me in a green bull's-eye.

Agitator lasers, the technology responsible for not turning me into North Sea fish food, are powered up and ready.

"One hundred and seventy-six miles per hour! Terminal velocity!" I shout to Puo. I check the clock spread out on the ocean surface to my lower left. "New record!"

Puo drops the music an octave, enough to shout over. "I can barely hear you! Twenty-one seconds to entry."

"Negative."

"Whadda you mean negative!"

"I made a mod!" I click on my leg thrusters.

The force on my legs pushes me even faster to my date with the North Sea surface.

One hundred eighty-five miles per hour.

Puo swears, "Neptune's balls, Isa! You need—"

"Shut it! And turn that shit back up!"

German techno music wraps around me, invades my consciousness, vibrates my helmet.

"Two hundred and five miles per hour!" I scream, grinning like an idiot. *Thirteen seconds.*

I ready the agitator lasers.

Here's where it all comes together. Either the lasers mix the right amount of air and water to decelerate me safely as I slide under the ocean. Or they don't.

And honestly, I'm not sure I give a shit at the moment.

Fifty feet to the surface.

Two blue agitator lasers shoot ahead. I barely have enough time to see a frothy white churn before I punch it.

It feels like an airy vice grip, gradually getting more forceful, and finally arresting my motion.

Bubbles swarm upward around me. The music continues to pump into my helmet.

Guess I made it.

I check to make sure I still have my backpack of goodies (I do).

Now, I'm already eighty feet underwater and sinking.

"Turn it off!" I shout at Puo. It's time to get to work.

The music cuts off. "They know I'm here?" I ask Puo.

"Yeah, they know," he says quietly. It's why Puo thinks this is so stupid. It's not possible to drop in on the underwater ruins of Amsterdam without alerting the authorities.

Yeah, they know—I feel the grin on my face get even larger.

I feel energy gathering in my stomach, quirks growing on my cheeks.

Chapter Two

TWO HUNDRED FEET below the surface of the North Sea is what's left of Amsterdam—I'm currently eighty feet down and sinking.

Amsterdam was one of the first cities lost when the mega-quake hit eighty-six odd years ago, when the new volcanic range at the bottom of the Atlantic Ocean reshaped, and continues to reshape, the earth's coastlines.

And since it was one of the first cities that was hit before the world fully understood what was going on, there's all kinds of good stuff down here for underwater reclamation specialists like myself to reclaim. Except, of course, for those pesky authorities tasked with protecting the "cultural heritage" of the sunken cities.

Which is really total bullshit, if you ask me. The mega-quake completely wiped out the Netherlands. Doesn't exist anymore, except under a thick blanket of the North Sea. *Who are they preserving it for? School kids on field trips?*

I'm one hundred feet underwater.

It's nearly pitch black under the ocean; barely any moonlight filters down this deep. I can't see anything of the city below me—the heads-up digital projected readouts have no surfaces to snap to, so they float out ahead of me. I feel weightless, devoid of senses.

It's a pretty trippy feeling. I delay turning on the nighttime overlays to enjoy it more. Fortunately, I don't have to worry about nitrogen narcosis—the anti-gravity suit is a closed system that protects me from having to equalize my ears and dealing with dissolved nitrogen in my blood—very, *very* handy for quick getaways.

And the single best invention in the dry scuba suits? Internal heaters. *So. Awesome.*

"ETA on any company?" I ask Puo for when the squiddies might arrive—they're the fast, gangly sentinels guarding the sunken cities. That would ruin the trippy feeling pretty quickly.

"Looks like they're only sending one to investigate your entry. Thirty-five seconds." Puo's continuing to drive around the skylanes in the area to monitor the situation and be close for my exit.

"Roger, that," I say. "I'm a hundred and ten feet down. Will be at the bottom in twenty seconds."

Puo denies me the pleasure of his surprise at being that deep that quick after entry.

"Oh, c'mon, Puo," I say. "Admit it, you're impressed—"

"You got a death wish, Isa," Puo snaps. "I am not impressed. Those thrusters were a reckless idea. We have no idea what the maximum speed of entry is with the agitator lasers."

"Those thrusters," I snipe right back, "got me down far enough under the water to get to the bottom before the initial squiddie shows up—"

"And how did you make the mod?"

"I replaced the flow jets."

"You did what!"

"I don't need them on this job—"

"You don't know that! They're there to outrun the squiddies. What are you going to do if they start chasing you? Rocket away?"

Sometimes there's just no talking to Puo, so I ignore him.

I turn on the nighttime overlay in my helmet with a flick of my eyes. Light doesn't travel very far in the ocean so it's not a great improvement over the previous situation. Only blue light travels down this deep, and what little light does penetrate at night has to be magnified so many times that any flare of real light this deep has the potential to appear like a sustained flash bomb and blind me.

One hundred and forty feet underwater.

I'm falling feet first, ready to stand and move as soon as I touch down. The suit allows me to move on the bottom of the ocean almost as if I were in air—it's a huge advantage not to have to deal with floating all over the damn place and dealing with buoyancy changes and trying to get the right leverage.

The tops of the nearest buildings below me start to get outlined in a blue haze. Most of the roofs are square, flat structures of right angles. There are a few peaked roofs with what look like patches of roof tile between the ocean crud growing on it. All of the buildings are in various states of decay. Some are mere rubble, while most have a series of cracks and holes in the roof—convenient for entry.

"What direction is the squiddie coming in from?" I ask Puo.

"South by southeast," Puo answers shortly.

I check the compass floating off to my right and mentally orient myself in the setting. I've got a runner in my backpack, but I don't bring it out; I should be safely inside when the squiddie swims through.

The runner is an overt misdirection. It's a piece of equipment that shoots through the water column emitting noise and a sonar cross-section similar to that of a human getting pulled by a diver propulsion vehicle (DPV) for the squiddies to chase. The problem is, once the squiddies capture it, they know it's a decoy and that something far more nefarious is in the water somewhere—which then brings more squiddies, authorities, and a whole bunch of other hot mess—you can't outrun the squiddies' ability to call ahead to other squiddies.

Best to just get inside and hide covertly.

"Isa," Puo says, sounding like he's gathering up for something, "this has got to stop. You're becoming increasingly reckless."

"I'm kinda busy, Puo," I say, trying to concentrate on subtly maneuvering myself toward my destination—the Pianola Museum.

"You won't talk to me any other time. Listen—"

"I talk to you all the time! But now is not the time for a counseling session, Puo."

"Ha! So you admit you need one."

"I admit you need to shut up. I'm about to enter the museum."

Two coasts, twelve dead bodies, and one broken heart. *Yeah, it's been a rough couple months.*

"Where's the squiddie?" I can see the blue pixelated outline of what's left of the street below me.

"Twenty seconds out," Puo says. "You launch the runner? I'm not reading it."

"Negative on the runner. I'm going to get inside and hide before the squiddie arrives."

"You have fifteen seconds, that's not enough time," Puo shouts at me. "Launch the runner now! It's useless if you wait too long and the squiddie makes you."

"The runner is overt," I explain, as I touch down to stand on the street in front of the brick Pianola Museum—*damn I'm good.* "No one's ever done a smooth lift before in Amsterdam. It'll be fine. I've got plenty of time."

Heists are rare in majorly protected sunken cities—there're just too many assets in place for the authorities, too much of a home field advantage. The crews that do attempt a major lift focus on misleading the authorities long enough to pull the job and get away. They don't actually try and hide their presence completely.

"And you want to be the first," Puo says rhetorically. "If you get arrested, I'm not coming for you."

"Yeah, you are."

Puo's silent, likely pouting on the other end.

"Yeah, you are," I say again.

"Oh, shut up," he finally says.

The nightvision is barely picking anything up down here. The blue pixelated surface of the three-story building is scarce on details. My heads-up readouts continue to float toward the bottom of my vision, not snapping to any of the ill-defined surfaces.

I can make out the door; it appears solid and intact. The windows on the first story are large enough to climb through, but also appear either intact or boarded up.

I can start to feel my chest beat inside the anti-gravity suit. I need to get inside; that squiddie should be here any second. I want to turn on my flashlights to get a better view, but that would be like shooting off a road flare for the squiddie.

I test the round door handle—it twists. I open the door several inches before it shunts to a stop.

"Squiddie's in the area," Puo whispers. "About a hundred and twenty feet above you—"

A bright-red digital arrow blips on in front of me pointing upward and to the left, announcing a squiddie-ping—an active sonar pulse the squiddie uses to map the area. The color of the arrow fades to a semi-transparent maroon.

"—He's going active," Puo so helpfully tells me.

The crack in the door isn't big enough for me to squeeze through yet. I apply the slightest amount of pressure to the door, and it starts to give with a slight scraping noise.

Damn it. Damn it. Damn it. I continue pushing.

There. Just enough room. I start to squeeze through.

"He's moving down in the water," Puo whispers in a rush.

Bright-red arrows start firing regularly in the lower right of my helmet, flashing over the semi-transparent maroon.

"It's coming fast," Puo whispers.

I slide the last bit of myself into the museum, and quietly but quickly shut the door shut behind me—an overturned bookcase at the entrance was blocking the door.

It's brighter in the museum than I expected. The nightvision is picking up all kinds of detail in the entrance of the two-story hallway. The heads-up readouts start snapping to the well-defined wall surfaces.

Then I realize the source.

The squiddie must have its search lights on looking through holes and windows. *Shit!*

If the squiddie has its search lights on, it's found something suspicious. And if I can see that light, it must be close—really, *really* close.

As gently as I dare, I slide the bookcase back to where it was blocking the door. The door, wall, and bookcase make a hollow triangle that I immediately climb into and crouch down in.

I make myself as small and silent as I can, curling up my knees to my chest and making sure the top of my helmet is below the edge of the bookcase.

Puo barely whispers, "It's right on top of you."

His voice through the comm-link in my ear sounds like a klaxon. There's no way a squiddie should hear him but still I whisper back, "Shut. Up."

Puo blessedly doesn't respond.

I turn off all the heads-up overlays in the helmet and the nightvision. Darkness envelops me.

Little rays of white light pop in and swirl through the building as the squiddie descends. Newly formed shadows dance in tandem.

Sweat drips off the end of my nose. I try to slow my breathing. My infrared signature should be masked by the anti-gravity suit, but safely masked at several hundred feet away doesn't necessarily translate to safely masked at five feet.

I can hear the squiddie on the other side of the door. They're like an octopus on growth hormones. The big, gangly, mechanical creature is swishing water around as it snakes its appendages loaded with sensors in various directions, looking for me.

The white light from the squiddie pours through the square, transom window at the top of the door, changes angle as it descends.

Oh, God. I hope the door will add some measure of protection from the infrared.

The door handle jiggles!

The door starts to slowly slide open and quickly shunts up against the bookcase. White light bleeds through the crack, pointed away from where I'm hidden behind the door.

The light shifts around, searching.

Something—an appendage—scrapes against the door. *It's trying to get in!*

A desperate plan starts to form. The runner is packed away in my backpack. But I could run farther into the building, gaining time to get the runner out and then set it off. Use the squiddie's size in the tight confines of the building against it.

But it'd be a disaster. The squiddie would call others. It'd destroy the building in its enthusiasm to capture and drag me to the surface. More than once, what the squiddie has dragged to the surface was freshly drowned as the mechanical creature proudly dumped off its cargo, unaware in the slightest it had killed its prize.

The questing appendage scraping against the door thuds to a stop. The crack between the door and its frame isn't big enough for the appendage to squeeze through.

I would exhale in relief if I could breathe.

Will it force its way through or not?

Squiddies are programmed not to disturb anything unless there's a high enough probability of a capture.

The seconds ache by. The white light continues to shine through the crack, dart up and down. It feels as if it's yearning to turn the corner and stare at me in the face.

The light strains for a second more before abruptly clicking off. The squiddie moves upward with heavy whoosh of water.

Puo whispers over the comm, "It's looking over the rest of the building. Sit tight."

I don't answer.

If the squiddie detected me, it would've already been through the door in seconds. Thank goodness for the anti-gravity suit's infrared protection.

I have a complicated relationship with the suits. I love them, I do, it's just— They are what caused us to flee from the U.S. east coast to the west coast, and strew bodies behind us on both coasts. As well as that whole broken heart thing.

I sit there for several more minutes, breathing shallowly once more. Sweat drips off of me in the suit. It's hot and moist in my helmet. The internal heater doesn't account for the internal stress of coming within five feet of being dragged to the surface and arrested.

Finally, Puo comes on the line, "It's moving off."

"Told you it'd be fine."

"You know it at least left a mini-squatter behind," Puo says.

"I know." It's what the squiddies are programmed to do if they assess a low probability that something might be in the water.

* * *

The Pianola Museum is a three-story Dutch building dedicated to the player piano—an early twentieth-century invention. A piano that played itself was all the rage back then, a precursor to record players. All you needed was a player piano and a piano roll, and this place is so helpfully full of both.

But I ain't moving no piano; the piano rolls on the other hand are nice and portable. And the early ones that are made in sheet metal are quite collectible—*quite* collectible. Most of the later piano rolls were encoded in paper, which obviously didn't survive the ocean rearranging itself, but the sheet-metal rolls (with a little restoration) do just fine.

I stand up slowly and try turning on the nightvision again, which is a total bust. It's too dark in here to be any good. I switch off the nightvision and kick on one of two helmet flashlights and reduce it to twenty percent power.

The controls in the helmet are all retina-tracking based, so it sometimes feels like I'm having a seizure, flicking my eyes all over the place to move through menus and trying to mimic strobing with all the blinking. But now that that's settled I take stock of my surroundings.

The inside of the museum may have been grand in its heyday, but now it's a debris-littered wreck with a thick layer of mustard-colored silt. A staircase doubles back on itself in the two-story hallway leading up. Rooms open up from the hallway on each side.

I step deeper into the museum and glance in the side rooms. Player pianos sit there silently, waiting to be played. It's an eerie feeling to imagine them playing by themselves, or this place once filled with music back when they held concerts here.

I can nearly imagine the people in old-time clothes with thick mustaches, drinking beers and leering at serving woman, hoping to catch a glimpse of their ankles. Now the pianos sit silently, brooding near one another as flecks of silt float by, disturbed by my passing.

The piano rolls, according to our research, are all held on the second floor. I step up the stairs carefully, testing my weight on each step before committing my full weight—I'm pretty sure the racket from a stairway collapsing would recall that suspicious squiddie, or alert the mini-squatter it probably left behind outside the door.

The stairs blessedly don't creak or crack as I slowly walk up.

"Approaching the second floor," I tell Puo.

"Roger, that," Puo says. "You got the leech bag for them?"

"Yes." Although if I didn't, there'd be absolutely nothing to do about it now.

The leech bag is how we're getting the piano rolls out of this place. It's programmed to sit on the ocean floor for several hours until the merchant, *Golden Delight,* drives overhead; then the bag will float to the surface and attach itself to the hull for us to easily pick up later.

If you're going to get caught trespassing in a protected sunken city zone, it goes a lot better for you if you don't actually have any stolen items on you.

The museum stairs dump me off on the second floor landing. The room we want is toward the front of the building and has a doublewide doorframe with no door.

"Bingo," I say. Straight ahead is the piano roll room with floor-to-ceiling little cubbies that once held the forearm-length piano rolls.

"You see the sheet-metal rolls?" Puo asks.

"Yeah," I say. They're the only ones that are still in the cubbies. All the rest have since disintegrated and all that's left is the wooden spool they were wound around.

I walk into the room that's the length of the front of the building and about half as wide. The windows on the outside of the building are covered by the cubbies—probably to protect the once fragile paper from the sun. There are maybe fifteen to twenty of the sheet-metal rolls in a room designed to hold at least several hundred.

But the buyer we're working with isn't interested in fifteen to twenty random sheet-metal piano rolls. He wants four specific, Igor Stravinsky piano rolls. And for the amount he's paying us, he's going to get those four, very specific, Igor Stravinsky piano rolls.

Except I don't read Dutch, which is what all the plastic-engraved name plates are in.

I switch on the text translator overlay in my helmet. I walk up to the nearest nameplate with an intact piano roll in it and read the text it projects over the nameplate:

>> Detecting language ...

I try not to move my helmet as the program works.

>> Does not recognize language.

Great. I try wiping off the nameplate.

>> Does not recognize language.

Damn it! I flip through the settings on the stupid program to tell it what language it is. *Where is the stupid default setting?*

"Your program sucks, Puo," I vent at him.

"That'd be because it's not my program," Puo answers matter-of-factly.

"Still your fault."

"Naturally. Have you tried telling it, it's in Dutch?"

I bite back my first response. "Yeah, I just found it." I select the Dutch option—

"Shit!" I snap. "Now it's all in Dutch." *Including the freaking menu!*

Puo tries to bite back his laughter, but is doing a poor job of it. "Can you now read the name plates?"

I try.

>> Kan niet lezen tekst.

"No! It's all in Dutch!"

Puo chortles more.

"What the hell are you laughing about?"

"Just look for 'Stravinsky.' It may be in another language, but they're not going to rewrite a proper noun."

"We do it all the time," I snap back. "Stravinsky itself is the English spelling of a Russian name. If they're going to honor the name, it's going to be in Russian. Do you know what it is in Russian?"

"Yeah," Puo says, "Stravinsky."

Freaking Puo.

I turn up one of the flashlights to seventy-five percent.

>> Bach: Goldberg Variaties. Opgenomen 1905 door een onbekende pianist.

"Fuck!"

Puo just snickers at my troubles. "Just slow down. Remember what you did to select Dutch and repeat—"

"Duh. Now shut up and let me think."

"Shutting up, boss."

I exhale deliberately and try to let my frustration dissipate. I think back through how I brought up that menu with the retina-tracking, focusing on what menus I selected and how many items in the menu from the top and whatnot.

I go slowly, taking my time.

"Well?" Puo asks.

"Alll-most there," I answer back absent-mindedly.

There. Finally, a list of different languages in their native languages pop up. I select English and swing back to translate the nameplate.

>> Bach: Goldberg Variations. Recorded 1905 by an unknown pianist.

Right. Not quite what I'm looking for. Fortunately, there's not many metal-sheet piano rolls in here, and it doesn't take too long to find the Stravinskys.

"Puo," I say, "There's five. Not four."

"Is there room in the leech bag?"

"Yeah," I say. I've already gotten the black leech bag out of my backpack and started to carefully pack the piano rolls into it.

"Then grab it," Puo says.

"Somehow," I say, "duh, just isn't the right response here. Suggestions?" I zip up the inner bag of the leech-bag and tie the outer one tight. The battery levels on the control panel are reading full.

"Mmm," Puo says. "How about, 'Puo is a genius,' or 'Golly, Puo was right. Puo's always right. I should—' "

"Golly?" I snort. "Gee whiz, wise guy. You giving me the business?"

"What?" Puo asks.

"Never mind, June." But I know what I'm making Puo watch when we get back home to the Seattle Isles after this job is over.

I continue, "The presents are wrapped. I'm headed out to drop them in the mail. Where's the squiddie?"

"Back at its original post," Puo says. "You're not going out the front door are you?"

"Of course not." That's where the squiddie likely left a surprise for me. "What do you take me for?"

Puo says seriously, "A reckless thrill seeker whose admittedly well-developed skills will one day not be able to bail her butt out."

"Way to suck the fun out of the moment." I head back down the stairs, once again careful to go slow and test the steps.

"Just sayin'."

"Well ... that's why I have you." I make a kissing sound at him.

Puo *mmmm*'s, but otherwise stays silent.

Puo is asexual, and when he is interested, it's in men. So even though we've been together for nearly two decades, there's never been anything sexual between us. We're just closer than brother and sister, thicker than thieves (which we *technically* are), two peas in a pod.

"I'm approaching the back of the hallway," I say to Puo. "Where's the exit?" The hallway on the ground level is dead-ending at a small servant's-type door. There's a sign on the door that the bright flashlight shines on and the language program translates for me.

>> **Museum staff only.**

"Through the door," Puo says, "is another stairwell. Push past that to find a gathering room or kitchen of some kind. There's a door on the back to the right. That leads out the back to the loading area."

"Roger, that." I push Museum-staff-only door open, and step past the stairwell. "You were wrong, Puo. It's a break room." It's a small room with half a kitchen along one wall, lockers up against another wall and a round table for sitting at.

"That's a gathering room," Puo defends himself. "Don't you remember, 'Puo is always right'?"

"Just make sure you're in place for my pickup in eleven minutes."

"I'll be there," Puo says, "I'm nearing my turn-around point."

The door to the back is a yellowish-green with a metal doorknob. "Stepping outside."

"Roger, that," Puo says. "Will you at least ready the runner?"

"No," I say. I don't want to tie one of my hands up. "The squiddie doesn't know I'm here. There's no point."

I turn the metal doorknob. The door swings outward with a whoosh of silt. My bright flashlight lances out into the back courtyard and falls on a knee-high miniature black metal trashcan looking device—a mini-squatter.

"Oh, shit—!"

The top of the squatter shoots up. Bright lights flash out at me, temporarily blinding me.

NEE-eu! NEE-eu! NEE-eu!

Chapter Three

*O*H, HELL NO.

    I move as fast as I can toward the mini-squatter. As good as the anti-gravity suits are, you can't really run underwater—only a kind of desperate shuffle-step in close quarters.

NEE-eu! NEE-eu! NEE-eu!

I can feel the sound waves pass over me. Its white bright light tries to blind me, but my meta-materials helmet is auto-adjusting the visor's tint to keep the worst of it out.

As for the annoying device trying to get a picture of me, go right ahead. All they'll get is someone in a black suit wearing an opaque helmet that in a digital photo will show a middle finger on my helmet flicking them off.

I get to the mini-squatter and drop to my knees. They have no defenses. Their purpose is to be loud and scare any quarry into not moving while the squiddies descend.

Fuck that.

I rip the access panel open at the base of the mini-squatter. I may not have Puo's technical abilities, but I do know how to destroy things: *rip, smash, pull, etc.*

The mini-squatter abruptly shuts off its annoying siren.

The courtyard blinks back into darkness except for my helmet flashlight.

Damn it, the flashlights. That's probably what the mini-squatter detected. I quickly flick it off with the retina-tracking.

There isn't time to dwell on it. I kick on the nightvision, and weak, blue pixelated surfaces emerge.

"Whoa," Puo says, "you've got a lot of company headed your way. And they're dispatching a cruiser. Squatter?"

Shit. "Yeah," I say, desperately looking for a place to hide. The runner is only of any use if they can't initially find you. "The squiddie must have dropped it." *Crafty mechanical bastard.*

It's a mark of seriousness when Puo doesn't reply with a smartass comment.

The back courtyard is closed in by buildings. The only ways out are either up and over, or through one of those buildings. The Pianola Museum is out. The mini-squatter got a picture of me leaving it, and the squiddies will definitely blunder through it. That leaves nine other mystery doors in the courtyard without time to make a decision.

"Puo—" I'm already moving. "—I'm headed toward the westernmost courtyard door."

"Roger. Bringing up building plans now. I've already turned around and am headed back near your area."

Good. Puo is driving overhead in the skylanes. He needs to be somewhat close for an extraction.

"They're going to be there any second," Puo says. "Hurry."

Like I need to be told twice. My chosen mystery door is a gray security door with a white, square vent in the top quarter of the door.

Locked.

My heart pounds in my chest. I feel along the frame of the door: rotting wood that's been sitting in seawater for eighty-six years.

I start ripping at the rotten wood with both hands around the lock, the wood flaking off easily.

I lean against the door and push. It gives, ripping out the rest of the doorframe around the lock.

I rush in and try to close the door behind me as best I can. As I do, I see the water in the courtyard lightening rapidly, more blue pixels spreading out over the courtyard surfaces from several approaching squiddies.

It won't take them long to find the evidence of the fresh gouges I left in the doorframe.

There are no blue pixelated surfaces in the building. Nothing once I closed the door. It's pitch black in here.

With no other option, I turn on one of my helmet flashlights to one percent, the lowest it'll go. One percent isn't enough to see anything; turning on the helmet lights automatically turns off the nightvision by default.

Even while I'm doing all this I'm taking slow, careful steps forward. "Puo, talk to me. Where's an exit?"

"Workkk-ing," Puo answers.

I override the default setting and turn back on the nightvision with one percent flashlight. Blue pixelated surfaces spread out before me.

"I'm in a kitchen," I say. "There's a double-hinged service door to my left—"

"Got it!" Puo says. "You're in *Zoe's Raw Bar*. Go through that door to the main dining room. From there you can exit to the street."

I follow Puo's instructions and step into the main dining room. It's hard tell in blue monochrome what kind of restaurant this was. But there's a bar in the middle of the floor, and square tables (most are knocked over) set up around it. The front windows are broken.

I head for the exit. When I'm halfway toward the front door and next to the central bar, I notice the blue pixelated surfaces in the street are becoming better defined by the second: *lights from a squiddie!*

I duck through the waitress entrance into the bar and get low; this time, I remember to shut off my helmet lights. I silently set the leech bag down and slide my backpack off to get the runner.

As I pull the cylindrical runner out roughly a foot long and a hand-span wide, Puo whispers over the comm-link, "They're sniffing around the back door. Another one is in the street out front."

Sweat drips off me inside the helmet. I really need to turn down the internal heater.

They're closing me in. My mouth feels as dry as sandpaper.

I reach out and open the nearest cabinet in the bar hoping to hide in it and praying it doesn't creak. It doesn't, but it's full of broken glass. I try the cabinet next to it—full of shattered plates.

That's when I realize two things: one, I can make those details out, which means the light is getting brighter. And two, the silt. The silt is disturbed from where I passed. It's like walking through snow.

I only brought one runner—seems so foolish now.

I ready the runner to head east, and set the delay to zero. I wish there was a way to tell it to kick up as much silt as possible. It has enough smarts to avoid debris and to try and avoid squiddies. But if the squiddies catch an image of it, recognizing it, it's over.

The back door leading out to the courtyard slams open.

Fuck! The squiddie out front is so close it's like blue pixelated daylight. And now another squiddie is coming through the back entrance I used, to sweep the space.

There's nowhere to go.

Oh, God—I hope they don't fight over me, using me as some kind of rag doll to pull apart between them in their enthusiasm to drag something to the surface for their masters.

Metal objects *clatter* back in the kitchen. Low light shines onto the ceiling from the direction of the service doors with circular windows.

Would the sudden depth decompression from a squiddie puncturing my suit be enough to kill me instantly? Damn—I don't think so. I'm only two hundred feet down.

A wedge of light on the ceiling from the service doors appears, getting larger—*the door's opening!*

I hold up the runner and let it loose. Immediately, it shoots off, sounding like a small engine.

I make myself as small as possible, tucked behind the bar.

The service doors *boom!* open, sounding like they fly off of their hinges.

The main dining room is bathed in a white light so bright the nightvision auto-shuts off to protect me. The light holds for a split second. There's a cloud of silt around me.

The gangly squiddie suddenly shoots off, knocking over tables and smacking against the bar as it scrambles after the runner.

I stifle a scream and squeeze down on myself, trying to make myself as small as possible. Broken glass falls around me.

My muscles ache from clenching. My heart pumps in my chest. Sweat pours down the sides of my face.

The bright lights of the squiddie fade quickly. The reverberations in the bar taper off. I want to wait longer, be sure it's safe, but there's no time.

Now or never.

I pop up slowly, the nightvision back in place. "Where are they?" I ask Puo. I can't see any.

"Half split after the runner. The other half are in the courtyard. Get out of there."

I'm already moving by the time Puo offers the unneeded advice. Once I'm through the broken window and on the narrow side street, I initiate the jump sub-routine.

It's the fastest way to move through the water while disturbing as little of the water column as possible. The flow jets are faster, but louder—and if I had them, I'd damn well be using them. Now isn't the time for subtlety. More squiddies, and other not-so-easily-fooled assets, are undoubtedly on the way.

I jump; the anti-gravity suit auto-adjusts my buoyancy and little water jets on my back propel me up and forward. I'm careful to stay below the three-story roofline.

I'm almost too afraid to look up.

Two jumps northward feel like an eternity to complete and bring me to a junction in the streets. I turn west.

The crusted-over cars all facing the opposite direction announce that I'm going the wrong way down a one-way street. *What can I say? I'm a rebel.*

I can make out just enough of the blue pixelated surfaces to avoid the big stuff. But the top of the buildings on my right hand side are far more defined—likely from the halo of lights in the courtyard I'm leaving behind.

Three more jumps and I come out where a canal used to be. And just on the other side of the canal, salvation: a tramline that connects back to the main railway through Amsterdam.

I take the opportunity to divest myself of the leech bag. I set it off to the side of the street, semi-hidden by laying it up against a parked, old-school land-car.

Puo interrupts in a rush, "They found the runner, and are doubling back—"

I leap toward the other side of the canal.

Puo continues. "—Half of the other half of squiddies back in the courtyard have stormed into the restaurant."

Shit. I land in the middle of the canal and leap again.

"I'm almost to the tram line."

Puo doesn't say anything, which only makes me feel even more panicked.

I touch down near the parallel metal tramlines on the ground. It's not that Puo doesn't have anything to say. It's that Puo's too scared to say something that would distract me. Or he's keeping even worse news from me that neither of us can do anything about.

My hands are shaking as I unshoulder my backpack and rifle through the bag for the rider—a heavy piece of powered equipment that Puo and I invented just for this job that's similar to a zip line trolley. The idea is based off of zip-lining, except using Europe's old railways instead of ropes as a quick getaway.

I clip the rider on, shoulder my backpack and make sure I have a good grip on the rider, holding on with both hands. "I'm linked up," I tell Puo. "Here we go."

Even with a tight grip the device nearly rips out of my hands. Zero to full speed in a second. *We'll need to change that.*

My forearms strain, burn from the effort of staying alive and out of jail. My legs splay up behind me.

The device itself is silent. But the sound of the rubber wheels running over metal sounds excessive in my desire to be invisible.

Shit. I zoom up to an abandoned tram on the track blocking the way. I slow down and stop. My hands tremble slightly as I unhook the rider and I'm constantly looking all around me for squiddies about to descend. *The squiddies can't hear the rider, can they?*

I tell Puo my situation and ask about the squiddies.

Puo answers in a dead-serious tone, "They've picked up the first of your jump sites."

Blood pulses against my ears for the twenty-foot journey past the eerie, silent tram. *Does using the rider kick up a silt trail squiddies can follow? It has to, doesn't it?*

The surrounding environment is painted in weak blue pixels as I hurry past the tram. I see no growing spotlights of blue pixelated detail emerge from any approaching squiddies.

Once on the other side of the tram, I clip the rider back on and gratefully zoom off. I'm moving north so fast that after a few short minutes I'm approaching the junction to the main rail lines.

I use the controls near my thumb to slow down. The main railways run through the center of the city. Where the tramlines connect to the main lines, there are at least twelve different tracks in a wide swath.

"I'm at the rail junction," I tell Puo. "Which railway?" The open space of the railways help the nightvision pick up more light. The rails are tight, parallel blue pixelated lines.

"Fifth one from where you entered, starting with the number one closest to you and twelve farthest from you."

"Roger, that." I unhook the rider, and mentally count out five to the right railway.

I lightly jump toward the right rail—

SCREECH! White light floods the railway. A squiddie explodes out from behind a crusted over railcar a hundred and fifty feet down the tracks.

BOOM! The railcar falls on its side.

I jerk in my trajectory downward. Sweat pours off my the sides of my head. I can feel my chest trying to burst through the anti-gravity suit.

The white light is darting toward me.

"Shhhit! Shit! Shit!" *I'm freaking descending way too slow!*

"What! What's going on!" Puo screams back.

"Squiddie made me!"

"Get to the surface!"

"Can't! Not going to make it!" I touch down to the side of the rail. I drop to my knees and fumble with the rider.

"Fuck!" My hands are shaking so bad I can't get it clipped.

"Isssaa!" Puo yells. "Get to the surface!"

I can hear the squiddie's massive body rushing toward me through the water.

Click. The rider, by the grace of God, connects. I hold on with both hands and kick it to full throttle.

I'm yanked hard. My rotator cuffs almost pop. I try and tuck my legs in behind me so the squiddie can't grab them, but I'm moving too fast, and they splay out wildly.

The white light of the squiddie shines brightly on me. It takes several seconds of hanging on for dear life to realize I have not been wrapped up by an overzealous squiddie. The light is slowly starting to fall behind.

"Puo," I say shakily, "The rider is outrunning it—"

"Oh, thank the sweet Lord!"

"But it knows I'm here. It must have already called ahead—"

"Yeah," Puo says, obviously looking at his displays. "Yeah, it did. Looks like they already calculated the optimum place to capture you."

"Where?" *Please God, don't let there be any abandoned trams on the line.*

"There's a bend in the railway tracks a mile up ahead. While you're on a straight line, none of them are in the right position to intercept you at that speed. But they can cut the distance at the turn."

"Okay." I gulp and try and think quickly. "How far is the squiddie behind me?" The nightvision kicks back on.

"Two hundred feet and opening."

"How fast am I opening?"

"Ten feet a second," Puo says.

"And how long does it take me to get to the surface?"

"In these freaking conditions, eighty to ninety seconds. I see where you're going. I'll figure out the optimum spot where you should let go."

"Roger, that," I say breathlessly. My back is starting to ache.

"Oh, crap!" Puo erupts.

"What!"

"The cruiser just launched a HiDAR. Ninety-five seconds to impact."

"Forget optimal, tell me when the HiDAR is fifty seconds out!"

"Roger!"

HiDAR is a high-resolution high-ping-rate sonar system. Imagine instead of your standard fixed closed-circuit camera system, you have multiple high-definition cameras in each room that can render the space for its masters in perfect three-dimensional detail. Oh, and they can push that information to all their gangly lackeys below the water.

The only weakness of the HiDAR is that it's downward looking (the "D" in HiDAR). So if you can get above its acoustic imagining beam, then it can't see you.

"Fifty seconds!" Puo shouts.

I let go, and increase my buoyancy to the maximum. I also curl myself into a tight ball. It probably won't help anything, but it feels like it should.

The water rushes over me as I tumble toward the surface. The sound of the rider continues on the track.

I'm one hundred thirty feet deep and rushing toward the surface with the depth readout floating and tumbling around me.

I catch blue pixelated glimpses of the track below me, increasingly becoming both more detailed and more distant.

Eighty feet deep.

I hear the splash down of the HiDAR, and its mechanical whir as it sets itself up.

"Puo," I say, "I'm forty feet from the surface."

"Roger, that," Puo says relieved. "As soon as you broach, initiate the subroutine for pickup."

"Where's the cruiser?" I ask. These anti-gravity suits were the catalyst for all this shit lately of moving coasts and dead bodies and broken hearts. I don't want anyone to know we have them. They're only supposed to exist as top-secret tech for a very small select Special Forces group.

"Does it matter?" Puo asks. There's an edge of worry to his question.

"No, I guess not." I broach the surface and initiate the pickup subroutine. If they arrest me, they'll definitely learn about the suits.

The counter for pickup routine lights up, snapping vertically to the distant horizon. Five seconds.

The night is still clear. The North Sea has a light chop to it. The half moon shines down on me, makes me feel small, lonely. It's like a whole different world up here.

Three seconds.

The air traffic is light in the region. One of those red streaking lights ten thousand feet above should be Puo.

Two seconds. One.

I always feel it first in my stomach, that something has gone horribly wrong in the world. And then I'm already several hundred feet in the air, falling *upward*, before I can force myself to reorient.

These anti-gravity suits are freaking *awesome*; at least when you're not about to get arrested or die in them.

If you close your eyes, it almost feels natural.

Chapter Four

TWO DAYS LATER, Puo and I are in south Essen, Germany, meeting our buyer, Vasily Kafarov, to make the exchange. It's early evening, but the sun has already set on account of Germany being further north than I'm used to, plus it's autumn.

It's also freaking cold—I was born and raised in the American south. Fifty degrees is *cold* damn it. Even buttoned up tight in a warm navy-blue winter trench coat with the fur-lined hood pulled up over my straight black hair, I still get unpleasant wafts of cold air sneaking down my neck—I should've worn a crew-neck sweater instead of the peach-colored v-neck I went with.

Puo and I are walking through the dirt parking lot toward *Der Kohlebergmann, The Coal Miner*, a chic, underground bar and a microcosm of Essen.

The city is a mishmash of three different cities in time. It was once an industrial center, but turned to technology after the manufacturing decline, and a number of corporations have their headquarters here. But after the mega-quake hit, it had to adjust to suddenly being a port city.

The result of this mishmash is *Der Kohlebergmann*, a failed coal mine repurposed with the newfound wealth the coast readjustment brought, and patronized by upper-middle-class techies.

What the *Der Kohlebergmann* owners hadn't counted on was how a bar two hundred feet underground with only one way in or out would appeal to a different kind of crowd—the kind of crowd that doesn't necessarily trust the person or people they're meeting with.

Specks of loose dirt crunch under my midnight-blue, knee-high boots, and Puo's scuffed-up yellow construction boots. He hates the cold as much as me. He's huddled under a honey-colored insulated down coat with the collar flared up for style. A bright purple leather satchel bounces against his fluffed-up coat as he walks—he looks like a walking beehive with some *flare*.

The entrance to the coal mine is lit up with a bright neon-pink sign, complete with a flashing yellow arrow pointing to a dark hole in the hill leading downward. I feel like I should be in an old Pee-wee Herman movie.

The leech bag worked as designed, and the pickup off the merchant's hull went much smoother than my near capture two days ago. Now, four of the metal-sheet piano rolls are tucked into my tan-colored canvas messenger bag slung around my chest, bouncing gently against my thigh—my black leggings are doing little to protect me from the little stabs of coldness—while the fifth piano roll is in Puo's garish purple satchel.

The bar's tunnel entrance is paved and gently slopes downward into the earth's gullet. The edges of the tunnel are rough-hewn and look authentic to what they were hundreds of years ago, which I think is supposed to make you feel the history of the place but fails miserably for me. I kinda doubt coal miners trudged to work under sparse, but chic modern lights that have been strung up and where every third light is a black light. But what do I know? It could've been a trendy place to work several hundred years ago, a forerunner to the tech sector.

At the bottom of the short walk is a metal elevator, closed off by a chain-link fence with old rusted and dented signs on it that say things like, "Safety First," "Caution," and "Help keep this place clean." The "Safety First" sign is a bit rich, considering that the metal elevator looks like a death trap. Of all the things to update, that'd be where I would've started.

A large German man is at the gate getting people to sign waivers and check identifications. He's an older individual with a scruffy beard and a potbelly, but looks like he knows how to handle himself, even if he looks like he was born on the stool on which he sits and is permanently entrenched there.

As for signing the waivers and recording our presence, we let two device-to-device transfers of five hundred quants (the preferred digital currency of ne'er-do-wells) sign for us without any problem.

I'm pretty sure that, as soon as the local mob learned of the utility of this place, they either inserted their own people here or leaned on the owners heavily.

Puo and I are alone in the shaky, death-trap elevator as it descends. I have to spread my feet apart and bend my knees to keep from getting jerked around. The only obvious modification to the elevator was that it used to be open to the raw tunnel walls around it, but now the openings of the elevator are covered in a very tight metal-mesh weave—probably to prevent drunk morons from losing a limb or a finger.

The air gets warmer as we descend. I relish the feeling of the burgeoning heat on my face, until I finally succumb to unbuttoning my trench coat some. Puo unzips his down coat.

The bottom of the elevator dumps us off in a level mining tunnel. The floor is nicely paved with cobblestone, but the owners left the tunneled walls and ceiling untouched. Regularly spaced rusty orange metal bracers that wrap around the walls and ceiling travel down the length of the tunnel. Between the bracers are wooden slabs that look to be haphazardly tossed in there—several are missing, many are not lined up properly. String lights with thick, clouded bulbs are tacked on near the apex of the tunnel, giving a warm light.

All-in-all it gives a weird feeling of: this place is nice, and: we're about to be crushed to death so let's drink and be merry. I can see why this place is popular on the dating scene.

We decline the coat check near the elevator entrance (we're not stopping off if we need to leave in a hurry), and pass by a group of people waiting for the elevator to leave.

The bar is laid out in a cross pattern, with the bar in the center and the tables and games set up along the four legs. We thread our way through the thin crowd and past the bar to the tunnel opposite the elevator.

Kafarov has already snagged us one of the railcar tables in the center of the tunnel that sits on the metal railway lines the owners kept—cool design feature. Puo and I climb on the tawny-colored bar seats. The bar is not yet packed this early in the night so we're relatively alone.

"Greetings," Kafarov says in heavily accented English.

Kafarov is not much older than us (I'm twenty-six, Puo's twenty-seven), with short, almost buzzed chestnut hair, and he doesn't seem to like to shave very much. He made a pass at me when we first met, but he's not my type (he has very dark, almost black, eyes that I don't trust, and slouching shoulders), and I'm just ... I'm just not ready for all that again.

I plop my tan messenger bag with the four desired piano rolls on the middle of the table. "Hi."

Kafarov restrains himself as a thin waif of a server with a narrow nose comes to take our order.

After she leaves, Kafarov asks, "Any problems?"

"Nope," I say sweetly, "It went as planned."

Puo wisely keeps his mouth shut. He's been a bit distant with me after the events two days ago in Amsterdam.

Kafarov nods his head with a small smile.

For some reason, there's no hint of what happened in the news. The authorities are keeping it quiet—probably while they try to conduct an investigation. The beautiful part is, even if it did get in the news, the original plan called for use of the runner and alerting the authorities anyway. So there's no way for Kafarov to know any differently.

"May I?" Kafarov asks, gesturing toward the tan messenger bag.

"By all means." I smile back.

Kafarov slides the bag toward him and makes to drop it surreptitiously in his lap.

"Ah-uh-uh," I say.

"Of course, of course," Kafarov says. His cheeks blush a bit—which is one reason I agreed to work with him. He's competent, but seems to be a bit unsure of himself at times, which means he's easy to read and may be easier to manipulate, if necessary.

Kafarov keeps the bag on the table and opens it to his vantage and reaches in. He spends several quiet seconds moving the piano rolls around, reading them. The sound of the bartender rattling a drink around with ice in a shaker fills the silence.

"Looks good," he says. He closes the bag and slides them back to the middle of the table. "Just in need of a little restoration."

"We can help you with that," I say. "If you like."

"Can you?" He looks at us inquiringly.

"Yes." It is what we used to do when we were on the U.S. east coast, before we had to shutter everything and flee. We had a topside business called Underwater Restorations that restored salvaged art, sculptures mostly.

"Mmm," Kafarov says, "A kind offer, but I already have something lined up."

"As you wish," I say.

We pause here for the thin waif of a server to drop off thick glass steins full of a heavy-looking dark beer, almost the color of espresso.

I dip my forefinger in the newly arrived beer and remove it after a slow count of five. My nail polish is still clear. No nefarious chemicals.

"So—" Kafarov takes out his tablet.

I take a sip of heady beer. It has a smoky flavor I haven't encountered before, like it was brewed near a campfire.

Puo's been watching me and takes a sip of his own without asking for me to test his. He doesn't like it when I stick my fingers in his food for some reason.

Kafarov continues "—same account number?"

"Yes," I say. We took a twenty-five percent deposit before starting the job—which was another reason to work with Kafarov, he was willing to make a deposit and pays promptly. Even with that and what Colvin gave us, we still weren't able to make a full payment to the Citizen Maker last time. It was only Colvin leaning on the Citizen Maker that kept the situation from getting out of hand with added interest and a longer payment schedule.

"But—" I continue.

Kafarov stops working on his tablet and looks up, his eyes narrowing.

"The contract," I say, "was for *four* Stravinsky's. We recovered five."

"Five?" Kafarov reaches out and looks through the messenger bag in front of him.

When he doesn't find it, Puo lifts up his purple satchel and pats it.

"Are you interested?" I ask. "Same price as the other four."

Kafarov leans back but quickly comes to a decision and says, "Let me make a call."

"You're not the buyer," I observe. It doesn't strictly matter, but it is what he presented himself as. So much for being easier to read.

Kafarov shrugs silently. "No. I'm afraid not."

"Make your call," I say.

As he gets up from the table I take a thick, heady sip of the smoky beer. "What is this?" I ask Puo about the beer.

Once Kafarov is out of earshot, Puo says, "We don't know who he works for. And the beer is a Rauchbier."

"No, we don't," I agree. "And how do you know that?" I flick the glass beer stein with a heavy *ting* to clarify the question.

"That's not good," Puo says. To my question about the beer he says, "I do this thing called listening. Powerful technique. Powerful—"

Freaking Puo. The server girl with her heavy accent must have mentioned it. I cut him off about Kafarov, "No, it's not. But they pay promptly, and there haven't been any shenanigans yet."

Puo's only response to that is to take a sip of his beer.

Kafarov returns quickly with a smile on his face. "Five it is. Same account?" He sits down and takes out his tablet and looks up at me.

"Same account," I say.

Puo takes out our tablet and logs into our account to verify the transfer.

For a few seconds the only sounds at the table are the bubbles of the beer rising to the surface and the sound of fingers tapping on screens.

"Annnddd ..." Kafarov taps the screen dramatically. "—done."

I look over at Puo, who's watching his tablet. A few seconds later Puo says, "transferred." Without looking up, Puo gets to work moving the money out of that account and through our laundering accounts. That should cover the missed portion of the last payment to the Citizen Maker, the late fee, and a good portion of the next payment.

Kafarov is grinning. "Come, let's toast."

I grin back. We just made a lot of easy money without all the bullshit of the last few jobs. I raise my glass. Puo raises a glass with one hand while continuing to work with the other.

"To profitable relationships," Kafarov says.

We *clink* our glasses together.

"Relationships" is an interesting word to use here. It's not one I would've used. This was our first job for Kafarov. It suggests that perhaps he has more in mind. Puo catches my eye to let me know he caught it too.

Instead of following up on that, I ask, "So what was your take in all this?"

"Heh," Kafarov laughs. "Don't worry about me. The buyer was very motivated."

"How much?" I can tell he wants to say it. He wants to brag, most men do, and probably to look cleverer than us for not taking as much of a risk.

Kafarov smiles again and leans forward. "Well, since you insist. Thirty percent."

Bastard. I keep the grimace from my face. Ten percent is the standard. "And how much of that do you get to keep?" I ask.

Kafarov scowls before he can catch himself and plant his grin back in place.

Yeah, I thought so. "Selevs?" The Selevs is the main Russian mafia. Kafarov's young, he's probably not that high up. His percent take will tell us that.

"I'm an independent contractor," Kafarov says.

I just stare at him.

"Well," Kafarov says, "never mind that. Are you open to more work?"

"Yes," I say. "What have you got in mind?"

Puo tightens. I wouldn't have noticed it, except I was looking for it. He's been lecturing me about lying low lately. *But we're going to need the money. So why not sooner, rather than later?*

Kafarov says, "I don't have anything specific right now—"

Puo loosens up a little.

"—But I am interested in forming a business relationship."

"I would be agreeable to that," I say, "on three conditions."

Kafarov cocks an eyebrow at me.

"One, we *are* independent contractors. We only take what jobs suit us."

"Of course, of course," Kafarov says.

"Two, we always need a deposit to start work. The percentage is negotiable, but twenty-five percent is a good ballpark."

Kafarov nods his head.

"Third, we get paid immediately upon delivery."

"Is that," Kafarov asks, "any different than how you operate now?"

"No," I say. "But you're going to guarantee payment."

Kafarov's eyebrows shoot up at that. "That's quite a condition."

"I think you can manage it," I say. If Kafarov is Russian mafia, which I think he almost certainly is, then they can act as a middleman, a clearinghouse of sorts. They can force the buyer to pay up front in an escrow account. This should winnow out any buyers looking to screw us over or play some bullshit shenanigans.

"I'll get back to you on the last condition," Kafarov says.

"Your answer on that," I say, "will mirror our own, on whether we enter a working relationship with you or not."

Kafarov shrugs his understanding.

Our business concluded, Kafarov finishes his beer with a flourish, makes another pass at me (which I decline politely), and then departs with the piano rolls.

Once he's gone, Puo says, "Should you have done that?"

"What? He's not my type," I say avoiding the subject. "I let him down easy."

"That's not what I meant," Puo says. "And you called him a slouching dark elfin man."

I did? Hunh. That's not that bad. Elves are theoretically pretty—not Kafarov, but there's something there to let him down easy. To Puo I say, "Look, it'd be the best working conditions we ever had if they agree to it all—"

"Yes, which is why I didn't interrupt, but—"

"But you think Winn leaving me has made me reckless and dangerous and I should sort that out before taking any more jobs."

Puo nods lightly, and looks at me with a bit of surprise. "That's right."

"I've been listening. You've been harping on it *forevah.*" Puo starts to say something more, but I talk over him, "Look, we can take only the jobs we want—"

"No," Puo corrects, "we take only the jobs *you* want. The only veto power I have is a walk-out strike, which usually only changes your planning, doesn't stop it."

Yeah, there's a bit of truth to that. "I don't know what you're talking about. But fine, we'll be more discerning in the near future in what jobs we take."

Puo looks at me in mock disbelief.

"I can show restraint," I say, a little defensively.

We're interrupted by the thin waif server *thunking* down another round of the thick mugs of frothy beer.

"We didn't order these," I say.

"They are gift from woman," she says in passable English. She points to a Chinese woman in a charcoal business suit sitting at the bar in the center.

I test the newly arrived beer with my forefinger again. "Mine's clean. Want me to finger yours?" I ask Puo.

"Just this once," Puo answers, while checking out our admirer.

"Yours is clear too," I tell him.

Puo switches his gaze to stare at me expectantly about our admirer.

I ignore him and finish off my original beer in one gulp. I pull the new beer close to me and do some people watching. More techies are flooding in. The tables around us, once empty, are starting to fill up. A low din of conversation in the bar is picking up.

You can tell techies by the way they dress. It's the ruffled casual dress of T-shirts and jeans coupled with expensive shoes, sunglasses, the latest gadgets, and/or an expensive timepiece that gives them away. The women almost always outdress the men, upgrading to a sort of business casual. So when you see the two together, it's always a dead giveaway.

There's also the casual disregard of prices, of ordering too quickly off the menu without looking at the price. Only people with money, who aren't worried about the final bill, do that.

"C'mon," I say to Puo. "Let's move somewhere else."

"What about the woman at the bar?" Puo asks.

"What about her?"

"What about her?" Puo asks in exasperation. "Drinks don't just magically show up without any prep from us. Don't you think we should figure out what that's about?"

"No."

"No?"

"I'm showing restraint, Puo."

Puo rolls his eyes.

"But all right," I say. "If you insist. Just remember this is your idea, not mine."

"Oh, shut up."

* * *

The Chinese woman is sitting at the main circular bar in the center of the cross pattern layout facing us. She watches us approach through dark eyes.

The bar itself is made of linked railcars, like the table we were just sitting at, continuing the coal-mining motif. The bar top is a dark, shiny stone, obsidian maybe. It's so dark that the Chinese woman's long hair only stands out because it's not as shiny.

I hold up my beer and smile my thanks at her.

She nods once. She has wide cheekbones with a narrow chin. She doesn't smile back.

Barf. I hate people who take themselves too seriously. I keep my face bright and cheery. You can conduct business without being an automaton.

"Thank you for the drinks," I say.

"They were a gift from my employer," she says in Chinese-accented, but otherwise perfect, English.

I raise an eyebrow at her. The bar has become crowded. There's a loud din making it difficult to overhear conversations nearby, but we're not exactly alone.

"Ne was impressed—"

Ne, nem, nirs, the gender-neutral pronouns. Interesting. It's a much smaller pronoun to hide behind. There are a lot more he's and she's in the world than ne's.

The Chinese woman continues: "—with your recent work for nem, and would like to meet you."

Puo subtly reaches out and taps me on the arm to get out of here. She's talking about a *recent* job that the authorities *know about* in a crowd of *unknown people.*

Before I can respond, she mistakes my silence for confusion, "Ne truly does love piano—"

I turn around with Puo and get the hell out of there. I drop the free drinks off at the nearest table and ignore the dirty look from the people sitting at it.

Puo and I instinctively head for the elevator.

We step in shortly with a crowd and spread out toward the back.

The Chinese woman runs on at the last second.

Damn it.

She threads her way over to us. "I'm sorry—" she says with genuine bewilderment.

Great. I'm not sure which is worse: nefariousness or incompetence. Well, probably nefariousness. But either can get you killed or arrested.

Puo steps between me and the Chinese lady, acting as a bodyguard. At six feet, three hundred pounds, he's good at the bodyguard role. "Ma'am. Please stay away from my client."

"Uh ..." the Chinese lady tries to gain her bearings.

I tap Puo on the arm.

"Ma'am," Puo says more forcefully. "I need you to take a step back."

The other people on the elevator are turning to watch the situation with interest.

"No cameras!" Puo barks as one of the women wearing too much mascara starts to take out her personal device.

The woman startles and drops the device back in her maroon Fendi purse that looks like a knockoff.

Puo needs to be careful. We just crossed the line from forgettable to starting to become memorable.

"It's okay," I say softly. To the group at large I say, "I'm sorry for Sebastian. He knows tight spaces makes me feel ... uncomfortable."

One of the guys, his cheeks flush from alcohol, asks in German-accented English, "Why do you need a bodyguard?"

I smile apologetically at him. "My father insists on it, I'm afraid."

The word *socialite* floats around with a bit of scorn, and just like that I slide back toward forgettable.

"I'm sorry—" the Chinese woman starts to say.

Oh, sweet mercy. She needs to catch a freaking clue and shut the hell up.

"—I'm just such a fan. I was hoping for an autograph."

And now I'm back to being more interesting and memorable.

Puo, without missing a beat, turns to me questioningly like this is the first time this has happened.

I look confused, then flattered. "Uh, sure. I think I have some headshots in the car." To the rest of the elevator I say, "I had a small bit part in a B movie last year. I didn't think anyone had seen that."

"Oh, yes," the Chinese woman says, "you were very good."

"Couldn't have been too good," I say. "I haven't had anything since."

"Well—" The Chinese woman smiles and blushes like a fan. "—I loved it."

"What movie?" the same alcohol-flushed-cheek man asks.

"It's really not worth mentioning," I say, acting embarrassed, which blessedly puts an end to the conversation as the elevator shutters to a stop.

* * *

"You're an idiot," I tell the Chinese woman.

We're standing alone at the edge of the dirt parking lot. The sky overhead is clear with sparkling stars blanketed over the passing hovercars, seemingly growing brighter in the cold October night.

The Chinese woman bites her tongue and looks visibly frustrated with me. "No one would've overheard us—"

"Oh, you've perfected acoustic cloaking?" I ask sarcastically.

"No. The bar was—"

"What?" I ask, stomping over her. "Is this your first time doing something like this?"

She confirms it by blushing.

"Freaking figures," I say. Lord save us from incompetent boobery. "Well, out with it. What's the offer?"

The Chinese woman looks around, "Is it okay to speak here?"

Puo says, "Yes."

"My employer used Kafarov as a middleman to distance nemself in case things went poorly—"

"How do we know," I ask, "that your employer is really the buyer?"

She repeats back the details of the piano rolls as well as the amount paid for each roll and the amount of the deposit— including all *five* of the rolls.

I nod that I accept that for the moment.

"Ne would like to discuss another opportunity with you directly."

I think of the deal we just tentatively made with Kafarov, but decide there was no exclusivity to it. If the buyer wants to cut Kafarov out, Kafarov and company can take that up with the buyer.

"When and where?" I ask.

"Tomorrow—" The Chinese woman looks relieved that this is going better for her. "—at St. Mary's in Oxford, England."

"Yes to tomorrow," I say. "But we set the place."

The woman nods her head once. "I think that'll be agreeable."

Chapter Five

THE LIBRARY OF BIRMINGHAM in the center of downtown Birmingham, England is a massive, sprawling complex, alleged to be the largest library in England and third-largest public gathering space. At least that's what the glossy brochure tells me.

Puo and I are leaning against the black metal railing on the third floor of the five-story book rotunda in the center of the sprawling twenty-first century post-modern monstrosity waiting for the buyer to show up. We got here early to watch the people below and see if we can identify the buyer before ne walks up.

I hate the building. According to the handy-dandy brochure, it was quite the postmodernist darling when it debuted ninety-nine years ago. Now it looks like a drunk toddler stacked three rectangles on top of each other and coated them in a metal skin, and then topped it all off with a gold chéchia cap.

Barf.

When I come to Europe (and England is part of Europe, don't let any hoity-toity smartass tell you otherwise), I want to see Gothic and neo-Gothic architecture. I want to see buildings several hundreds to thousands of years old—the stuff I can't see in the States.

Since the buyer is addressed with the gender-neutral pronoun ne, Puo and I are not sure what to expect. It could literally be anyone. Unlike the other pronouns, there's no physical expectations attached to the pronoun, which I guess, is kinda the point.

"Hey," I say to Puo, "How come you use 'he,' and not 'ne'?" Puo's asexual. I'm not sure how other asexuals identify themselves.

Puo gives me a sidelong glance before answering. "Because I identify as a man."

"Uh ... right," I say, trying to search for the right way to ask my questions.

Puo interlaces his fingers and answers my unspoken questions without looking at me. "Gender and sexuality are two separate things. You can identify as non-binary and be attracted only to women, or you can identify as a man and not be attracted to either. Or any of the other combinations. It's fluid. And neither is it set once forever. It can change with time."

I look out over the rotunda and think about what Puo just said. It was never much of a thought for me. I'm a woman, and I like men. Done. "Seems awfully complicated," I say.

"Life's like that," Puo says with a little bit of snap.

"You mad at me?" I ask.

Puo looks over at me. "It's complicated," he says quietly.

"Yes, it is," a voice says from behind us.

We both whirl around to see a Chinese person standing there observing us.

Puo and I both give each other I-thought-you-were-watching-our-backs looks as ne eloquently says, "This place smells like a dump."

That's the code phrase. Ne's the buyer.

I answer with the code reply, "That's because Puo farted."

Puo scowls at me.

Ne is shorter than me (I'm five-nine). Ne's wearing a white blouse and a knee-length gray skirt. Nir skin is smooth and graceful looking, and nir long black hair is tied up in a crisp bun. Ne doesn't look much older than me.

Ne smiles a friendly smile with white teeth. "I am Shǐ Guìyīng. You may call me Shǐ." Ne holds out nir hand.

I shake it, though it's limp, and Shǐ holds on a second longer than I'm used to. Ne then shakes Puo's.

"Shall we?" Ne gestures with nir palm down toward the left of where we're standing to talk somewhere more private.

"Yes," I say. "But this way please." I head off to the right, which really was where I was planning on going.

We cut through some library stacks and emerge out on a long hallway that we stop halfway down in.

I politely ask, "How can we help you?"

Ne smiles again at us and looks up and down the hallway. "I will try to be as discrete as I can—and I am sorry for Chén the other night. She's ... new."

Puo and I wave it off.

"The previous task was a trial run. We needed to make sure—"

"We?" I ask.

Ne smiles a small embarrassed smile at me again. "I work for a larger organization that would like to hire your services."

"Which one?" Puo asks.

It could only be one of a handful of transnational organized crime syndicates. They're the only ones with deep enough pockets and reach to go through a trial run like the one we went through in Amsterdam.

"It would be premature," Shǐ says, "at this point to reveal that information. We would like to first know if you're interested and whether you think it can be done."

"And what specifically would that be?" I ask.

Ne hands me a piece of paper.

It's a library call number. I show it to Puo.

Ne says, "Pull the book. I will be in the Archives on the fourth floor if you're interested." Ne starts to move off.

"Wait!" I call after nem. "We're in one of the biggest libraries in the world. Perhaps a little hint of where we can find this?" *So we don't have to traipse all over the place.*

Ne points past us down the hallway opposite the way we had come. "At the end of this hallway." Ne smiles a small smile again and turns away the way we had came.

Damn it, did ne just play us? After Shǐ's gone I ask Puo, "Coincidence?"

"I don't think so," Puo says, sounding a touch worried.

Well, that's unsettling.

Puo and I head in the opposite direction toward the end of the hallway. We emerge into a quiet, long rectangular room with regularly spaced floor-to-ceiling bookshelves. There's a waist-high, holoscreen self-help console near the entrance. We enter in the call number and a map floats up to show us the exact location.

We find the right bookshelf easily enough.

"Oh, balls," Puo says. He sees it before I do. He pulls it off the shelf and hands it to me.

Oh, balls is right.

It's a book about the British Museum. One of the most protected underwater real estate sites in the world.

* * *

"Do you have a plan?" I ask Shĭ in the archives.

We're alone in the small, closed-off space. The air is cool, the humidity carefully controlled. Olive-green boxes line the bookshelves, each one carefully labeled.

"No," Shĭ says. "However, with your ingenuity and our resources, we're sure you can think of something."

"We'll have full access to your resources?" I ask for clarification.

"Pending approval, yes." Ne nods nir head.

"Wait," Puo says. "This doesn't make sense." Puo spent the entire time on the walk to the archives telling me how stupid hitting the British Museum would be. "That place has been evacuated clean. There's nothing left."

A point Puo has already brought up with me. *But if there's nothing left, why is it so heavily guarded?*

"Are you going take the work?" Shĭ asks.

"I'm very interested—" I say.

Puo does his best not to scowl.

"—But Puo's right. We can't say for sure until we know what it is you're after."

Shĭ thinks to nemself for a brief second before saying, "It's true. The display areas for the most part have been recovered by the British Government. But there are vaults underneath the museum, some of which are airtight, whose opening would destroy the contents. We would like certain objects in one of those vaults."

"What objects?" I ask.

"Chinese jade," Shĭ answers. "Enough to fill five trunks full."

"What about the other objects?" Puo asks. "The ones that would be destroyed."

Ne shrugs. "The vault only contains our jade, which the British Government stole in the first place and refuses to give back. If other vaults are destroyed in the process, what do we care what happens to their stolen goods?"

"That's a little self-righteous," I say, "coming from an organization such as yourselves."

"We are not," ne says, "without our national pride."

Puo and I just stare at nem.

"But," ne says, "the manner in which the jade has been kept out of Chinese hands has made it rather valuable."

"How much we talking?" I say.

Shǐ doesn't answer.

"You know," I say, "the first thing we're going to do is look up the value." What I don't say, but which the ensuing silence implies, is: then use that information to see if it's worth skimming off the top. It's an empty implied threat. Double-crosses aren't worth the added hassle.

"Yes, well," ne says. "About that. There is one condition on taking the work. One of our agents will be assigned to your team and accompany you."

"No," Puo and I both say at the same time.

"Very well." Ne extends nir hand. "Thank you for meeting with me. A small fee for this meeting has been deposited into the same account you gave Kafarov. We trust you to keep your silence."

When I don't take nir hand, ne turns and walks away.

Puo exhales. "Good riddance," he mutters.

"Wait!" I call out.

Puo groans.

Ne returns.

"How much?" I ask. If it's enough to cover the rest of the next payment to the Citizen Maker or more, we're hitting that museum.

Ne hands me another piece of paper—*it better not be another library book.*

It's not. It's a math problem. It's given as a percentage of the Chinese national GDP.

Holy shit.

Chapter Six

THREE WEEKS LATER Puo and I are in Hampstead Village, England, starting more serious preparations for, as Puo and I have taken to calling it, the BM job—which accounts for a considerable amount of snickering between us. Three weeks because that's how long it took Shï's organization to buy and close on a very squat, two-story dark-brick home here.

Hampstead is a pretty little village that used to be in a northern London borough. Now it's pretty much the closest piece of dry real estate to a submerged London. Before the mega-quake made Hampstead remote lakefront property to the Sea of London, it was some of the most expensive real estate in England. And it's still damn high despite the capital being relocated to Birmingham. Puo and I never would've been able to secure a house here without first selling our Queen Anne home back in the Seattle Isles and having to take out a loan.

The house itself isn't bad. I just don't like the exterior. The front of the brick house is flat, with a barely sloped roof that makes the house look squat, and the windows and door are off center. All that together makes the house look like it has a squished nose and flat hair with a dark-orange pimple door. *Ugly.*

But it's detached, and has a bare concrete-floored basement with cinder block walls that sits directly over what used to be the Northern Line running directly into London, right past the British Museum.

And while I like the house, except for the exterior, I'm not as keen on the third occupant, Liáng Jūn. He just showed up fifteen minutes ago, and after he dropped off his bags and pocket tablet upstairs we immediately hustled him down to the basement to put him to work.

Liáng's taller than me, but not by much, and thick with muscle—but in an appealing, balanced way, not in the strutting I'm-so-thick-I-have-to-hold-my-arms-out kind of way. Normally, I'm a fan of the look, but he's also covered in tattoos (which I don't like—it's like covering a nice piece of art with stickers), and I'm still not in a good place after Winn.

All three of us are standing around a core drill, and there's a power auger in the corner for the earth underneath.

"After you," I say to Liáng, and gesture toward the core drill.

Liáng stands there with his arms crossed in front of his body, one hand propping his smooth face up. He looks at me through the finger-length black bangs hanging down in his eyes—I think he might spend more time grooming himself than I do. "Why me?" he asks. He sounds like a native English speaker, making me wonder about his true background.

"Because," I say, "you're the strongest." *And we have to find something for you to do.*

"No—" He shakes his head without lifting his hand from his face, and indicates Puo. "—I think that honor goes to your friend here."

"And don't you forget it," Puo says. "But I have more important things to do. Can you write code?"

Liáng scowls. "Fine."

Puo heads back upstairs, leaving me alone with Liáng.

Liáng unbuttons his black- and dark-green-striped shirt and tosses it on a foldout table near the stairs. His well-defined muscles and "V" shape are hard to ignore in the tight white tank top he has on underneath.

Lotus and dragon symbols are heavily featured on the tattoos covering both his arms. The tattoos mark him as a member of the Chang'an, a dangerous Chinese international gang.

"Nice tattoos," I lie, trying to draw him out and into conversation.

He eyes me suspiciously, but then decides I pass his sincerity test, "Thanks."

Score one for my ability to lie. "How long did they take?"

"Long enough," he says dismissively.

Grrr. If there's one thing most tattoo people love to talk about, it's their freaking tattoos. How long they took, how they chose the design, their meaning, their placement, blah, blah, blah. But Liáng is giving me none of it. *Why so reticent?*

Liáng wheels the chest-high core drill over to the prescribed spot and fumbles around trying to set it up. His face starts to burn a little red after several minutes.

I'm just enjoying the muscly show.

The core drill looks like a drill press only much larger and with a fire-red pressurized air tank attached. The goal is to drill enough connected holes in a circle through the concrete to make a large enough hole for us to fit through.

Liáng eventually says, "Do you know how to set this thing up?"

Yes. "Nope," I say with a shrug. But I come over anyway and pretend to look it over.

After several more minutes of leading him by the nose, we have it set up.

"All right," Liáng says. "Ready?"

"Let it rip," I say.

CA-CHUNK, CA-CHUNK, CA-CHUNK!

Liáng cuts it off right away, but the horrible sound seems to bounce around the concrete basement.

My ears are ringing.

"We can't," I say my voice elevated from the ringing in my ears, "run that thing like that." Even in a detached home, that sound is going to raise questions.

The basement door flies open and Puo hurries down the steps.

I repeat my assertion to Puo.

"What d'you suggest?" Puo asks, his voice sounds distant, much too soft.

"Make this place an anechoic chamber," I say. Keep the sound from traveling out. A real anechoic chamber, not the electro-magnetic variety we just recently dealt with in Seattle.

Puo nods a couple times. "That could work."

* * *

"We need to be careful—" Puo says quietly in the way he always says be careful. Which is to say it as a matter of fact, like commenting on the weather when running out of conversation topics.

Puo and I are standing in the small white kitchen on the first floor, upstairs from the basement, divvying up the Italian takeout food from *Rotta's Cucina*, while Liáng's in another room on the phone with his handlers okaying buying the materials needed to make the basement an anechoic chamber.

Puo continues softly, "—You saw Liáng's tattoos right?"

"Yeah," I say.

Chang'an is financing this operation. They certainly have deep enough pockets to, but they're not someone you want to get on the bad side of. Let me put it this way: if the Bosses back home got in a war with the Chang'ans, it'd be all kinds of ugly, but the Chang'ans would eventually roll over the Bosses with just pure manpower and resources.

"And who do you think they're going to come after," Puo says, "to recoup their investment if we're not successful?"

That would be very, *very* bad, to owe both the Chang'ans and the Citizen Maker. This job just became the worst kind of double or nothing. If we're successful, our cut will be enough to pay off the Citizen Maker once and for all with a little cash to spare. If we're not, our debt will more than double to two different and dangerous entities.

"I know," I say lightly. *Best not to dwell on it.*

Puo eyes me over the narrow, light-gray glass countertop that extends out from the metal sink, separating the dining area from the kitchen.

"We need to drill that hole," I say. It's the key to our entry and exit.

"I agree," Puo says. He takes his gnocchi in a red puttanesca sauce, pops off the plastic top from the metal container and pours it carefully onto a plate.

A strong whiff of cooked tomato and savory garlic make my stomach rumble.

Puo continues, "All I'm saying is be careful."

Duh. I pop off the clear plastic top from my chicken fettuccine Alfredo. A billow of steam rushes up, bringing with it the smell of melted Parmesan in a creamy butter sauce. *Yum.* I pilfer a black plastic fork and twirl some pasta around it and take a bite.

Hot! I suck an inward cooling breath. The sauce is rich and creamy; the pasta is handmade and perfectly al dente.

"Oh, for the love of Neptune," Puo says. "What are you an animal? Gimme." Puo holds his hand out for my container so he can properly arrange it on a plate.

I scoop the metal container closer to my body with one hand while brandishing my plastic fork with the other hand at him and *hiss*.

"It's—" Puo says.

"Oww!" The metal container burns my hand! I drop my food on the counter with a heavy plop. The white, precious Alfredo sauce spills over the side.

"You are an animal," Puo says. While I'm shaking my hand and going to rinse it under cold water, he slides my food over and starts to get a plate ready. He switches topics, "We still don't know entirely what we're dealing with."

"What don't we know?" Liáng asks, walking into the kitchen.

"They approve the materials?" I ask.

Puo opens a third container and says at the same time, "We got you rigatoni with Italian sausage, hope that's all right." He starts to arrange it on a plate. "I have gnocchi if you're vegetarian."

"Yes, they approved the materials," Liáng says to me. "The materials should be here the day after next. The rigatoni is fine, thank you. What don't we know?" He directs this last question back at me.

Puo starts ferrying the plates and metal silverware (apparently only animals use plastic silverware) over to the white circular table. "We are not entirely sure of all the museum's defenses," Puo says.

I walk over and sit down, pulling my left leg up on the chair, and lean my shin against the table. "We know most of them, but not all."

"What do you know?" Liáng asks as he sits down. He sits with his back straight, elbows off the table, and begins to eat with the utensils in the Continental style. "Would you please pass the pepper?"

What's with Mister Manners all of sudden? And the fancy-schmancy eating style? Did we just slip into some Lord's eighteenth century castle dining hall? Who is this tattooed-covered guy with perfect table manners that was trying to shirk work only an hour ago in the basement?

Puo hands him the store-bought peppershaker. "Squiddies for one."

Liáng raises his eyebrow at us, unfamiliar with our vernacular.

My heart rate spikes suddenly at Liáng's simple reaction—Winn used to complain about my and Puo's use of private vernacular. *It still happens*—little, innocuous things will bring the memories back against my will, make Winn's leaving fresh all over again.

I take a deep breath to give myself time to recover.

"Most governments call them underwater sentinels," I explain. "But they look like overgrown, mechanical squid—"

"No they don't," Puo says. "They look like giant octopi—"

"Yeah, well," I say, "Squiddie sounds better than octopi-ie."

Liáng is bouncing his gaze between Puo and I, his face confused.

"Mmm," Puo says. "I do like pie though."

"Are there any pie shops around here?" I ask. *I like pie too.*

"What," Liáng asks with a hint of exasperation, "are you talking about?"

I snort laughter, a piece of fettuccine flying out of my mouth and landing in front of Mister Manners Liáng, who looks at it in disgust.

Puo covers his own mouth as he tries to prevent spurting out his own food while laughing.

Liáng just stares at us in undisguised disgust.

I reach over all shifty-eyed and snatch up the errant piece of fettuccine like I was palming someone's wallet.

"So," Liáng says, eying me, "Sentinels. What else?"

I can't get a handle on this guy. But if he wants to be all prim and proper at the moment, I can run with that.

"Aerial surveillance," I say. "Both visual and radar." So coming in from above is out. There's no way we're going to let Liáng in on the anti-gravity suits anyway, but there's more than one way to enter a site from the air.

I raise the errant piece of fettuccine to lower it onto my outstretched Alfredo-coated tongue.

Liáng's face falls further into disgust.

"And the always fun," Puo adds smiling, adjusting his speech to show his food in his mouth while he talks, "mini- and regular-sized HiDARs, squatters, and very likely air-gap sensors."

"You're like teenagers," Liáng quips, distaste pulling down the corner of his mouth. He shakes his head and asks, "And you have a plan for these defenses?"

Liáng has been asking about the plan since he first showed up, but we hustled him down to the basement to shut him up and tried to put him to work.

"Some," I answer evasively.

"Some?" Liáng asks, clearly put off at the answer and wanting clarification.

"There's no point," I say, "in forming detailed plans without first understanding the whole picture." It's just wasted mental energy to start planning before all the facts are in.

Liáng exhales through his nose. "And the drilling in the basement?"

"That doesn't count," I say. "That's getting a head start—"

"We know," Puo says, "that's the way we need to get in and out. We know the defense grid around the British Museum. And we have some educated guesses about what's in the museum, but we don't know exactly."

"Why don't you know that?" Liáng asks.

"Because no one has ever made it that far," I say.

"And," Puo adds, "that information is classified."

"Is that something you can help with?" I ask.

Liáng shakes his head no. "We've tried before and have been unable to gain access."

So then why freaking ask us like we should know? First the guy is lazy and surly in the basement, then he's mister perfect manners, and now he's an ass.

"So that's where we are," I say a bit huffy. "We're confident we can get to the museum. We're just not sure what's in it." *Or if we can get out of it.*

Liáng takes another prim bite of his rigatoni, spearing a carved slice of Italian sausage in the process.

"If you can't get us the information," I say, "that leaves us with either running a game on the Muppies—the Ministry of Undersea Protection," I explain for Liáng's benefit, "—or running a desensitizing campaign, or fielding an unmanned intrusion into the museum."

Puo holds up his hand and ticks off his fingers as he says, "Risky, stupid risky, and impossible."

Liáng asks, "What's a desensitizing campaign?"

"Basically," Puo says, "you throw annoying pebbles at the defense grid to see how it responds. The problem is—"

"The authorities," I say, "know what you're doing. But not always." Puo and I did something like this with rats on one of our early jobs together.

"I don't think we can direct fish to go where we want," Puo says, clearly thinking of the same memory about the rats. "As for the intrusion, that's the whole problem to start with. Whatever we send in there isn't likely to come back with the data we need."

"Can you make the device look like a fish?" Liáng asks.

Damn. That is a good idea. But it sparks a better one.

Puo says, "No. There's not enough room to hold the sensor package and getting it to move like a fish isn't trivial."

"What about a squiddie?" I ask.

"What about a squiddie?" Puo asks in return.

"That'd be big enough, wouldn't it?" I ask.

Puo stares at me like I've sprouted another set of teeth in the middle of my forehead. "I can't build a squiddie. They have all their own encoding schemes—"

I give him a knowing look. We exploit those encoding schemes all the time. It's how we talk to each other underwater and how we know where the squiddies are.

Puo continues answering my thoughts. "—It's a little more complicated than that. I can't just manufacture one from scratch."

"So," Liáng says, "you're thieves. Steal one."

"Party foul!" I spit out at him. *Prim turd! That was my idea.* I open my mouth of food at him.

"What?" Liáng asks, visibly perplexed and disgusted at my outburst.

Puo is trying poorly to keep his laughter in. "You stole her idea."

"Oh. Sorry?" Liáng says in a tone that's anything but sorry.

Puo alternates between laughing and talking, "Isa, you're not going to be able to sandbag for the dramatic reveal anymore. Liáng, I think you and I are going to get along just fine."

Harrumph!

Puo watches us for a few more seconds, his face starting to fall from mirth to disbelief. "Wait. You're not serious? That's a terrible idea."

Chapter Seven

AFTER PUO REALIZED I was serious and Liáng was on board, Puo then started explaining how stupid this idea was: squiddies are not dainty things; it *has* to be a London-based squiddie, which means the authorities are going to notice if it goes offline; and one does not just swim up to one of these gangly beasts and tickle its belly to subdue it.

And when Puo starts explaining how stupid my ideas are, then I know I'm really onto something—he even left his thoery about Winn affecting me out of it this time, further convincing me I'm on the right track. I'm not sure Puo's ever been entirely on board with one of my utterly brilliant ideas.

Liáng and I are on Wembley Island, an abandoned dime of an island a quarter-mile west of Wembley Stadium the very next night. We're in dry scuba suits cloistered behind a brick fence on a one-way street lined with two-story row houses that dips down into the Sea of London.

The skylanes to the north are just visible in white and red lights streaking by. Delivery drones in small green and blue lights copter by overhead fairly regularly. Hovercars aren't allowed to drive over the Sea of London by English Law, but delivery drones? No, no. That's just fine. *I need my package, damn it.* I can't decide if that loophole is a product of selfish desire or successful lobbying—probably both.

It's clear but windy tonight, with the silver orb of the moon high overhead. And cold. A typical English October night. I hate the cold. I'm huddling against the brick wall in my suit sans helmet, dreading getting in the water. The internal heater in the dry scuba suit will warm me up quick enough, but the first minute is miserable.

"Puo—" I say.

Puo is flying around above in a hovercar the Chang'ans provided. He's sticking to the lower skylanes running over the northern shore of the Sea of London three miles north of us.

"—the next job we take," I continue, "is going to be someplace tropical."

"Roger, that," Puo says, "Miami, Nassau, Havana?"

Miami's too close to our old stomping grounds in the sunken state of Florida. And I'm not aware of any good loot in Nassau. "Havana might be fun," I say. It's a partially submerged city like the Seattle Isles.

I was really thinking Bangkok, but that's close to the Chang'ans territory and with Liáng listening in, it's best not to tip them off—which I'm sure is why Puo only mentioned things in the Caribbean.

Liáng breaks in to chide, "Perhaps we should focus on this job, before planning the next."

"Buzzkill," I say. I keep my teeth from chattering. The wind is cold on my face, but my body is actually quite warm from the internal heater in the suit. "How we doing on the squiddies, Puo?"

"They're scattered around the area. The closest is on the other side of the stadium."

"Is that close enough for it to hear our bait?" I ask.

"Only one way to find out," Puo says.

We've been sitting here for the better part of two hours waiting for a squiddie to get close enough to make sure it'll follow our bait. The time hasn't been the most pleasant. It's cold, and though Liáng is willing to chat some, it's not much. And certainly not about where he's from or anything like that—neither am I, for that matter. So that's two hours of awkward small talk with Liáng alternating between arrogant and pleasant responses. I was about ready to flick him in the throat and tell him to be nice.

But for the record, he likes Chinese comic books. At first he wouldn't stop talking about his favorite, *Huángdì de wàikē yīshēng*—it's about a surgeon to the Emperor, or something like that. Liáng was less willing to elaborate after I clarified that he was in fact an adult that read comic books.

"Let's go," I say. I've been patient enough tonight.

Liáng and I stick our heads up over the brick fence to make sure it's clear.

The frigid water twenty feet away has some heavy chop to it tonight. Waves are regularly crashing against the street, traveling up the paved lane a ways before reversing direction.

We latch our helmets on (turning on nightvision), and grab our flippers. Liáng hefts our equipment bag and I carry the two stunners attached to two four-foot aluminum poles. Staying out of the street, we leapfrog over the brick fence into the next yard that's halfway under water, sloping downward.

The water in the lower yard has only small ripples on the surface from the wind, buffered from the greater sea by the fence.

The cold wraps around my feet and calves as we wade in. I hate this part. We leapfrog again, and in the next yard, we're up to our waist. This is where it's the worst. Wading up to your waist is tolerable, but something about plunging your vital organs under is what makes your heart thud.

I land in the next yard and sink down to my bellybutton. At this stage, there's no point in delaying the inevitable. I drop down under the water and work to control my breathing after that first icy stab of a breath.

Liáng follows my lead, and we both put on our flippers over the dry scuba suit boots. By the time we're swimming toward the next brick fence line, the cold is already starting to fade as the internal heater does its job.

The water just barely comes up over the next brick fence. We set the equipment bag and stunners on top of it and gently roll over the edge. On the other side, we finally submerge for good.

It can be difficult to modulate the buoyancy in the dry scuba suits as air is trapped in the suit, but it gets easier the deeper you get. We're down about eight to ten feet in the bricked-off row-house yard.

"We're under," I tell Puo. I use the retina displays to turn on my heads-up displays. Digital readouts spread out on the blue-pixelated surfaces around me. The bright moon is providing just enough additional light for the nightvision to pick out some good detail.

"Roger, that," Puo says. "Squiddie still hanging out on the other side of the stadium. Careful of any squatters."

"Duh," I say to Puo. "Liáng, follow me."

I gently kick over to the paved, submerged street, outlined in blue pixels. We go slowly. Very slowly. Careful at every yard opening to look around the corner and make sure there isn't a nasty surprise waiting for us.

"Puo," I whisper getting frustrated at our slow progress, "We need a quiet runner. A silent scout. Something we can send in to map out the way."

"Hunh," is Puo's response. "The quiet bit is the hard part. That and the communication link back to us could be traced if it's captured."

Liáng breaks in, "What about a dead man's switch?"

Fuck yeah, Liáng. A dead man's switch is a device that if it doesn't receive our regular signal in the event that it's captured, it automatically self-destructs.

"Damn, Liáng," I say. "You keep it up, we're just going to have to hire you."

"You couldn't afford me," he says dismissively.

"Gah!" I snap. "What is with you? You're worse than Dr. Jekyll and Mr. Hyde. Pick a freaking mood and stick with it—"

"Isa—" Puo says.

I continue: "—This bouncing between being helpful and an arrogant ass is annoying—"

"Isa!" Puo cuts me off. "Not now. You have a candidate location? It looks like a squiddie may be heading toward you."

Grrr. "Negative on the location. Depth is forty feet, continuing to get deeper. As for you Liáng, pick a damn mood and stick with it. Got it?"

Liáng is silent for a few seconds before saying in a perfectly normal voice, "As you wish."

I want to whirl around and strangle him, but resist the urge.

The street is transitioning from one of row houses to a row of brick businesses with broken windows and crusted over signs. I head over to a narrow, brick alley on the right.

The alley has some fire scaffolding on the upper floors, a dumpster, some side entrances. I test one of the doors—it's unlocked. "Found a good spot," I say to Puo and Liáng.

"Liáng," I say, "hide in the dumpster. I'll hide in the side entrance there. We'll put the pinger between us. I'll draw its attention when it descends on the pinger, you stun it from behind."

"Understood," Liáng says. He situates himself inside the dumpster and then reaches into the equipment bag to hand me one of two stunners on a four-foot pole.

"Puo," I ask, "how we doing?"

"Squiddie's still on the other side of stadium," Puo says.

"That squiddie was never heading over here was it?" I ask. "You were just trying to get me to shut up."

"I don't know what you're talking about," Puo says innocently. "It looked like it to me."

Liar.

Liáng hands me the large, soup-can-sized cylindrical pinger.

I swim toward the unlocked side door and set the pinger down outside the door. "About to go active," I say to Puo. "Keep an eye on all squiddies in the area."

"Roger that," Puo says. "Standing by for you to go active."

I flip the switch and set it down.

The pinger isn't technically a pinger. It's an active source that's designed to mimic the kinds of sounds that interest a squiddie without necessarily reporting in. Sounds like rubble settling, or objects hitting the surface.

The pinger alternates making its noises as I get in position on the other side of the unlocked door.

The plan is simple. Lure the squiddie down here, zap it with the stunners, drag it to shore. Not all plans need to be eloquent to be effective.

Puo says nearly immediately, "Looks like the squiddie picked it up. It's headed in your direction."

"For real this time?" I ask.

"Oh, yeah," Puo says in his dry, nervous voice. "ETA in ... two minutes, sixteen seconds."

"Liáng," I ask, "get ready."

"I'm ready," Liáng says.

I check to make sure my stunner is on. It looks like an oversized bottle rocket, a thick cylindrical package attached to a long, thin tube. Except the long, thin tube is made out of rigid aluminum and the thick cylindrical package is a Puo invention that looks like a cattle prod but emits a scrambling, localized magnetic field where it connects, not an electrical shock—since I don't fancy being electrocuted when I use it.

The waves crashing fifty feet overhead travel down, a kind of soft lullaby in the dark, blue-pixelated alleyway. Coldness seeps in around my neck, where the suit is thinnest. The rest of my body is comfortably warm. The suit smells of rubber and seawater.

"Squiddie is in your vicinity," Puo whispers.

I can't see anything or hear anything beyond the active pinger.

My fingertips tingle in anticipation. *Or is that sweat sliding down them?*

Still no sight of it.

"It's right on top of you," Puo whispers.

A red arrow flashes in front of me to point upward. "Squiddie going active," I whisper. "No visual."

My heart thuds in my chest.

Puo whispers, "It's hanging out above the alleyway. It's not descending."

Damn. The pinger is still making noise, but it's not drawing the squiddie in. How long before the squiddie recognizes the sounds aren't natural? Or will it just dismiss the sounds as nothing and move off?

We need that squiddie.

"Liáng," I say, "time to do something stupid."

To Puo I say, "Puo, watch for activity with the other squiddies."

"Why?" Puo rushes. "What are you—?"

I push myself out into the alleyway and turn over on my back. "Hey squiddie, squiddie, squiddie! Abracadabra, you metal bastard!" Yelling of course does nothing, but it's the spirit of the thing that counts.

The squiddie is covered in blue pixels directly above the roofline over the pinger. Its many appendages extending out of its teardrop-shaped center swish around toward me.

I kick my fins in the direction of the dumpster where Liáng is hiding.

"It sent an alert—!" Puo yells

The squiddie barrels down the alleyway toward me.

Screaming, I alter my panicked trajectory away from the dumpster so the squiddie will have its back to the dumpster.

Centipede-segmented like appendages lash out toward me.

I shove the stunner with two hands at the wiggling mass descending on me.

It connects at the armpit of one of the appendages.

The appendage goes limp. The squiddie rolls away from it.

Another appendage shoots down blindingly fast and grabs my left calf.

"OWW!" It feels like someone took a bat to my calf and is now shoving it downward.

"Isa—!" Puo screams.

It reverses direction and jerks me upward by the leg.

"Fuck! It's got me by the leg!"

I try to use the stunner again, but the squiddie's gotten wise. It swats the stunner away with a forceful smack that reverberates in my hands.

It's got me. It's pulling me upward—

Oh, God. I can feel cold water seeping onto my throbbing leg. It punctured my suit.

Suddenly the squiddie's grip on me goes lax, and I snatch my leg back.

Liáng's stunner is smack on the spherical part of the teardrop-shaped center of the squiddie.

The squiddie stops its terrifying motions and reverses course, falling toward the bottom. And I happen to be under it.

I quickly kick to get myself out of the way. Cold water leaks in through the tear in my suit, searing my open leg wound.

"Squiddie is down," Liáng tries to say calmly, but you can tell his heart is pumping.

"I'm free," I say.

Puo's response is a relieved exhale followed by a rushed, "You need to get the heck out of there. Every squiddie in a two-mile radius is zooming your way. The authorities have been alerted."

"Roger, that," I say. "Liáng, the DPVs."

Liáng sprints over to the dumpster.

"Puo," I say, "I don't want to alarm you, but—"

"What now—?" Puo asks worried.

"My suit has been punctured in the leg. Water is leaking in."

"Can you breathe okay?" Puo asks.

"Yeah," I say. "It was just on my leg." The breathing system is airtight to my helmet.

"Soooo ... what?" Puo asks, all his concern gone. "You're just cold?"

Liáng retrieves the equipment bag and two DPVs—the hand-held propeller devices that look like a thick pair of motorcycle handlebars but with enclosed propellers. The squiddie is too large for either one of us to carry alone, but strung between the two DPVs we can drag it to Wembley Island.

"Yeah, Puo!" I say. "Hypothermia!" *Yeesh. You'd think there'd be a little concern there.* "*And* it throbs where the squiddie grabbed me."

I work with Liáng to string the lifeless squiddie between us in a fish net.

"Roger, that," Puo says. "I'll get some band-aids and have Liáng kiss your boo-boo when you get back—"

"Puo—!" I start.

But Puo cuts me off. "You need to get the heck out of there. They're almost there."

Liáng and I start up the DPVs and hang on. The DPVs strain against the squiddie, but we increase our buoyancy and lift up with our muscles. Once the squiddie is off the bottom of the alleyway, we start to move forward, picking up speed.

We glide back up the street, adjusting our buoyancy as we go to keep the squiddie from slamming into the paved street. Once we're near the surface we turn into one of the row houses with the brick fence sticking up out of the water.

"The first one is at the alleyway," Puo says.

I stand up in the yard and jog up the steps of the two-story row house. I push open the front door. There's about a foot and a half of standing, frigid water in the house. Just deep enough to leak into my suit.

Liáng and I work as quietly as we can to pull the squiddie into the house.

"We're in," I say to Puo.

"Roger that," Puo says. "Get the squiddie upstairs and sit tight. I'll see you in the morning. Behave yourselves," he adds.

I grind my teeth at Puo. That last line is a bit too reminiscent of our jobs with Winn. Puo is going to have to get disabused, vehemently and quickly, of the notion of doing that again.

Chapter Eight

THE NEXT DAY, around noon, I'm toweling off after a long, luxurious hot shower in the steam-filled upstairs master bathroom at the house in Hampstead. By the time Puo got to us in the morning on Wembley Island, I was shivering near constantly.

Freaking Puo. Not worried at all about me and hypothermia.

Wembley Island was crawling with authorities within hours. They used the island as a base to conduct their investigation under the water. Searching the island was secondary—they were doing it, but weren't dedicating enough manpower to it to do it fast enough.

There were so many vehicles coming in and out of Wembley Island at that point, I think Puo may have been able to just drop down and pick us up without any subterfuge. As it was, he acted as a food delivery truck ordered by some unknown cop and brought them hot coffee and breakfast sandwiches—*isn't that nice of us?*

But the bastard didn't even freaking save me some hot coffee! *Freaking Puo!*

I blow-dry my hair, enjoying at first the fresh blasts of hot air. It soon starts to get a little warm in the small space—don't let the term "master" in *master bathroom* fool you. It's a closet with a stand-alone shower, a toilet and a single-sink vanity shoved in it with taupe walls. But after the night I just had, I force myself to enjoy the growing heat, a mini-sauna. I slip into olive-green cargo pants and a long-sleeve black sweater and step out of the bathroom into the master bedroom.

Puo is waiting for me, sitting on my bed, facing the bathroom. *Great.*

"You got lucky," Puo greets me with. His face is serious.

"I get lucky a lot," I say defensively from the bathroom door. There's nowhere to go in the sparse, but similarly painted taupe bedroom.

"What the heck was that?" Puo asks not letting up.

"What?"

"That leap-out-in-front-of-a-squiddie suicidal stupidity. Are you suicidal?" He asks that last question seriously.

"No!" I answer, getting annoyed. "The squiddie wasn't coming down. I had to do something. What would you have suggested?"

"How about trying another time? How about waving the stunner around past the door to get its attention?"

The stunner idea makes my mouth drop. I stare at him for a brief second. "Well, you didn't suggest those things!"

"You didn't give me a chance! You didn't give anyone a chance! You just leapt out there like a selfish idiot."

"Selfish?" I yell at him.

"Yes, Isa! Selfish! What would happen to us if you got arrested, or killed?" Puo's chest is rising and falling, causing the bare metal bed frame to *creak* in rhythm. Red blooms on his cheeks.

I can't think of anything to respond to him with when he's all worked up like this. And the *creaking* of the bed frame suddenly reminds me strongly of my bedroom back in the Seattle Isles. It too was sparse when Winn shared it with me. No bed frame. No furniture. Cheap plastic stacking drawers—kinda like the ones that double as nightstands on one side of the bed Puo's sitting on.

"Look—" he says more calmly, pulling me back into the present.

"Ugh. You're not going to tell me a story are you?" Puo likes to tell stories with morals, or at least what he thinks are morals, to them.

"No!" He looks annoyed, but plows on, "You've been ... different ever since Winn left—"

"Damn it! Not this again."

"Yes, this again! You refuse to even acknowledge anything has changed." He pauses here for me to retort, but I don't give him the satisfaction. "It's like whenever something reminds you of him, you get reckless. Whenever you're in the anti-gravity suits—"

No. Those are just plain fun.

"—And last night when Liáng mentioned *Huángdì de wàikē yīshēng*. You then suddenly decide to jump out at a squiddie."

Puo's mention of Liáng reminds me of his dumbass line about Liáng kissing my boo-boo, but I bite my tongue. Somehow I think unloading on him will play into Puo's whole corner-store psychology diagnosis. So instead I correct him, "I don't even know whatever that comic book thing is."

Puo stares at me. "*Huángdì de wàikē yīshēng* is a comic book about a *surgeon*. Sound like anyone we know?"

Winn was a surgeon that fell in with us after a malpractice suit left him with no alternative but crime. When I don't respond, not trusting myself to speak, he says, "You do this. You have this weird selective memory. Like you're trying to erase all memories of Winn."

I use the opportunity to pick up my wet dirty clothes from the night before off the floor, pointedly ignoring him.

Puo watches me for several seconds and then says, "Not going to talk to me, hunh?"

"Yup," I say. "It's a new strategy. Analyze that." *Asshat.*

"I kinda like it," Puo says. "I can finally get a word in edgewise and explain in far more detail what is going on with you—"

"Oh, shut up." I get a towel from the bathroom to wipe up the puddle of water that had formed around my crumpled clothes on the floor. "What have you learned from the squiddie?"

"That you and Liáng successfully scrambled its electronics. It was dead-on-arrival. I can't do anything with it."

I stop my cleaning. "Whadda ya mean?" *My leg still stings, damn it.*

Puo explains, "Where Liáng struck the squiddie was right over the SFID chip. That chip is one of several that acts a lynch pin. Once scrambled, there's no putting humpty-dumpty back together again."

"Can you order a new one?" I ask.

Puo leans back a bit and smiles at me.

"What?"

"Nuthin'," he says with a little smile.

"What!"

"Look at you," he says. "Ordering something, instead of planning some elaborate job or game. I think Winn rubbed off on you."

"Puo—" I start, my heart lurching in my throat. "Can you just ... let it go? I just don't want to hear about him right now."

Puo screws up his mouth and looks like he's moving his tongue around inside his mouth. "All right," he finally says. "Yes, we can order another chip, but it's not straightforward—"

My first thought is that Liáng should be here to hear this if we need to buy something. My second thought is what Puo would make of me asking for Liáng to be here.

Puo switches topics seamlessly, apparently reading my mind. "—I already talked to Liáng. He's on board." He gives me a small knowing smile for anticipating me and switches back to his explanation. "The company that makes the chips will only sell them to government agencies, so I have to spoof an order, which is actually a lot easier with the squiddie in hand."

"So you put the order in?" I ask, suspecting I already know the answer.

"Yup," Puo says.

"Good," I say, feeling suddenly drained. "Anything else?" I ask, dismissing him. "I'm going to lie down for a bit."

"No," Puo says quietly. The box springs *creak* as he gets up from the bed. He makes to say something else, but shuts his mouth and rubs at his face as he leaves.

"Wait," I say, "When does the acoustic dampening material get here?"

Puo says, "This afternoon."

"Okay." I pull back the sand-colored cotton bed sheets. I don't normally nap, but it just seems like less effort right now than going downstairs and dealing with Puo and his constant reminders of Winn.

The bedroom door clicks shut as I lie down, the sound echoing in the empty room.

Chapter Nine

I WALK DOWNSTAIRS groggy and bleary-eyed six hours later. It's now dark out and early evening. I think I could've slept longer, but I became paranoid about screwing up my sleep schedule.

I hear slow classical music as I head down the cold bare wooden steps. But the music has a distinctly Asian feel to it. There's a mournful erhu woven throughout along with something else I can't place.

The stairs empty out on the first floor foyer; the family room is to my left and empty, while the sitting room (with no furniture) is to my right and contains the source of the music.

Liáng is streaming music from his pocket tablet that he set on the fireplace mantel. He also built a small wood fire in the yellowish brick fireplace. Red flames lick the dark-purple bark of the logs. Small cackles fill the gaps in the classical music.

Liáng momentarily has his back to me and is moving throughout the room, pretending to dance with a nonexistent partner. His back is straight, and he holds his hands high; his left hand would be on the back of his partner's shoulder and his right hand is held out. It takes a second in the fog of my nap, but I recognize a waltz. He stops when he sees me.

"It's pretty," I say. I can't help a small yawn escaping. "What is it?" I step into the room and make a beeline for the fire. It's chilly in the house. I'm still in my cargo pants and sweater but the cold seems to seep into everything in October in England.

"It's the Chinese Waltz," Liáng says. After a second's consideration, he asks, "Would you like to dance? To help me practice," he adds when he sees my questioning look.

The throbbing on my leg has subsided to a dull ache that reminds me it's there every time I take a step with it. "Sure." *Why not?*

"Have you waltzed before?" Liáng asks.

"It's been awhile."

I step into the middle of the room, and Liáng comes to stand about half a pace away in front of me. I hold out my left hand and rest my right hand on his muscled back. *Whoa*—he's got to have like zero body fat. He directs my right hand higher up on his shoulder, and I feel suddenly like I was in junior high trying to cop a feel or something—*oh yeah, baby, nice middle back.*

Liáng is wearing heavy tan corduroy pants with a forest-green waffle sweater—I'm sure we look like a jumbled mass of colors, but Liáng's sweater is soft, and I like the waffle texture.

Liáng takes me through the steps. Right foot back. Left foot back and to the left. Bring right foot together with the left. Left foot forward. Right foot forward and to the right. Bring feet together again.

Pretty basic dance. The key is timing your movements to your partner. When I step back, Liáng steps forward in the space where my leg used to be. It takes us a few laps, both of us staring at our feet, but soon we're in rhythm. It helps that we're almost the same height.

"So why waltzing?" I ask.

Liáng looks up and grimaces at first.

The grimace makes me self conscious about my breath after napping for six hours and not brushing my teeth before I came down.

Liáng eventually answers, "They say, never trust a religious man that won't or can't dance."

"And you're a religious man wishing to give advice?"

"One thing I've learned is that we're all not what we appear."

Ugh. I break eye contact and don't try to hide my eye roll.

"You don't like that answer?"

"I'm not in the mood for mysteries," I say. Or for potentially brooding men. *I've had my fill of those, thanks.*

"Hmm," Liáng says. "You'd think mysteries are at the heart of your chosen profession."

I don't know how much choosing of my profession I had. Puo and I are legacies. We were born directly into a crew without citizen chips. The only choice we had was deciding what kind of criminals to be. It was only recently that we were able to purchase modified citizen chips that allowed us some normal freedom of movement with hacked CitIDs.

"If we're doing our job correctly, there should be no mysteries," I say. "Where's Puo?"

"Downstairs putting up the acoustic tiling. He asked to be left alone."

We dance in silence for a few steps.

"Keep your eyes up," I say.

Liáng keeps alternating between looking at me and looking down at our feet.

"If I didn't know any better," I say, "and was wearing a sexy dress, I'd think you were constantly staring at my breasts."

Which, of course, is directly where his gaze lands for a half-second before he looks up at me with a slight blush.

"Sorry," he says. "Are you and Puo ... ?"

"No," I say. "We're like brother and sister." But closer than most brothers and sisters. A shared life of crime will do that.

"Ah, I see," Liáng says. "That makes sense. So, then, you're having a sibling squabble?"

I stiffen in the dance, but then force myself to relax. Well, Liáng is living with us. He could hardly not notice us not talking to each other and yelling at each other behind closed doors. "Yeah," I say.

"What about?" Liáng asks, surreptitiously trying to watch me.

Puo's voice breaks in from the foyer, "None of your business."

We break off the dance, and step back awkwardly from each other like junior high kids, again, whose father had just walked in the room.

Liáng looks between us and says diplomatically, "It's my business to make sure our investment isn't poorly placed. You two clearly have a disagreement. It was clear the moment I arrived there was a tension between you. I need to know if that disagreement is going to affect our bottom line."

"No," both Puo and I answer at the same time.

Liáng looks like he's about to say more, but I cut him off, asking Puo, "How's the tiling coming?"

"I could use some help," Puo answers. "With all three of us, we might be done by morning."

Liáng turns off the music and slides his tablet in his pocket.

"What about dinner?" I ask as we walk out of the bare living room toward the kitchen at the back of the house and the stairs leading down to the basement.

"Pizza," Puo suggests.

Italian again? "What about Chinese food?" I blurt out. "Oh, wait," I say, blushing at Liáng. "Is that okay?"

Liáng looks at me in confusion. "Why wouldn't that be okay? Because I'm Chinese? I can't eat Chinese food?"

"Jeez, Isa." Puo shakes his head at me.

"What?" I say getting frustrated. "I don't know what you want to eat!" I swear the more you try to be sensitive, the more you put your foot in your mouth.

"C'mon," Puo says to Liáng.

Liáng walks ahead with Puo, each of them shaking his head at me.

How did I get to be the one on the outside? "Fine," I say. "I'm going to order Chinese food then."

Their self-righteous non-response confirms that I will be ordering one tasty dish for me, and two dishes that I think are absolutely disgusting with all the pepper flakes the restaurant owns for the two self-righteous asshats.

Chapter Ten

TWO WEEKS LATER, we're finally ready to send the stolen and refurbished squiddie into the British Museum for reconnaissance. The acoustic tiling went in fast enough, but punching a hole through the concrete floor down to the flooded underground tube beneath us took more time than we thought.

We had to drill slow and set the core drill to a slow rate of turn to try to mitigate the noise that traveled down through the concrete and earth and possibly into the flooded tube. But even with the slow rate of turn, that core drill made a lot of noise.

As soon as we punctured down through to the tube, water flooded upward to turn the hole into a muddy, goopy mess— which then caused our paranoia about being detected from below to peak, which in turn led to a brief detour while Puo sent out sensors small enough to fit through the initial hole to try and figure out what's down there. Then, after all that, we had to give Puo an extra couple of days to practice driving the rogue squiddie around down in the underwater tunnel once we determined it was safe.

Of course, it didn't help that after my stunt with ordering terrible Chinese food for Puo and Liáng, both Puo and Liáng separately returned the favor. Now, no one can be trusted to get food alone anymore. We all have to stop working and go together.

But we're *finally* ready—it's been a dull two weeks.

All three of us are in the basement after dinner. Puo is sitting at a foldout table he set up near the hole with his custom, retro-looking computers that he dragged down from upstairs on it. It's the monitors that give them the retro feel: four wide touchscreen physical monitors stacked two by two. Puo eschews the more modern float screens. He says he likes to be able to slam his finger against something solid when things get hairy and he needs to act quickly.

There's a distinct chill to the room. The water in the hole is dark and quiet, not a ripple on the surface. All the dirt we dug up is in the corner farthest from the stairs, giving the room a cold earth smell—like a graveyard at night.

Liáng and I are standing behind Puo watching the stacked widescreen monitors. It's all gobbledygook to me—a bunch of open screens with a black background and color coded text. I'm decent at programming, but I'm no super user—that's why I have Puo.

The rogue squiddie is unceremoniously lying on its side on the other side of the hole, appendages splayed out like a drunk frat boy in the street. It has hand-sized circular lenses, regularly spaced around the main sphere, that dully reflect the basement around us. There's no light behind the lenses, just dark voids that I swear are staring at me.

Dark voids just waiting for Puo's code to get overwritten. Gaping. Dark. Voids. Staring at me—

Puo snaps his fingers at me.

"What?" I ask, abruptly realizing both Puo and Liáng are staring at me.

"We're ready," Puo says. "What were you daydreaming of?"

"Never mind," I say. "Okay, go ahead."

Liáng walks over to the squiddie to lower it. Both Puo and I watch him.

"Uh ..." Liáng says and stares at us.

"Isa—" Puo says at the same time I say, "Well, go ahead," and gesture for Puo to go help Liáng.

"I'm doing all of this." Puo motions over the computers with two hands.

"And lowering the squiddie takes away from—" I mimic his motions. "—all that? You're stronger than me. Go help Liáng."

Puo starts to argue then stops himself. "Yeah, all right." He gets up and helps Liáng lower the squiddie into the water.

Not sure what that was about. The last two weeks has been like that. Puo switching between moments of things being normal between us, and then being uncharacteristically easy, as if he were walking on eggshells or cutting off his remarks like he thought better of it. He hadn't brought up Winn again at all, or said any dumbass things about me and Liáng—of which there is nothing more going on than two attractive people living and working together in close proximity.

I'm tempted to ask him what's going on, but I suspect I don't have the heart for that conversation at the moment.

The squiddie sinks down into the water, lowered in a net between Liáng and Puo. Small ripples push outward and lap up against the rough concrete edge. Once they remove the net, it sinks down to float just below the surface, barely visible in the muddy water.

Puo slides back in his chair at the computers. "Okay," he says, drawing the word out as he types on the keyboard. "Here we go." He hits a button with a flourish.

Nothing changes that I can see. The squiddie is still floating near the surface. Nothing but gobbledygook code is on the screens in front of me.

I wait a few seconds, still nothing. "I'm not sure you understand that phrase, Puo," I say.

Puo blushes and starts banging around on his keyboard more.

"Did you remember to plug it in?" Liáng asks dryly.

Heh.

I'm about to add another helpful comment when Puo slaps himself in the forehead. "Damn it!"

"What?" I ask.

"I, uh, forgot to 'plug it in.' "

"What?" I can't help but laugh at him.

"The infra-sensor needs to be in the water to communicate with it." Puo gets up and goes around to the other side of the table. He fiddles with a PVC pipe that has what look like wires and a pressure vessel shoved in the end and puts it into the hole.

The squiddie responds to the sensor in the water by sinking out of sight.

"Uh—" Puo is stuck there holding the PVC pipe. "Liáng, come hold this."

Liáng does as asked. "Glad you could find something for me to do."

As Puo sits down back at the computers, I say, "Nice planning."

"Shush," Puo responds. "I'm working."

"What'd you do while you were practicing with the squiddie?" I ask about the infra-sensor.

Puo glances at me out of the corner of his eyes. "I just tossed the infra-sensor on the wire in the water—it floats. It needs to be deeper when the squiddie ranges out farther. Which is why I put it on the PVC." Puo continues to work on his computers. "Is that okay with you?"

"Yes," I answer guardedly. *What's with him?* I watch him for a bit, growing bored. "Nothing is happening," I say to be helpful.

Puo answers without looking up, "I'm going through the checkout process to make sure everything is up and running properly."

Well, that's exciting. "I think there's some c-clamps upstairs," I say to Liáng while Puo continues his anticlimactic checkout process. I head for the stairs to go grab the clamps.

"Grab some wood and some screws as well," Liáng says.

I fetch the required materials and have a makeshift stand built shortly.

"How we doin', Puo?" I ask when Liáng and I are done.

"Almost ready," he says. He continues banging away on the keyboard and then suddenly snaps at me, "*Hey—!*"

"What?" I ask annoyed at him.

"You sighed," Liáng answers for Puo.

"I did?"

"Yes," Puo says. "Look, the squiddie emits a coded signal that identifies it to other squiddies. It's what makes the other squiddies and any other defenses know it's one of them. It has to be *perfect*, or we're screwed—"

The screen on the left blips into a detailed blue pixelated surface of the tube.

"All right," Puo says, "we're ready."

"Wait," I say. "What do you mean screwed?" There was something about the way he said it.

"If the squiddies," Puo explains, "think this is a fake, they'll capture it and drag it to the authorities, who will then trace the chip we ordered to our delivery point. They already know a squiddie went missing. They'll be on alert."

"We have an identification gap," I say about tracing the chip.

We spoofed the order so the authorities shouldn't even know about the new SFID. And even if they do eventually learn of it, we opened a post office box in another resident's name without their knowledge. The authorities will track down one Jay Chadwick Brewer, and if they pull the video data from the post office all they'll see is a scrambled mess from our digi-scrambler we wear whenever we go there.

"Yes," Puo says. "But how long do you think before they pull the data stored on the squiddie and figure out where it entered the underground tunnel."

Whoa. I don't show my discomfort, but I'm rapidly thinking of a quick exit plan.

"Suddenly," Puo says, "I didn't take long enough to do the checkout, did I?"

Freaking Puo. "Finishing prematurely is your own problem," I say.

The tube is very detailed in the blue pixels. Way more detailed than I would expect. "Is that active?" I ask.

Active sonar. Almost as good as light underwater. It works by bouncing sound waves off of stuff to get a picture. The problem is anything that's between the max distance you can "see" and twice that max distance can detect you without you detecting them. Which is why we don't use it.

"Yup," Puo says. "We're one of them now. Nice, right?"

Indeed.

The tube is empty, a cylindrical path with a railway running along the bottom. It curves to the left a bit and comes up to an underground station.

The cylindrical walls expand out. An empty platform extends down the length of the station on the right. It's all outlined in the same blue pixels. Nothing out of the ordinary. Regular gaps in the wall lead off the platform to stairs that head up.

"There," Puo says. He taps on the keyboard and brings up a separate window.

It's a screen capture looking into one of the gaps the squiddie had already passed. It's a full-sized squatter; it looks a few inches taller than my waist and resembles a vertical pill.

"What'd you call that?" Liáng asks.

"Success," Puo says.

The squatter didn't react to the squiddie—we're good.

Our rogue squiddie ducks into the tube tunnel leading out of the station.

"A full-sized squatter," I tell Liáng.

Liáng bobs his head in small motions and sticks out his lower lip. Eventually he lets slip, "Hunh."

"What?" I ask.

The squiddie scoots up near the ceiling of the tunnel to pass over a railcar frozen in time. Fortunately, the sonar can't penetrate into the closed windows to see if there is anything on the train—actually, that's pretty interesting. Squiddies can't see past windows.

I tap Puo on the shoulder to make sure he saw it too.

"Yeah," Puo says, "I got it."

Liáng answers my earlier question, "I figured you'd have a more inventive name."

"Like what?" I ask.

"Well—" Liáng crosses his arms in front of him. "—Suppository seems the most likely direction you two would go—"

"Hey—!" Puo says.

I bark a laugh. *That's great.* "How'd we miss that, Puo?" When Puo doesn't respond, I say, "Okay, suppository it is."

Puo says defensively, "Doesn't have quite the right kind of ring to it."

"Plopper?" Liáng suggests in a perfectly dry voice.

Puo turns around looking disgusted.

I can't help myself from snorting laughter. I have to hold my hand over my mouth to try and get a hold of myself—*plopper*. Man, I haven't felt this great in a while.

"You know," Puo says to Liáng, "for someone who accuses of us being teenagers with junior-high maturity levels, you're spending a lot of time down here in the muck with us."

Liáng *mmm's*, and continues to stand there with his muscled arms crossed.

The squiddie passes into another tube station. There's a plopper at every entranceway off the platform we pass. Again the ploppers don't react. The mood in the basement is turning more and more positive. Even Puo's barks have a little less bite to them.

The squiddie silently passes through four more tube stations in the next fifteen minutes and finally enters the last station, Tottenham Court Station. Puo instructs the squiddie to turn on its flashlights so we can read the sign.

Bright, white light lances out ahead to form two broadening beams. The orange circular with blue rectangular text box in the center confirms it's Tottenham Court Road Station.

There's little growth down there. The little thumb-sized tiles that the wall is made of are mostly clean. There's only a little crud starting to grow in between the cracks. A layer of silt is on the platform, but it's thin, and we can still tell where individual floor tiles are.

The squiddie approaches the plopper, squatting guard at the base of the steps that lead up and out. All three of us hold our breath.

The rogue squiddie squeaks by above it, and continues on its merry way up the stairs.

"Score!" Puo says. "We are definitely using this trick again in the future."

The throbbing on my left leg has long since subsided in the past two weeks, but I think I'm going to have a scar there now. "You can be the one to nab the squiddie in the future," I tell him.

"Bah," Puo says, "We can think of something."

Glad to see him so confident in our abilities.

The squiddie continues its journey up through the various levels of the underground station. The connection is getting weaker as it travels up. There's more ploppers strategically placed to cover different entrances, but all of them continue to leave our rogue squiddie alone.

Eventually, our squiddie emerges onto the street and we lose contact briefly until the squiddie releases a relay that floats up to the surface. The sounds of waves breaking overhead announce the link has been reestablished, and the active sonar has already painted the street's four- and five-story buildings in wonderful blue-pixel detail. The distinct shapes of London land-cabs line up across the street, and other various types of hover- and land-cars and even a double-decker bus are on the street. Bikes are locked to metal fence posts; cafes sit empty with tables and chairs knocked over. Most of the windows are broken. The street is stock-still, unmoving under a hundred feet of seawater that was never meant to be there.

The mega-quake hit so fast that by the time people realized the waters were steadily rising, there was nothing to do but get your ass to high ground. It was the single greatest disaster in human history. And many that did survive had to leave everything behind. Some experts still think, eighty-six years later, that we haven't fully recovered yet.

I shake off the mood. Seeing the leftover ghosts of a sunken city always gets me contemplative.

The British Museum is a thousand feet northeast of the underground station, which the squiddie covers in two to three minutes.

There's a lot more noticeable activity around the museum. We can see at least one other squiddie swimming along the back of the museum. There are several ploppers scattered around the property and on the building itself that we can see.

"Whoa," Puo says.

Yeah, is all I can think. *Come in from below somehow?*

Puo says, "They're going to have seismic sensors."

I grunt. "Wait," I say, "was that out loud or did you just know me that well."

"Both," Puo says.

I look at Liáng.

He mouths *out loud* at me.

Our rogue squiddie heads down in the water column toward the museum's southern entrance.

Now this is the kind of architecture I love and expect to see when I come to Europe. Not that postmodernist rat's nest crap library in Birmingham.

Even in the blue pixelated view provided by the squiddie, I think it's gorgeous. The original building was built in the Greek revivalist style as a quadrangle, four separate rectangular buildings with an open courtyard in the center. The entrance has eight soaring stone columns in two rows each that form an impressive portico, while the stone columns continue to wrap around the front of the building.

I do wish, though, I could've seen the pediment—the triangular upper part of the front of the building—for myself, not in blue pixels. It reportedly held some gorgeous stonework, but those fine details are lost in blue pixels. I can tell the statues are there, but not the detail. I can't see their fingers, what they're pointing at, what they're holding. I can't see the stone come to life in their eyes.

Our squiddie glides down the center of the portico. A plopper sits in front of the closed doors to the museum.

"Look at that," Puo says. He points to two balls attached to the walls on either side of the door.

"What—?" Liáng asks.

"Squiddies," I answer.

Two squiddies are attached there, ready to deploy and grab anything the plopper spots. Squiddies aren't exactly cheap enough to just be sitting around completely ineffective.

This security isn't messing around.

The window to the upper right of the doors is broken. "Through there," I say.

"Yeah," Puo says in the distracted voice he uses when he's thinking about something else. He brings up another window on a different computer screen and starts fiddling with it.

The squiddie pivots in its course toward the broken window.

Puo is staring at the screen in concentration.

"Puo," I say, "What's going on? We're about to enter the museum." I need him focused on the task at hand.

"I'm—" Puo says. "I'm not sure. There's a signal coming from the plopper— Is that really what we're calling it now?"

"Definitely," I say. "What's the signal mean?"

The squiddie pushes it's way through into the entranceway of the museum—*dang. Now that's an entrance.*

Square columns rise up twenty, maybe thirty feet up to coffered ceilings to separate the entrance into two parts. The doorways off the entrance are maybe twelve to fifteen feet high, nearly as wide and framed in decorative stonework (at least I suspect it's stone, hard to tell in monotone blue pixel). A gorgeous wide staircase splits and doubles back on itself up to the second level. Empty stands for statues are symmetrically placed—empty except for the center stand on the staircase landing, which holds another plopper.

"I don't know," Puo answers my question about the signal from the plopper. "The signal is outside of our normal usable band in the helmets. It's like they're trying to hide it. We wouldn't have seen it if we weren't using the squiddie. That one has it too." Puo indicates the plopper on the staircase landing.

The rogue squiddie moves through the tall doors leading into the Great Court—the courtyard created by the four original Greek-revivalist buildings and circular reading room in the center that was closed in by the crisscrossing metal and glass ceiling (which now has several broken gaps). There are more empty stands where sculptures should go.

For years, the authorities regularly returned to the museum to loot (sorry, recover—maritime rules of salvage need not apply) so that most of what was on display is long-since gone.

There are more ploppers scattered throughout the Great Court, including one right in front of the entrance to the east building where we're headed. Our rogue squiddie manages to scoot over the plopper and into the east building through the door which is large, but comparatively much smaller than the doors in the southern entrance.

The rogue squiddie is now in the King's Library, known later as the Enlightenment Gallery. It's a long, open-spaced room split into three connected sections. The middle section the squiddie is in has smooth—presumably once-polished—stone columns all the way up to the ceiling along the back and front walls. The walls in all three sections are two stories high and split into two levels with the lower level marked by wall-to-wall wooden display cases from the floor up to the bottom of the balcony walkway that wraps around the halfway point of the room.

The large, once-impressive room is in a state of disarray. The display cases look ransacked, opened in a hurry with drawers left half-open, some pulled clean out of the display case and left lying on the floor. Display stands are empty. The glass in the display doors is broken in several places.

Puo says, "Looks like the ploppers are all transmitting the same signal."

"Dead man's switch?" I speculate. The technique has been on my mind since Liáng first suggested it.

"Maybe," Puo says. "But I think it's more than that. The signal is very high frequency, which doesn't travel far underwater— which means the signal doesn't have to travel far to accomplish its purpose. I think they're all networked together, as one huge, defense super-organism."

Great. None of the ploppers we encountered in the underground tunnels (or elsewhere) have had this networked signal.

Our rogue squiddie heads up to the balcony level where windows and display cases alternate along the wall, broken up by thick wall protrusions that jut out into the room where the room sections butt up against each other. The balcony walkway passes through these protrusions through matching wooden doors on each side.

"Wait," I say. "If they're all networked together, can they identify that we're not a part of their system?"

"Maybe," Puo say.

"That's not an inspiring answer," Liáng says.

"The squiddies on the wall," Puo explains, "weren't transmitting the signal. So ... I don't know."

Liáng and I share a look.

"We're approaching the stairwell," Puo says.

The squiddie swims up to one of the closed wooden doors on the balcony that leads into the wall protrusion. Inside the wall protrusion is a stairway that leads down to the much more interesting lower levels.

"Check the other doors," I say. There are four, two on each level.

All the doors are closed. This isn't the main way down; that's accessed through the North building and has a large elevator to move heavy sculptures up and down. But that way is likely to be heavily guarded, and we're searching for a more covert way in.

Puo stares at the screens while the squiddie just hovers there dumbly.

"Force it," I say.

"Right," Puo says. He continues to stare at the screens not typing.

"Do you know how—?" Liáng starts to ask.

"Yes! Just deciding how. I think I've seen the squiddies use their appendages to turn doorknobs. I'm just not sure—"

Liáng continues, "Can you just give it a command and let it sort it out?"

Puo's mouth falls open a crack. "Yes. But ..."

I smirk behind Puo's back. He really hates not being the smartest person in the room. "But what?"

"Never mind." Puo taps on his keyboard.

The result is immediate: the rogue squiddie bashes, claws, rips, and shreds the door down with four of its appendages with ferocious precision.

The sound is deafening in the silence of the museum.

"That's what!" Puo yells and then growls his frustration.

All that's left of the door are the pieces around the hinges and the doorknob.

Puo swivels the view of the squiddie back toward the plopper that sits at the entrance.

The piece containing the doorknob falls off the doorframe and floats down to a soft *clatter* on top of the rubble of the door.

Puo groans under his breath.

The plopper has raised up from its sentinel position and is looking in our direction. But what it hasn't done is set off the alarm.

"It's sent another signal," Puo says.

"Do you know—?" I start to ask.

"Nope," he says.

Liáng starts to say something but Puo cuts him off.

"We've had enough of your ideas!" Puo snaps.

"Three options," I say, "bolt home, bolt down the stairs or pretend nothing's wrong."

Seconds drip by in silence.

"Right," I say. *Pretend nothing's wrong.* With the greatest risk comes the greatest reward. "Puo, make it look like we're investigating the disturbance. Can you do that?"

Puo nods solemnly, and issues a command to the squiddie.

"For the record," Liáng says, "that was going to be my suggestion."

Puo *grrs* under his breath.

Another squiddie swims through the entrance and over the plopper.

The air in the basement goes still. All three of us aren't breathing, or blinking. Staring at the screen at the impending meeting. A cold sweat forms on my palms.

I ask Puo breathlessly, "Do you have the get-the-hell-outta-there routine installed?"

Puo responds by pointing at the screen where he has the command, **>> SaveQueenBeeButt(1190625,true)**, queued up only waiting for him to hit enter.

I punch him on the shoulder at the function name.

"Ow—!" he says and starts to say more.

"Shh!" I say.

Puo mumbles about them not being able to hear us, but shuts up all the same.

We all stare at the screen as the new squiddie swims up to ours.

Puo has a window open that mirrors the rogue squiddie's internal commands and dialogs. New commands are flowing down the screen. Puo's interjecting his own commands at times.

"They're talking," Puo translates quietly. "The official squiddie is querying ours for any data about what happened. I told it we got nothing."

"Tell it we're investigating the noise," I say.

Puo shakes his head no. "Can't. Don't know how. I only know the basics— It's querying our purpose."

Puo types more. "I told it we're on a standard patrol."

The cursor blinks at us in the window as we wait to see if that's an acceptable response.

Suddenly a stream of text flows down the screen rapidly.

"Crap!" Puo swears, and then starts typing frantically. "It's taking control of our squiddie."

"It can do that?" I ask in a panic.

"Apparently, yes!" Puo answers.

Puo continues his rapid typing.

Liáng stands there with his arms crossed in front of him, his dark eyes intense as he stares at the screen.

"Wait." I shoot my hand out to arrest Puo's typing. "Look," I say, and point to the other screen that shows the squiddie's point of view in blue pixels.

Our rogue squiddie is following the official squiddie through the broken door into the stairwell.

"Sweet," I say. "An all expenses paid tour."

"So long as we can go our separate ways at the end," Puo says. He looks grim, staring at the wall of text and scrolling back through it.

Both squiddies turn on their flashlights in the stairway—interesting. Apparently when the squiddies are investigating—

"Has it notified the authorities?" Liáng asks.

Puo nods his head and taps his nose. "The squiddies notify them any time there's a disturbance and the squiddies are investigating."

"Can they tell—?" I start to ask.

"That we're here?" Puo annoyingly finishes for me. "No. Our processes are masked from inside the kernel. They would have to get their physical hands on the squiddie—which brings a whole set of other previously discussed problems."

I exhale, annoyed with Puo for completing my sentences, but don't say anything more. At least that way he can't complete my sentences for me.

The screen starts to flicker. Puo answers before I can ask, "The signal's getting weaker. All we'll be able to stream is the video. The rest of the data will be recorded."

The staircase is bland compared to the King's Library the squiddies entered from—just a steep, circular stone staircase that leads down. No windows. No railings. No art. Just stone steps with some green signs with white stick figures running for the exit, and a thin layer of ocean crud settled on everything.

The squiddies descend rapidly to the ground level of the King's Library, stopping to inspect the two wooden doors that lead out and the green stick figure sign next to each door.

The doors apparently pass inspection and the official squiddie leads our rogue squiddie farther down the circular stairs. The walls abruptly shift from the smooth stone walls of the first and second levels to brick laid in the English style of alternating rows of long and short bricks.

The squiddies continue down into the bowels of the building. They pass one brick landing, pausing only briefly to look on an empty room beyond, peppered with brick columns, column-vaulted brick ceilings and deep shadows that look like they're cowering from the squiddie's flashlights, waiting to return to their rightful place once we pass.

The stairs bottom out at a long brick tunnel. The screen becomes pixelated, downsampled to try and maintain the stream. I can still tell that the tunnel is wide, maybe twenty feet across, and high—I'd guess twelve feet—with a rounded brick ceiling. At first, the tunnel strikes me as strange. Why such a big tunnel that dead-ends at such a small staircase? But the answer becomes apparent as the squiddies swim down the center of it.

There are several arched brick doorways leading off the hallway into hallways of their own. It's a maze down here, a crisscross of tunnels for moving, rearranging and storing various artifacts.

"You recording this?" I ask Puo to make sure—the screen continues to degrade. The squiddies take a couple of quick turns through identical looking hallways.

"Yeah," Puo answers. "Including the active sonar pings, which should let us piece together what's down some of those hallways."

Good.

"Look," Puo says. He pushes his fingertip against the screen, distorting the pixels around the spot, and pointing to a pixelated but discernible starfish-shaped sensor that all underwater reclamationists are familiar with: air-gap sensors.

Those pesky little devices detect the presence of air, either from scuba divers (which is one reason we use closed systems) or a belch from opening an air-filled vault door in this case.

I explain all this to Liáng, which he listens to stoically.

Puo and I continue to study the computer screens. There are no vaults yet. But the presence of the air-gap sensors indicates we're on the right track. Why else would they be concerned about the presence of air down here?

More turns. How many turns is hard to tell as now the screen freezes for seconds at a time before updating. Ploppers are starting to show up at junctions. Inactive squiddies attached to walls ready to be unleashed sit near some of the ploppers.

Yeah, I think we're getting close.

"Hello," I say. The rogue squiddie just passed the first vault door on the right.

There's no mistaking a vault door. The pixelated rectangular metal door and frame is set into the arched brick entryway. The metal is probably steel—but I'm no metallurgist—and the door is draped in beige ocean crud, pooling on top of the metal spin handle and lock. An air-gap sensor is attached to the brick ceiling directly over where the door opens. We also catch a black oval sign on the door that identifies this vault in white letters as Vault ASVT-4: the fourth vault of Vietnam. The first two letters denote the continent, the second two letters denote the country.

The squiddies continue their rounds. Swimming by more vaults, all with the black pixels above their doors that indicate air-gap sensors. We see more ploppers and inactive squiddies.

Oh, man.

"Please tell me," I say to Liáng, "that you know which vault we need."

Liáng says, "Vault ASCH-17."

Puo chimes in, "It looks like we're headed in the right direction, the numbers and letters are decreasing."

That and the security is going from paranoid to overkill.

The brick entryways off the hallway are getting larger, holding larger vault doors.

There. Vault ASCH-17. It's one of the larger ones and has a circular door containing what looks like a spin wheel in the center, but it's hard to tell in the pixelated surface. An air-gap sensor squats above it all (pretty sure that's what those black pixels are).

"Well?" I ask Puo. Safe cracking, vault doors, that's his gig.

Puo shakes his head back and forth several times, thinking. "Uh, no idea based on that image. But honestly, that's the least of our problems. Just getting to the door is a bigger issue."

I nod absent-mindedly. He's right. But now that we know what we're dealing with, some ideas are starting to form and being summarily rejected (you have to start somewhere).

The squiddies continue their patrol through the vaults and then eventually make their way to the main basement entrance/

exit in the North Building where the signal starts to improve. Large elevators mark the main entrance, along with more air-gap sensors, ploppers, and inactive squiddies.

"Yeesh," Puo says. He points to the elevator doors themselves.

There are contact sensors at the top and bottom where the doors meet. If those doors are opened, those sensors are going to trip, not to mention the plopper sitting directly in front of it.

Yeah, I don't think we want to come in that way.

The official squiddie leads our rogue squiddie through a stairwell, nearly as heavily guarded, near the main elevator. Once we emerge into the main level of the museum the official squiddie returns control back over to us with the instructions to go back to our regular patrol.

"Whew." Puo exhales. "Now what?" he asks me.

"Now we get to work," I say.

"Got any ideas?" Puo asks.

Some. Others are starting to form. We have knowledge now, and a working layout. I think we're in a good spot.

Chapter Eleven

W E'RE SCREWED.
Puo, Liáng, and I just spent several hours back at the house trying to solve the defenses at the British Museum. It always came back to those damned networked ploppers. There's no way to take out a node without alerting all of them.

So now I need a drink. Because that's what you do when you're screwed: you drink.

Generally I prefer beer, at a bar, or since we're in England, at a traditional pub. What I'm not as fond of is this place: a goth bar ... or club—or whatever the goths refer to this place as. I'm going with bar.

"Nice choice, Puo," I say.

"Thanks." Puo beams at himself.

The beaming is completely out of place at The Bridge Between, described as "England's most ethereal alternative night scene." The stone Gothic structure the bar sits in is at the southern entrance to Highgate Cemetery in Hampstead and rises up to form a bridge over Swain's Lane that divides the cemetery in half.

The three of us are sitting in a U-shaped booth of dark red leather in the middle of the building—smack over Swain's

Lane below us—facing out toward the black painted wood bar that runs down the length of the wall. The exposed brick walls are painted black with a yellow mosslike material worked into the mortar. Multiple candelabras and lighted lanterns reflect off the decorative copper tiles on the ceiling to give the dark, gloomy room a soft glow with plenty of places for shadows to hide.

The moody bar smells of candle smoke and incense with a layer of anise and licorice that pervades it all. Two rather strong flavors I hate, and the key components of absinthe—which is the specialty of the bar. Absinthe ice-water fountains are on every table (including ours) and spaced down the bar—they're glass and dark-metal containers with five metal spigots evenly spaced around it.

The absinthe might be the bar's drink specialty, but the bar is also known for straddling Highgate Cemetery, a sprawling Gothic nineteenth-century cemetery that has the bonus of being reputed to be haunted. The bar even gives nighttime drinking tours of said cemetery.

Our server, a young guy in a striped black silk shirt with matching black skinny pants and black boots walks over to our table with a bored look.

Black, black, *black*—the boring requisite color for anything and everything goth. The bar is full of these characters draped in black. I think they think they're hiding in shadows, except for, ya know, when it's daylight out. I like to think they're just sad at the current state of entertainment and wish for the nicer, cleaner periods of black-and-white television—like all they need is a good old-fashioned hug.

Our server sets the tray down on our—you guessed it—black wooden table top and stares at us from behind shoulder-length black hair like, if we tried to hug him, he'd try to bite us (not in a scary vampire way, but in the petulant toddler way).

Yeah.

Liáng and I kinda stick out since we didn't know where Puo was leading us. I'm in white capri pants with a pink v-neck shirt and a gray sweater for extra layers—turns out capri pants in November in England can be cold. Fortunately, all the candles in the place make the bar feel comfortable and warm. Liáng is in khaki Chinos with a form fitting charcoal long sleeved shirt. He'd almost fit in except that the shirt makes his muscles look good, not the pale pasty limp look Goths like to sport. Honestly, I'm surprised they let us in through the door.

Puo is in black jeans and a slate, almost purple buttoned shirt with his sleeves halfway rolled up. Apparently the turd knew where we were headed tonight and forgot to share that with the rest of us.

"Pinot noir," our server says softly and sets a tall red wine glass down in front of me with a *clink*. It's hard to hear him over the brooding slow rock music with an emo male singer that's being piped in everywhere. Or maybe it's the ring in the server's lower lip that causes a speech impediment.

The server sets down a tumbler with etched spider webs on it and a bone base holding a red liquid in front of Puo. "Brain hemorrhage."

What? But I keep my mouth shut as the server sets a small absinthe glass, a type of short-stemmed shot glass with a spherical bottom half and fluted top half, down in front of Liáng. The spherical portion is filled with a bright green liquid (looks like radioactive liquid to me). The server then sets down a small plate with a flat ornate silver slotted spoon and a cube of sugar.

Before the server can leave, I ask, "What's in the brain hemorrhage again?"

The server stops in his tracks and pauses while the bartender creates a racket shaking a drink. Once the bartender stops, the server says, "Peach schnapps, grenadine, and Irish Cream." The server turns on his heel on exactly the last syllable, afraid perhaps that we'll infect him with our non-black color.

"Mmm," I say, and look at Puo with a slight nod of my head. "Manly."

"Cheers," Puo says and picks up his tumbler to take a sip.

Liáng sets the flat slotted spoon that resembles a squat dagger on top of his absinthe glass, sets the sugar cube on top of it and slides it under the absinthe fountain in the center of our table. The ice water from the spigot melts the sugar cube as the water dribbles over it. The bright radioactive-green liquid inches up above the spherical portion and turns to a sickly yellowish-green (like infected pus—*yum*). The scent of licorice is overpowering.

I slide my wine glass toward me and breathe in the aromatic wine to try to cleanse my palate from the unfortunate licorice scent. The smooth wine pleasantly smells of light oak with an undertone of cherry.

"Have you had absinthe before?" I ask Liáng.

"No," he answers, focusing on the drink before him.

"Then how'd you know what to do?" I ask.

"A gentleman," he says, a bit of airs creeping in, "knows how to properly consume alcohol."

Ugh. "Why do you do that?" I ask. "Bounce between being a normal, helpful person and an arrogant prig. It's like you can't decide who you want to be."

Liáng actually blushes, mumbles an apology, and then says cryptically, "There may be some truth to that."

I start to follow up on what he means when Puo interrupts me, "Don't take it personally, Liáng. She's just frustrated, both about our network problems and, ya know, ... sexually—"

"Puo!" I yell in surprise. Then against my will, my cheeks burn.

I think of several more things to say but reject them. There's no way after what happened with Winn that I'm ready to jump in the sack again. *Where the fuck did that come from!*

Puo sniggers into his manly peach schnapps drink.

Fucking Puo.

"Why are you such an ass tonight?" I ask. "And unless you and Liáng have something on the side, it's been even longer for you! And we're still screwed on the network."

"We're always screwed before we figure something out." He shrugs. "I've learned to just enjoy the ride." Puo toasts himself and takes a sip of his red drink.

Grrr. I reach over and tip the bottom of the glass he's drinking upward spilling it down his chin.

He sputters and drips the red liquid all over himself.

"It's okay, Puo. Just enjoy the ride," I snark and slide out of the booth. I take my pinot noir with me to go find a less irritating spot.

What the fuck is with Puo? I am not sexually frustrated.

Am I?

No. No, I'm not. Fucking, Puo.

Then why did my cheeks burn?

I move down to the empty end of the black-painted wood bar that's standing room only. This part of the bar is out of our booth's line of sight, but I turn my back to Puo and Liáng all the same.

Winn and I were ... we were like two peas in a pod. Well, more like a pea and a ... uh ... nut of some kind, but still in a pod.

It was just— *Ugh!* I run my hands through my hair, pulling on it to distract me.

A small group of people are congregating for the midnight cemetery tour on the far side of the bar near the entrance, five goth types and a normal-looking couple. I'm not sure what goth people refer to normal people as—muggles? The normal couple looks like they just came to the bar for the tour. Most of the group looks like couples. *Isn't that sweet?* I take a swig of my wine and roll my eyes at the thought.

The pinot noir is smooth, warm on the tongue. The oak taste gives it an aged flavor while the cherry is sweet on the finish. The flavors linger in the front of my mouth asking to be replenished which I oblige with another sip.

I know what Puo's doing, or at least trying to do. He's trying to piss me off under the belief that I have better clarity when I'm irritated. *Bastard.*

"If it's any consolation," Liáng says walking up, "he said he thinks he went too far."

"It's not true," I say more to my own thoughts than to Liáng.

"He didn't go too far?" Liáng asks confused.

"Oh, no. He went way past too far." I explain about Puo's theory about my working when pissed off. "He thinks I have flashes of insight when I'm too pissed off to worry about the consequences."

"Do you?" Liáng asks, interested.

I study the congregating group at the end of the bar while considering my answer. One of the goth chicks is sporting a small skeleton handbag that looks to be made of ribcage bone. It caught my eye because I can see everything in there, including exactly where her brown-leather wallet is—helpful information for a pickpocket.

"Yes, and no," I finally answer Liáng. "I think my dynamic with Puo is that it just often seems that way. But it has to be organic, not contrived. I'm just not in the mood for it tonight."

Liáng doesn't say anything at first. He leans his back up against the bar. "What was this Winn like?"

Fuck. I don't want to talk about Winn. I gently rest my forehead on the warm black-painted bar—it's kinda sticky, which is really gross. "He was a law-abider right before we met him. A welder." I start lying my ass off and lift my head up, my forehead peeling off the bar. Winn was a surgeon. To Liáng I continue lying. "He was funny though—" No he wasn't. He was more like a brooding piece of man candy. "—a short little Argentinian man that was nearly as round as Puo." Winn is a white southern gentleman, clean-cut, six foot and all muscle. A very delicious piece of man candy I clicked with on multiple levels.

I shrug off the memories. I am not ... frustrated. I mean, I may, possibly, miss him—

Damn it, Puo!

"You okay?" Liáng asks in concern.

I'm seething. First Puo is all like "I'm worried about you" and "you act like nothing's wrong." And now he's purposefully stirring shit up. I'm really tempted to go unload on Puo.

Liáng stares at me like I'm a caged animal.

"I'm fine," I bite off. "What about you?" I ask.

"What about me?" Liáng asks.

"I don't know," I say, getting annoyed. "Ever loved and lost? Isn't that how conversation works? We just talked about me. Now we talk about you."

"I didn't realize we were done talking about you," he says.

"Yes," I say. "That's what the question signals: a shift in

conversation. Your turn. Go!"

"I ... uh ..." Liáng stammers. He trails off into silence and sips his absinthe instead.

Men. Prying into everyone else's business, but the moment you ask them about theirs, they clam up.

Liáng continues to stand there awkwardly, looking like he's trying to decide how best to proceed.

The tour at the end of the bar is getting ready to leave.

I suddenly decide I don't want to talk about relationships. "C'mon—" I walk toward the tour group and tuck my arm into Liáng's arm to pull him along. "—Let's go on the cemetery tour."

Liáng's arm is as I remember it from dancing, very well muscled indeed. Winn is gone. *I have to start getting over him somehow, don't I?*

Liáng hurriedly sets his drink down before he's out of reach of the bar. "What about Puo?"

What about him? He can stay right where he is. To Liáng I say, "He can enjoy his ride alone."

* * *

After picking up our coats from our booth and telling Puo to piss off, Liáng and I now stand near the entrance to the west portion of Highgate Cemetery only a hundred feet or so from The Bridge Between.

Our tour guide is a goth server from the bar. She's wearing a long dark trench coat with the hood up that looks to be made of a shiny felt material. She's also painted her face white for that extra pasty-white-goodness contrast. But it's her calf-high ash-colored laced-up boots and dark-gray jeans that have me really jealous. Capri pants at midnight in November in England—I really should've known better. Wafts of cold air snake up the gap at my cuffs.

We form a semicircle around our tour guide who is handing out candle-lit dark lanterns out of a cardboard box at her feet to a select few—all of them goth chicks. I think this is less nepotism and more the fact that all four of us muggles are standing in the back behind the goths.

"Highgate Cemetery," our tour guide starts, "was founded in 1839 to house the overflow of dead bodies from London." She says all this in what I think is supposed to be a disembodied voice, but sounds to me like a bored monotone. "It was immediately associated with the paranormal, becoming a favorite spot, then and now, for occultists to perform their rituals."

She continues: "The most famous inhabitants aren't necessarily those who are buried here. Those like Karl Marx, Douglas Adams, and Charles Dickens's parents and brother. The most famous are those that only come out at night." She then lists off those nighttime inhabitants, pausing after each one. "The Highgate Vampire. The Insane Old Woman. The Dark Shrouded Figure. The Floating Nun. And the long list of nameless ghouls."

The group isn't moving, fixated on our tour guide. The cold wind stirs at our feet (and my freaking exposed ankles, *damn it!*).

"Be watchful," the tour guide continues, "be mindful of things in the corners of your eyes. Heed the chill creeping along your spine—"

"I feel a chill creeping up my leg," I whisper to Liáng.

Liáng doesn't react to that verbal joust of genius, but the other muggle woman near us snickers.

The tour guide stares at us in silence. The other goth types turn to give us the stink eye, or maybe it's just their makeup, and they give everyone including themselves the stink eye—hard to tell.

I press my lips together and raise my eyebrows at them to let them know I'm done for the moment, while inching myself closer to Liáng to try and leech off some of his warmness. He leans his hard warm hard body into me.

The tour guide goes over how the dark lanterns work—they're just lanterns with sides that can be lowered/raised to turn on and off the light. She then dips into the box at her feet and brings out black shrouds.

"These are funeral shrouds-"

Oh, good Lord.

The group once again stops to turn at look at me.

Whoops. "Was that out loud?"

"Yes," Liáng says, giving me a look. To the group he says, "It's how you can tell she's nervous."

"Sorry." I grin helpfully at them and cling to Liáng's arm.

"As I was saying," the tour guide says, "these are funeral shrouds. We must wear them so that the inhabitants leave us be, thinking that we are part of the graveyard itself."

The group shuffles forward to claim their ridiculous disguises. I don't let go of Liáng.

I am not wearing one of those stupid shrouds. "Uh, excuse me," I speak up. "I think my friend here is right. I— Maybe another night."

"Another time then," our tour guide says, surprisingly graceful. "Happens all the time."

I back up, pulling Liáng with me, toward The Bridge Between and bump into the goth chick with the skeleton purse. "Sorry," I mumble apologetically and make a beeline out of there.

The group silently turns back to donning their funeral shrouds.

Liáng pulls himself even with me. When we're far enough

away he asks, "What was that about? Were you actually frightened?"

"Good Lord, no." I snort. "I didn't want to actually go on the tour."

"Then—?"

I hold up skeleton-purse-girl's brown-leather wallet. "We needed to pay for our drinks. It's tradition to never use your own cash to pay for your beverages." I grin at him.

Liáng actually smiles back. I decide it's a nice smile. "Sounds like a fun and potentially dangerous tradition." He closes his free hand over my arm in his.

"Yeah." The cold air causes me to blush. But that's not all that's put me in a sudden good mood. "I also think I know what to do about the ploppers."

I hold onto his arm and huddle close all the way back to The Bridge Between.

Chapter Twelve

Y OU WANT TO DO WHAT?" Puo asks me incredulously.

Puo and I are alone in the common bathroom upstairs back in the house the following morning. Liáng is already downstairs going through his morning calisthenics. I'm perched on the edge of the white porcelain tub in my pajamas and a zipped-up forest-green cashmere hoody, while Puo's in the process of brushing his teeth after a hot shower.

"Put funeral shrouds on the ploppers," I say again like it's the most obvious thing in the world. I'm still pissed with him, but we need to get moving on this.

Puo spits out the frothy white spearmint toothpaste into the sink and looks at me through the fogged mirror. "I—I don't know what that means."

"The Cleaners' software, Puo." I leave off the *duh* and manage not to roll my eyes. Well ... not roll them completely.

Cleaners' software is the tech that allows one to break into, and more importantly escape from, a smart home without the system ever knowing you're there—like you're a ghost.

Puo pulls his head back in surprise. He lowers his voice, "Even if we could. Do you want to clue Liáng into the fact that we have a copy?"

The tech is so valuable that it's controlled by the Cleaners Guild, who by definition happen to be a bunch of pricks. Which is why it was so damn satisfying to skim off their code three months ago without them knowing.

"He doesn't need to know that it's Cleaners' software," I say and unzip my hoody—it's too warm in here. The sweater is part of my standard morning complement along with charcoal pajama pants, a random T-shirt, and thick, fluffy rainbow socks. "You can take full credit for writing your own code, customized to the ploppers."

Puo looks like he likes the idea of that. He always loves to look smart. But his pleased look falls off suddenly. "It's not that simple, though. We have to install it at the central hub point and we don't know where that is."

"Well," I say thinking. "How do we find the hub?"

Puo rolls his eyes.

"C'mon, Puo," I say getting miffed, my frustration from the night before bleeding over, "I can't think of everything." Although sometimes it certainly feels like I do.

I get up to flee Puo's presence and head downstairs for my delicious, absolutely required morning cup of coffee. I only forwent it this morning out of extreme discipline and a need to catch Puo alone without Liáng knowing, to discuss the Cleaners' code.

Before I get to the bathroom door, Puo says, "Listen, about last night. I was out of line."

I stop in my tracks, my stomach dropping out from under me and my hand still on the door handle. "Yeah, you were," I say guardedly.

Puo pauses, searching for his words before continuing. "I'm sorry. It's just .... I feel like one minute you're fine, and we're back to our old selves, and the next minute you're acting like supergirl to prove nothing's wrong, and the minute after that you're extra-sensitive to any reactions to the previous two. I misjudged last night."

"Puo," I say quietly looking back at him. "I'm all three, all the time. Except I'm not sure things will ever go back to the way they were."

Puo takes this in silence, his face somber.

"I don't mean," I say, to correct what I said, "that we won't get back to normal. It'll just be a new normal."

"I know what you meant," he says. "Does this mean you're finally ready to admit things have changed?"

I cock an eyebrow at him.

He stares right back at me.

I say, "That's the best you're going to get out of me." His apology has me feeling better, like a weight I didn't know was there is gone.

"I suppose I'll have to take it," he says with some of the swagger we use with each other entering his voice.

And then, because I want to, I skip over the bathroom tile to hug Puo. We've been through everything together since kids. We may fight—a lot—at times. But he's always there. I know he didn't mean it last night and feels awful. Puo's a big softie.

He hugs me back, lifting me a few inches off the tile, and sets me back down.

"And I haven't gone supergirl in a while have I?" I ask.

"No," he says. "Not since the squiddie."

"But you're still worried about it?"

"Yeah." Puo pulls back from the hug and asks me, "Anything happen with Liáng last night? You two seemed awful cozy."

"No." I don't need to add to Puo's corner-store psychology.

Flirting all night and almost kissing a little doesn't count. But it did feel good to feel normal for a bit.

* * *

I pass by the empty sitting room as I come down the stairs on a mission to find my blessed coffee in the kitchen. Liáng is in the sitting room on a yoga mat, a small fire kindled in the room where we waltzed several weeks ago. It appears he's wrapping up his morning workout routine—some kind of yoga/tai chi thing.

He's in gray, almost white, loose cotton pants and a black wife-beater. His green tattoos flow down his arms. Sweat gleans on his body, but his movements are slow and deliberate, winding down.

I head into the kitchen and am greeted by a blast of cold air. I zip up my sweater and pull the hood up as I make my way to the espresso machine.

I grind the beans, once again vowing to do this in advance as it's a horrible sound first thing in the morning, like sandpaper on the ears. I pack the portafilter, attach it, and hit the button.

The machine chugs once and then beeps at me. I check things over.

Son of a bitch. It should be *illegal*, punishable by twenty public lashes, to use the last of the water in an espresso machine and not refill it.

I get a water glass to fill it up.

Liáng walks in, and then pauses awkwardly upon seeing me, unsure of where to look. He then mumbles, "Good morning—"

"Refill the water when you're done using the espresso machine," I say with a little bit of heat caused by delayed coffee consumption.

"Uh," Liáng says, "I don't drink coffee." His voice settles into a more normal tone, although he's still acting like he doesn't know where to look.

Damn it. Puo doesn't drink coffee either. It should still be illegal though, with grandfathered exceptions for people named Isa Schmidt.

And then, as if to underscore the point, Liáng retrieves a mug and starts to make himself a cup of pu-erh tea.

I scowl at Liáng. I pour the water into the espresso machine and hit the button. The hot, light-brown creamy liquid streams out the two sides of the portafilter. The color darkens into a dark-brown, almost black, liquid pool of deliciousness.

I microwave, rather than steam, a cup of skim milk to make a latte—there's no time to waste. I'm already behind on my caffeination schedule.

"What were you and Puo talking about in the bathroom?" Liáng asks.

"Nothing," I say. "I wasn't in the bathroom. Why?" Lying is a requisite skill of criminals of our type. The trick is all in the tone.

Ding! The microwave announces it's done. I mix in the espresso and then blow on the top to take a sip, the edges of the mug burning my left hand as I cup it.

"I heard voices," Liáng says. It's clear he's not sure if I'm telling the truth or not.

"Oh," I say. "That was Puo. He does that."

"Talks to himself?" Liáng asks.

"His poop specifically," I say in all seriousness—it's all in the tone. Tone informs body language, which in this case, is the body language of a girl in need of her coffee.

"What?" Liáng asks bewildered. All the awkwardness from before evaporates at the weird turn of conversation.

I shrug. "He says it helps get things moving. Me—" I hold up my latte. "—I need a cup of coffee. You?"

Liáng shakes his head.

"Oh, sure," I say, having fun with Liáng and purposefully misinterpreting his reaction. "Coffee snobs everywhere hate it when I use the terms coffee, latte, and espresso interchangeably, but I don't care—" About the terminology. They are all different, but pissing snobs off is sort of a bonus. "It does the job though."

"You can be so strange sometimes," Liáng says while taking out his tea bag and throwing it in the trash.

"No, the strange part is that Puo's poop talks back. And the voices tend to have a French accent for some reason. So what about you?" I ask, not letting up.

"We are not having this conversation," Liáng says in disbelief.

"Hmm," I say thinking, "I'd guess calisthenics and a cup of tea, based on how religiously you follow that morning routine."

Liáng blushes, but then raises his mug and says dryly, "Cheers." He then turns around to leave when Puo walks into the kitchen.

"You talk to your poop?" Liáng asks like he can't help himself.

Puo without missing a beat, in dead seriousness says, "Everybody needs encouragement from time to time. I'm trying to get back to a morning schedule. Haven't you heard of positive reinforcement? You should try it some time."

Fortunately, Liáng is facing away from me as I have to bite my lips to keep from laughing. *Yeah, Puo and I are going to be just fine.*

Liáng says, "You two are really like teenagers." He starts to leave again.

"Nonsense," Puo says, his head buried in the refrigerator retrieving some apple juice, "no teenagers talk about their pooping schedules. What kind of teenager were you? This is an entirely adult conversation."

"All right," Liáng says, "that's it for me. See you two in a bit." Liáng tries to leave the kitchen for a third time.

"Wait," I say calling him back.

But he ignores me and pushes his way out of the kitchen.

Puo says in a horrible French accent, "Some people, eh?" Puo pours himself a glass of apple juice.

I burst out laughing.

Puo grins at me. "What?"

I tell him what I told Liáng, which causes him to burst out laughing as well. I clink my coffee mug to his glass. "Sometimes, I think we know each other too well."

"Indeed." Puo stops and looks like he's thinking of things to say and throwing them away. Perhaps it's growth from our mending in the bathroom.

Eventually Puo says, "We do work well together don't we?"

I raise my mug at him.

"I think," Puo says, "that I thought of a way to find the central hub."

"Yeah?"

"Yeah," Puo says uncertainly. "But I'm not sure if I should tell you."

"You don't think I'm going to like it?"

"No, quite the opposite. I think we just need to be absolutely sure and think through all the implications before moving forward."

Yeah, whatever has Puo this reticent sounds right up my alley.

Chapter Thirteen

"I KNEW I SHOULD'VE kept the idea to myself and thought of something else," Puo says.

"What are you talking about?" I ask.

It's the following evening, and Liáng and I are in our hovercar flying in the uppermost skylane over the northern shore preparing for our plan to find the central hub while Puo's back in the basement on his computers.

The plan is actually pretty simple, but brilliant. Purposefully trigger the alarm system in the museum while hacking into the power company to monitor the power consumption in the surrounding area and see which handy-dandy plain-looking building has a power spike at a time of day when it shouldn't.

"I knew you took to it too fast," Puo says. "We need to trigger things, but this is crazy."

"What are you talking about, Puo?" I ask, mildly frustrated. "I'm not in the water. No supergirl antics. Nice and safe."

Puo starts to sputter.

I *shush* him while sitting in the back of the hovercar in the open-spaced trunk with the drone and its cargo. "Preparing to launch the drone. How's it look out there," I ask Liáng who's up front driving.

"We're as alone as we're going to get," he says.

"Roger, that," I say. It's nine in the evening. There's some traffic, enough to provide cover but not enough that we're likely to be spotted and reported.

I open the trunk. Cold wind *roars* into the cabin. *Damn, that's cold!* The cold stings my nose. I can't smell anything except the sharp cold of nothing.

The drone is an octopus-looking thing that's roughly the size of me. But the big-ass stone it's latched onto is what makes it really difficult to move.

If we need to alert the authorities, then there's no reason to be subtle about it. A big-ass stone crashing through the glass roof of the British Museum's Great Court should get their attention.

The real trick is making sure the stone can't be traced back to us, which is why we're using a co-opted delivery drone and keeping our hovercar over land. For added security, after dropping the stone, the drone is instructed to pivot and drive over the Atlantic until its battery fails somewhere in the middle of the ocean.

I put one foot in the center of the drone and my other foot on the stone itself. Then I brace myself and push against the back row of seats. The stone moves several inches. I repeat this process until enough of it is over the edge to fall out on its own.

The hovercar immediately jerks upward from the sudden loss of weight. I squirm over to the edge of the trunk and look for the drone in the darkness.

"It's out," I say, "but I can't see it."

"I got its vitals," Puo answers. "Everything's working. It's en route."

Sweet. I push the button to close the trunk and climb up front. My part's over. Done. Now we just go back and let Puo do his thing.

It's kinda nice to be done so early in a job. *Is this what it feels like to be Puo?*

Easy peasy.

Chapter Fourteen

"WE'RE SCREWED," Puo says.

Liáng and I are back at the house after releasing the drone and in the basement where Puo has all his computers set up. We never moved them after the squiddie museum excursion—it's become Puo's de facto spot.

The special-delivery stone has long since made its splash. *Ka-boom!*

I kinda wish I was there to see it, but we didn't want to risk our rogue squiddie getting hijacked again.

"Why are we screwed?" I ask. Puo's an alarmist. According to him, we're always screwed. And honestly, if that's true, we'd be in no different a situation than we were in before.

"Did you find the building?" Liáng asks.

"Yes," Puo says. He taps on his keyboard and brings up a map of St. Albans, a city about ten miles north of here.

Shit. Puo hasn't pointed it out yet. But the map of the area and his tone of voice makes it clear.

Puo zooms in and then reaches out and points to the building I was thinking of. The "V" shaped building of the Muppies—the Ministry of Undersea Protection.

Not a huge surprise. But shit.

Liáng nods his head with a tight look in his eyes—he's familiar with the building as well.

"So," Puo says, "back to screwed?"

Yeah, back to screwed.

"Infiltrating isn't an option?" Liáng asks.

"Do you want to wait a year?" I ask. "We'd have to case the place, find the patterns just to gain an entry point. There might have to be personnel ops to ghost a badge, and to find the right people who would know where the central hub is located and how to get to it. Then of course we'd have to get out. And do everything while making sure they don't record us."

"Which ain't trivial," Puo chimes in. "These secret government types have digi-scrambler detectors. So that stunt we played at the post office ain't gonna fly."

"Nothing's impossible in the limit of time and money," I say. "But how much of either do you want to spend?"

"Unless," Puo suggests, "you can help with some of that."

Liáng clarifies, "You need to find this central hub to install code that will mask our arrival into the museum?"

"Yes," Puo and I both say. *He's not actually thinking—*

"Is the central hub known by any other name?" Liáng asks. "It's not your vernacular is it?"

"I don't think so," Puo says. "But I can do some research to be sure."

"You think your organization can help?" I ask.

"I have no personal knowledge," Liáng says, "on this particular matter. But that doesn't mean someone else doesn't."

I ask, "You couldn't tell us what defenses were in the British Museum, but you can help with this?"

Liáng answers, "It doesn't hurt to ask."

Puo and I share a concerned look behind Liáng's back.

* * *

Puo and I are eating breakfast at The Red Swan the following morning while Liáng is set to meet with his contact in thirty minutes to discuss the situation with the Muppies.

The hotel-attached restaurant is half-empty on a Tuesday midmorning—the business travelers staying at the hotel have long since eaten and dashed, and tourist season is over. Puo and I are occupying an aged brown-leather booth in the corner that's pushed up against the ten-foot windows running down the wall facing the street.

All the windows and natural light are nice, but the ceiling is what really sets the place off. It's an antique. The ceiling is engraved and painted red with looping scrollwork in white, while the symmetric swans grouped in fours are painted in gold. Blue metal chandeliers with curved upward lights dot the space. It's one of the reasons I love Europe; they know how to do ceilings right—which, I'm starting to realize, I kinda have a thing for.

We needed to get out the house to discuss things privately—Liáng's seeming belief that his organization could penetrate the Muppies set off all kinds of alarm bells. If that's true, his organization isn't the Chang'ans as advertised. As powerful as the Chang'ans are, nation/state-level espionage like that in a short time frame is out of their reach.

Our server, a dark-haired French woman in her early twenties, swings out from behind the bar carrying a tray with our food. She steps quickly over to us, her black flats scuffing lightly on the thick, slightly uneven wooden planks that make up the floor.

I slide out of my warm navy-blue winter trench coat and set it beside me in the booth before she gets here. I've learned my lesson from the other night and am properly dressed for the cold weather this time in warm ivory corduroy pants and snug dark-brown boots with no heel and a purple long-sleeved sweater.

"Zee full English Breakfast." She sets a large plate down in front of Puo which looks like a pile of bland fried food.

I try to keep the distaste off my face—it's Puo's food. But there's no color to it. Brown beans, brown toast, brown fried hash browns, pink ham patties with brown fried marks, brownish bacon, and a nasty looking black circular patty. It's like a color spectrum in brown. The only things on there daring to be different are the white and yellow eggs, which kinda matches Puo's honey-colored insulated down coat draped over the back of his chair.

"Zee muesli." She sets down a bowl in front of me and then continues to set down little cups of brown sugar, honey, fresh raspberries and blueberries and a miniature carafe of milk.

"Can I get you anything else?" she asks.

We politely decline.

After she leaves, Puo rolls up the sleeves on his gray buttoned shirt and says, "What are we going to do about Liáng?" Puo goes for his hash browns first—no need for a fork, a perk of fried food.

I pour a dash of milk in my muesli mixture to soften it up and then add some berries. "Well," I say, "we took the job. We're committed now."

If Liáng doesn't work for the Chang'ans, then he either works for a bigger illegal organization, in which case we're still on the hook for the capital we've been burning through. Or he works for a foreign government entity engaged in illegal activity, in which case we may not be on the hook, but that brings its own unique set of challenges—mainly how not to get arrested or end up indentured to them. Either way, we still have to scrounge up the rest of the next payment to the Citizen Maker.

"But if they acted in bad faith misrepresenting themselves," Puo says.

True. That may provide a way out, but ... "There's no Boss over here to police things." We're purposefully staying under the local crime lord's notice. We couldn't risk offending their national sensibilities of stealing from the British Museum and having them alert the authorities to their advantage. The Brits can be strangely nationalistic, which is ironic given how much they've looted and stolen from other nations and refused to give back.

"We are also," I say, "starting to rack up quite a debt. So whoever is funding this has deep pockets." *And committing us even further.* But I leave that unsaid. Either we come out of this debt free (finally) or ... *better to leave that unthought.*

"Mmm," Puo says. "So we need to know who's actually funding us." Puo picks up a stiff piece of bacon. "Which brings me back to, what are we going to do about Liáng?"

I eat a spoonful of my muesli, which has an interesting texture. It's smooth from the oatmeal in it, but has a number of crunchy, lightly salted seeds and nuts mixed in. The raspberry I scooped up with it crumbles into a tart, tasty emulsion.

While I'm savoring and swallowing, I start to take out my pocket tablet from my tan canvas messenger bag with my other hand when movement catches the corner of my eye near the entrance of the restaurant. *Winn.*

My breath catches in my throat. My heart pounds in my chest.

I almost throw up. I can't see properly. *Is it really him?*

I set my shaking spoon down quickly to keep it from clinking like an alarm clock. I blink several times to try and get a good look at the person. *Why can't I focus properly?*

This isn't happening.

Puo is blissfully unaware, consumed in preparing his breakfast beans with salt, pepper, and now ketchup.

The apparition's tall form steps out from behind a wooden support.

It's not Winn. I can breathe again.

Sweat breaks out all over me.

My brain auto-filled the tall, white-complexioned, muscled form with Winn.

Relief floods in.

What the hell was that reaction? And why is a part of me disappointed? And why is a part of me feeling guilty?

I exhale heavily and continue to retrieve the tablet. I set it on the table queuing up a map of the area while keeping an eye on Winn's doppelganger, triple checking it's not him.

"You mean," I say perfectly normally, "Liáng who is off meeting with his contact in about twenty minutes?" *What would Winn be doing here anyway? Does he know we're here? Did he—? Would he even follow me?*

Puo nods, chewing on some more bacon he just picked up.

"You mean, Liáng," I say, trying to shove Winn out of my mind, "who is off meeting with his contact unknowingly wearing a tracking bug with audio enabled?"

Puo grins conspiratorially at me, still unaware of the turmoil roiling inside me.

"You mean, Liáng," I say, glancing down at the tablet between us putting on a show for Puo, "who currently just left the house on foot and is headed east?"

Puo silently toasts me with his half-full glass of apple juice.

* * *

The man in The Red Swan is definitely not Winn. I got a good long look as we left after finishing up breakfast to get a visual of who Liáng is meeting with.

Liáng is moving east from the house into Hampstead Heath, one of England's oldest, most idyllic parks, full of rambling hills, ponds and woodlands. Although the park is a shadow of what it used to be.

After the mega-quake hit, large parts of the Heath were reclaimed to settle the survivors. Which, in typical British "chin-up" fashion, pissed off a lot of people who didn't need to be resettled.

Even now, as Puo and I walk into the Heath from the North past the stone fence, there are flyers decrying the encroachment of civilization on the natural wildlife and calling for a town meeting. *Yeesh.* It's been eighty-six years—let it go.

I have more important things to consider then the silly selfish people prioritizing animals over people, like: *even if Winn did know I was here, why would he come? Do I want him to come?*

The morning is brisk, but not unpleasantly so. The sun is shining through sparse but fast-moving clouds above. The glare makes it difficult to see the tablet screen and where Liáng is. It smells fresh here, distinctly of autumn with decaying leaves heavy on the wind.

Birds chirp off in the birch trees in the woodlands to our right. The loose gravel crunches under our feet as we walk. A runner trots by on our left.

Puo waits until the runner passes to ask, "Where does it look they are?"

I squint at the screen. "Parliament Hill."

"I don't suppose you brought—"

"Auto-binoculars?" I reach into my tan messenger bag and bring out a pair. "Yeah."

"Anything you didn't think of?" Puo asks in good humor.

Everything about Winn comes to mind as an answer to Puo's question. Like what would I say, or act like, if we ran into each other? Instead, to Puo's question I say, "What we're going to do about those ploppers if this idea doesn't pan out."

"Spoil sport," Puo says, but without any heat.

We walk through the peaceful woods; the pedestrian traffic is minimal this time of day, midweek. It only takes a few minutes to reach the edge of Parliament Hill.

The hill is so-called because it used to offer views of downtown London (and the parliament buildings in the long, long ago); now it looks out on the Sea of London and the tombstones of those buildings left that jut up above the waves. The north skylane passes by almost directly overhead while the south skylane is visible in the distance and, of course, a steady stream of delivery drones zoom over it all.

The top of the hill is an open brown-green grass expanse. Puo and I stay ten to fifteen feet inside the tree line halfway down the hill, the leaves around us a mixture of gold, red and fading green. I retrieve the auto-binoculars and scan ahead of us.

A narrow, paved walking path crests over the hill, with no

cars on it this morning. Benches are scattered on the other side of the path from us—only a few of which are occupied.

"Got 'em," I tell Puo. I can make out Liáng's head and broad shoulders, but not who he's meeting with. His contact looks to be a diminutive person with short dark hair similar to Liáng's. "Shit," I say.

"What?"

"We're staring at the back of their heads," I explain.

"And you miss seeing Liáng's face?" Puo asks dryly.

"What? No." I feel a flutter at Puo's needling. Followed immediately by a sense of guilt. "The auto-binoculars can't read their lips and translate for us. And I can't see who he's with."

Puo looks at me quizzically. "I thought you said he has a tracking bug with audio enabled?"

Oh, right. Whoops. Stupid Winn occupying all my brain space. "Heh." I turn on the audio on my pocket tablet. While I do that, Puo takes the auto-binoculars and scans out to find Liáng.

Puo says, "It's nem. It's Shǐ Guìyīng."

"How can you tell?"

Before he can answer, the audio pipes in. It's a woman's voice speaking in rapid Chinese. If there were a desk around, I'd bang my head on it. *Damn it!*

I express my extreme frustration in sighs and growls.

Puo again looks at me strangely. "What's with you? You still have the translation program you uploaded to your helmet?"

"Yeah."

"Gimme." Puo holds his hand out for my tablet. I hand the tablet over and he starts tapping on it. "You're acting funny. Something happen?"

Fortunately, Puo is focused on the tablet and doesn't see me relive an echo of what happened back at The Red Swan when I thought I saw Winn. A pang rips through my hollow stomach all over again, and my heartbeat thumps through my neck. A light, cool wind brushes over my hot face.

I have to swallow before I can answer him. I think about lying, but we've had a bit of clearing the air after the night at The Bridge Between. Things have been better. But ... it's just worse to talk about it.

I fidget for a few seconds before saying, "I thought I saw Winn." I try to sound nonchalant and fail miserably.

Puo stops what he's doing and looks up at me.

"It wasn't him, obviously," I say.

Puo regards me heavily for another few seconds and then finally asks, "Want to talk about it?"

I shake my head no while avoiding eye contact.

"Okay." Puo goes back to typing on the tablet. "Promise you'll come talk to me when you're ready?"

"Yeah," I say a little shakily. "Look at us," I say once I'm calmer, "having an adult conversation. I don't like it," I add conclusively.

"It does feel a little weird," Puo says. "There." Puo shifts the tablet so we can both see it. The chatter of Chinese continues, but now a less than perfect English translation is writing itself across the bottom.

>> **I do not forget.**

"Do not forget what?" I ask. "Which one said that?"

"Shh," Puo says, trying to ignore me.

We can provide building layouts and access badge. In addition, you must create your own opportunities.

Okay, the text marked with "##" is Guìyīng. Well, it might be nir voice, but it's kinda hard to tell. They're speaking a foreign language, and I only met nem once. But it's definitely Liáng's contact.

Puo and I share a silent look. Providing the layout of a government building isn't trivial, but it isn't earth-shattering either. It's the blasé mention of the access badge that's raising our eyebrows.

But if that's the contact, then what doesn't Liáng forget?

>> **They might prefer it that way.**

We need a copy of their code.

Puo growls at the attempt to copy his code (really the Cleaners' code). "Not going to happen," Puo finally says. To which, I heartily agree.

>> **I have told you before. I cannot copy their code on their systems.**

Puo's low growl turns into a string of benign pejoratives.

A grim feeling swirls in my stomach. This isn't entirely unexpected. It's why Puo has been going through the encryption lengths he has. But ... life would've been much nicer if Liáng hadn't been trying to steal from us. *Freaking thieves.*

This will help.

Shit. I yank up the auto-binoculars, but I can't see anything change hands. "No visual." I alternate between looking at the tablet and through the auto-binoculars.

"We have to know what they just passed," Puo states the obvious. "If they're a bigger player than the Chang'ans, then whatever that was may be able to break in."

Anything else?

There's a pause in Liáng's and the contact's conversation. I can feel the tension between the two from several hundred feet away.

>> **Have you thought about my earlier request?**

Another awkward pause.

I gave it a lot of thought and a decision has not been made.

All these damn pauses and Chinese accents make it difficult to figure out who is saying what. It sounds like they're in high school and one of them is trying to ask the other one out. But is Liáng asking the contact out, or is the contact propositioning Liáng, or ... what?

I suddenly find myself intensely more interested in this contact. *What kind of person is Liáng interested in? And what was with that "I do not forget" line?* The tension at the start of the conversation was much different than this tension.

The contact stands up but continues to face away from us as they say their goodbyes.

The contact walks away from us down the hill so we can't see them.

I make a split second decision and shove the auto-binoculars and tablet in my messenger bag.

"Isssaa?" Puo looking at me with an alarmed questioning look.

"I'm going to tail the contact." I start moving off.

"What about Liáng?" Puo asks. He leaves the question of the very dangerous software program that Liáng was likely just handed unvoiced.

"Get back to the house," I say over my shoulder, "don't leave him and the system alone until we can figure something out."

Puo stands there dumbly watching me disappear. Finally he calls out, "Be careful." But not in his usual way of commenting on the weather. He says it in an unsettling, quiet, I'm-actually-worried-as-shit-about-you way.

Chapter Fifteen

*B*E CAREFUL.
  When am I not careful? What the hell was that? Puo's never said it that way to me before. Not like he really means it.

It's like saying tie your shoes. *Duh.*

I keep inside the tree line working my way around, practically running since I have to take a circuitous route. The fallen leaves rustle under my steps, but even in my haste, and out of pure habit, I avoid any sticks or twigs that might snap.

The smell of the dead leaves and fresh earth is pleasant, the cold air against my face chilly. It's nice. *Is this what everyone in the North always raves about?*

I grew up in the South. It can get cold there (but rarely enough to snow). And we don't have the changing of the seasons the Northerners are always blathering on about.

The crisp November weather puts me in the mood for warm apple pie. Or maybe pumpkin.

And then like a middle-school bully, the thought of Promontory Pies back home in the Seattle Isles hits me from behind like a smack to the back of the head. Winn, Puo and I found the place together right before all that crap went down and Winn left.

Be careful. Puo's warning floats to mind.

Is that what Puo's worried about? That I thought I saw Winn?

This isn't reckless. I'm not going supergirl here. We need to confirm that the contact is Shǐ and then, more importantly, figure out who is bankrolling this job and trying to steal our code base—two key pieces of information we need to know so we can get paid and continue to be able to work.

I connect to a path leading south in the direction the contact went.

But where is the contact going? All I have is a general direction and because I had to circle around, I'm pretty far behind. There are only really three types of transportation out of here: on foot, hovercar or train.

It's unlikely the contact is staying in Hampstead while we're here. So that rules out on foot. Hovercars can't take off and land in the immediate vicinity that the contact left in (ruins the view for the park goers). So the best probability is the trains.

But which train station? There are two equidistant from Parliament Hill, either of which could've been where the contact was headed when they left.

I come out on the western edge of Parliament Hill. Brick apartment buildings and town homes line the edge of the park behind a brick fence. Several back yards are dotted with the glass tops of greenhouses.

There isn't time to dither so I listen to my instincts and continue on the trail on the edge of the park moving south.

The cold air is starting to bite into my cheeks. I wrap my arms closer to my body as I hurry along, keeping an eye out for the contact.

As I near the southern tip of the park and the entry point back into the urban sprawl, I see the contact's diminutive form moving west toward me on the southern edge of the Heath.

Puo was right. It's Shǐ.

* * *

So now the real question is: was Liáng asking Shǐ out, or was Shǐ asking Liáng out? Or have I completely missed the mark and it was about something completely different (but I seriously doubt it). And then, why do I care?

The Hampstead Heath Overground station was hastily expanded several times after the mega-quake hit, from a small regional stop to a main station that serviced the edge of the Sea of London and connected the new coastline back to the rest of England to the north. It's still technically an Overground station even though the rail lines are below street level and pass through several underground tunnels at points.

Shǐ enters the station from the south street entrance for the trains moving north. Ne walks purposefully into the brick building and through the black-and-metal pay turnstiles.

I've been following at a comfortable pace but stop briefly before entering the station, watching for my opportunity, which doesn't take long.

A college-aged woman carrying her weight in her thighs and stomach comes out of the station looking frustrated. She's wearing tight jeans and a black hoody, and carries a black shopper-style purse with red straps that she just shoved her metro-chip into the inside pocket of. She then helpfully shifts the purse, whose design is intentionally open at the top, behind her as she's walking away.

The metro-chips are supposed to be wireless, but don't always work great. All I needed to wait for was someone to have problems with their metro-chip and take them out to swipe right next to the reader to reveal where they kept it. *Thanks frustrated college girl. Or should I thank the metro-chip company for a subpar product?*

I cross the street but keep my head turned away, focusing down at the end of the street and keeping college girl in my peripheral vision.

"Hey!" she startles as I bump hard into her and slip her white metro-chip out of the inside pocket and slide it up my sleeve. "Watch where you're going."

"Sorry," I say apologetically in a French Accent. "Is zis 'ampstead Station?"

"Yeah," she says still annoyed with me, "can't ya read?"

"Not well. Sorry." I make off after that, lest annoyed college girl decides to try and be more helpful.

I jog into the station like I'm late and use my body to conceal my new metro-chip from the direction I just left college-aged woman behind.

Once I'm through the turnstile, the brick station walls with yellowing paper maps hung on them abruptly switch to a modern look of clear and fogged glass walls with embedded electronic displays of maps and directions.

The hasty expansion after the mega-quake gives the station a haphazard feel, as the design isn't consistent and switches off in places.

I find myself in a central holding room where multiple exits head off depending on where you're going. The station is at the end of the Overground line, but there's still a path back to the other platform to the left.

I head down the stairs to the platform that services the northbound trains, making my way slowly and cautiously in case Shĭ doubles back, or stopped off in the bathroom.

The platform is a dirty concrete slab with scuffed up and fading paint. The metal-and-dirt stink of the railways is offset by the fresh air from the open air above. The cold air greets me as I step out of the stairwell.

The 11:10 morning bullet train to Northampton is boarding and leaving in eight minutes.

I don't see Shĭ on the platform anywhere so I hurry to the back of the red-capped silver train and step on to look for nem. I can always get off before it leaves if ne's not on it; but I can't get on it once it leaves.

The back railcars of the train are the coach sections. It's unlikely Shĭ would ride here, but then I don't know what kind of budget ne's on—Puo and I are burning through an alarming amount of capital.

People are stowing their bags and looking for seats, clogging up the narrow walkway. It takes a supreme amount of self-control not to be lifting wallets and other valuable goodies as I rudely squeeze by. Well—it'd be rude in the United States where our personal buffer space is more reasonable; in Europe where people are packed nut-to-butt, it's not as rude. Quite useful for pickpockets in retrospect.

No sign of Shĭ yet as I exit the fifth coach railcar and enter the first of two service railcars that are marked by a bar running down the long side of the railcar, standing room only. There's only a smattering of people here, and a quick inventory reveals Shĭ isn't a morning drinker.

Nor is ne in the next service railcar which includes two columns of cafeteria-style seating.

The first class railcars are beyond. I check through the

window between the railcars before entering. Most of the seats are facing forward, but I don't want Shĭ to see me.

The first class cabin is half-full; the seats are wider, spaced farther apart. Each seating section has it's own white plastic table. A couple of the sections have the chairs reversed to make a group of four.

Shĭ's sitting up near the front. Near the front exit.

I text Puo my situation, sit in the back seat and take out my pocket tablet to pretend to read in case ne bolts.

* * *

Why Northampton? I can't stop thinking.

It's not exactly a hopping spot. There are other closer locations to Hampstead that fit that smaller-city feel.

It just doesn't feel right to me.

The train doors close with a pneumatic hiss and a pleasantly generic female voice announces the doors closing and to "mind the gap."

The train gives a deep chugging sound followed almost immediately by the train levitating an inch or so over the magnetic tracks. It's a small amount to levitate but, believe me, you feel it every time.

The train moves forward slowly, but smoothly, the platform sliding by behind us.

We start to pick up speed once we're clear of the platform for the eighteen-minute journey to Northampton.

But something still doesn't feel right. I feel it in my gut. Something's off. Something in front of me is not the way it should be; it's like one of those games were you pick what's different between two pictures.

It doesn't take long for me to zero in on two British guys sitting next to each other halfway up the train from me. They're alternating their gaze between their tablets (which they're not playing with at the appropriate cadence) and Shĭ.

They're dressed in nice jeans, buttoned shirts. Both still have their coats on, but unzipped.

Shĭ is either unaware of them, or much more practiced at being covert.

After several minutes, the British man on the aisle seat gets up and walks back toward me and the service car. He has a crisply trimmed black beard with wisps of silver in it, and a narrow nose. His brown leather shoes are scuffed on the inside of the toes as if he shoves his foot into doors to stop them from closing.

As he passes, his thin black jacket flaps open and I see the top of a rectangular badge holder in his inside pocket.

He's a cop of some kind. Following Shĭ.

I studiously stare at my tablet that I'm pretending to read as he passes. His cologne washes over me. It's muskier than Winn's, I can't stop myself from thinking. *Winn's had a more spicy, woody element—*

The memory of Winn's cologne brings back a powerful memory of us together in the basement of the Skyline Hotel back in the Seattle Isles after the solid-state job. When the rush of the completed job and being alone led to—

The full memory hits me all at once. *His warm wet skin. The cold air. The smell of rubber from the scuba suits.*

Shit. I try to shake the memory off, my heart beating rapidly.

I get up to follow the cop. His jacket is open, and the badge is visible. I can make that lift; figure out who exactly is following Shĭ, and is possibly onto Puo and me.

Be careful.

Fucking Puo.

I am not being reckless. I can make this lift.

The cop is just on the other side of the doors out of first class in the service railcar with all the tables. He's on his comm-link—likely calling ahead.

I walk past him, making my way toward the railcar with the bar to get a drink. I'll make the lift on the return trip, spill the drink near him as a distraction.

I pass through into the second service railcar and walk up to the bar and order some club soda and cranberry juice, keeping the cop visible through the windows between the railcars.

I can make this lift. The cop is still on his communicator.

But once he realizes his badge is gone they're going to pull any available video. They'll zero in on me as suspect number one causing a disturbance.

I dig into the bottom of my messenger bag and pull out my digi-scrambler, a single-pearl necklace on a thin metal chain. A gift from Winn.

The bartender plops my small plastic cup filled with carbonated water colored red on the bar in front of me.

The pearl from the necklace is oblong, more flat than round. Cold from being in my bag. It shimmers blue as I stare it.

It was early in the morning when Winn gave it to me. Still dark out. Our bedroom was cold from running the air conditioning in the summer just after we moved to the Seattle Isles. He brushed my hair back and whispered my name to wake me up. The day-old scent of his cologne enveloped me. His warmness comforted me. He told me he wanted me to wear something special. There was no reason for the gift. No other reason than he wanted to.

I take a deep breath and slip it on, working the clasp with a small shake in my hand. There was a time I never took it off. I press the pearl along the sides activating the digi-scrambler.

I'm not being reckless. *Am I?*

No. *I can make this lift.*

I realize I've never left the house without the necklace since Winn left. I've never gone to bed without it near me. But the necklace is useful. That's why I carry it. *Right?*

I take a sip of my drink. The carbonation tickles my tongue, the cranberry is sweet but not strong. Perspiration beads on the side of the plastic glass.

Be careful.

Is Puo really that worried about me? He's never been worried about me like this before. He was practically frantic in my bedroom yelling at me after the squiddie incident.

Winn really was different. Even Puo knew it. Puo probably knew how I felt about him before I did.

Oh, God. This is not the time for this.

I pick up my plastic glass to take another sip to steady myself, but my hand shakes so bad I set it back down. *How am I going to make a lift with a tremor in my hand?*

The lift. Shǐ. The British Museum.

I brush the bangs out of my eyes—*just like Winn did that morning.*

What if he really is gone for good?

It all comes crashing down on me. The situation I'm in. The loss of Winn. I feel paralyzed. Like I can't catch my breath. Like no matter how hard I run, I'll never get away. Even standing still, my heart is racing so hard that it's ready to break through my ribcage and flop on the bar for everyone to see.

This can't be happening right now.

Shï can't see me. The cops following nir can't learn of me.

What if that really was Winn at the The Red Swan—?

Oh, God. What is happening to me?

I force myself to breath slowly, inhaling through my nose and exhaling through my mouth.

I have to get out of here. This was a bad idea. Puo was right.

I sloppily drink the last of the carbonated cranberry juice and try to think of how to get out of this mess.

The pleasant generic female's voice announces our impending arrival in two minutes.

How long have I been here at the bar?

I look back toward where the cop should've been. He's gone.

I wander forward into the next car, feeling like a ghost, like watching through someone else's body. The train feels like a dream sliding by me. I'm aware of pounding in my neck. Sweat slicks my skin.

The train is pulling into the station.

Shï is gone. So are the two cops tailing nem.

Where the hell did they go? The train hasn't even stopped.

I don't even care anymore. *I need to get out of here.*

The air is stale here. Filtered. Dry. My mouth is parched. *Why is the air so stale?* The train feels so small, the walls so tight, like I won't be able to raise my arms up. The ceiling feels like it's breathing down my neck. The people crowding around me at the exit are all violating me. *Just give me some space!*

The train comes to stop. It drops down onto the tracks.

The doors are taking forever to open.

My heart pounds in my chest.

The doors finally *hiss* open.

Strong scents from the station assault me: the overpowering scent of curry from the Indian restaurant across from me, the smell of baking bread from the cafe next to it, people smoking, the smell of asphalt from the platform. Over-piled trash in the trash bins.

I think I might vomit.

I stumble out of the tiny train, keeping my head down and looking for a place to sit down. My legs are jittery.

I make my way over to one of the metal benches facing the train and nearly collapse onto it.

The metal is cold against the back of my legs. I sit with my head in my hands, leaning forward.

Breathing. Just breathing.

Chapter Sixteen

IT'S EARLY AFTERNOON as I blow through the dark-orange front door into the house, locking it shut behind me.

I sat on that metal bench in Northampton for an indeterminate amount of time. But slowly, my thoughts turned from panic and flagging down medical help to coming up with a plan to get me back to the house in Hampstead.

I don't know how long I sat there. But I do know that one of the first coherent thoughts I had was this: *This is Puo's fault.* It was a galvanizing thought, immediately ruling out calling him for help.

I used college-aged girl's metro-chip again and took the train back to Hampstead. The whole way back I continued to improve, the cause and object of my ire coming into laser-like focus.

The house has a settled-in feeling for the afternoon. No movement or lights on.

I walk down into the basement to find Puo sitting at his system and Liáng standing behind him.

"Liáng," I say, "get out of here. I need to talk to Puo."

Liáng raises his head up from staring at the screens to regard me. What he doesn't do is make like he's going to listen and leave.

Fine.

"Puo," I command, "with me then."

"Does this—?" Liáng starts to ask.

"No," I snap. "Now, Puo!"

Puo locks his system and gets up, studying me, alarm in his eyes.

We head upstairs.

Liáng follows.

"Go away," I say to Liáng, stopping at the top of the stairs.

"What is going on?" Liáng asks suspiciously.

"I followed Shǐ," I say in an angry flash of inspiration. "Chang'ans my ass."

Liáng's face gives him away. He knows the truth—*whatever that happens to be.*

"Puo," I say, not taking my eyes off of Liáng, "outside."

All three of us walk to the back door. I open it and motion for Liáng to go first.

The goob falls for it, and I shut the door behind him and lock him out there.

"Let me in!" Liáng yells through the door, trying the doorknob.

"Learn to pick a lock," I answer right back.

I lead Puo back down to the basement.

"What's going—?" Puo starts to ask.

"You asshole!" I swear at him. "*Be careful?* What the fuck was that!"

"Isa," Puo says, visibly shocked at how angry I am, "What is going on?"

"I freaked out, Puo! Your stupid warning got into my head and fucking *crippled* me. Next time keep that shit to yourself—!"

"Are you okay?" Puo asks, studying me intently.

"Yes, I'm okay! *Now!*"

"Then what happened?" Puo asks.

"I was on the train, following Shĭ, ready to make a lift on the two cop/agent types also following Shĭ—"

"There were agents following nem? Who did they work for?"

"I don't know, Puo! Your stupid warning started making me second-guess myself—"

"Stop yelling at me!" Puo roars over me. "I am on your side!"

"Then what was with the 'be careful' shit? You've never said that before."

"Yes, I have—!"

"Not like that! What the fuck was that?"

Puo sidesteps the question and instead asks, forcing himself to be calm, "What were you doing when you freaked out?"

Technically it was a panic attack—at least, that's what the internet informed me it was on the way home. "I was putting on the digi-scrambler, getting ready to make the lift."

"Where you thinking of ... ?" Puo dances around his name, visibly unsure of how I might react.

"Winn?" I ask. "It's okay to say his name, Puo," I say sullenly, and then answer his question. "And maybe."

"Maybe?" Puo stares at me.

"Yes. But it was your stupid warning that got it all started. Made me second-guess what I was about to do—"

"And there was nothing else that led up to that besides possibly seeing him earlier this morning?" he asks annoyingly.

I stick my tongue out at him and choose not to tell him about the memory flashbacks of the Skyline Hotel basement and receiving the digi-scrambler—he does know me too well. "What was with the warning?" I ask in a more normal voice.

Puo exhales. "I'm sorry it freaked you out, but you looked shaken. I haven't seen you like that since that ... that morning—"

That morning.

The morning Winn left. The morning I woke up and he was just gone.

"—We're getting in deeper here," Puo continues, "and I didn't want—"

"For me to do something stupid," I finish for him. *Getting in deeper.* Yeah, that's a polite way to put it.

Puo nods, and watches me for several seconds before finally saying, "I'm sorry it got to you, and contributed to your freak out—"

Not contributed. *Caused.* But I let it go.

Puo straightens up and raises his hand like he's in the boy scouts. "—I hereby retract all warnings and any inhibitions it may have unduly placed on you." Puo waves his hands and flutters his fingers over me in a mocking fashion. "Go forth, and do your crazy, seat-of-the-pants, unbelievably-lucky-there's-no-way-that-should-work lunacy."

"Thanks," I say. It's stupid, but it does make me feel better.

"But I'm not going to stop worrying about you," Puo adds seriously. "It doesn't work that way."

I give Puo a small smile.

Before the moment gets even more awkward, Puo says, "So what was with the line you fed Liáng about Shǐ and Chang'ans."

Heh. "Some of that seat-of-the-pants lunacy. Nothing I said was untrue—" Not that lying would bother me. But I think it's an extra stroke of genius here. "—But I think I can get Liáng to reveal who he's working for."

"Right," Puo says, sticking out his lower lip and nodding lightly. "Except, now, he's outside, unsupervised and possibly rattled with a perfectly plausible excuse to contact Shǐ."

Ah, shit. "Go get him," I tell Puo.

As Puo clomps up the steps to retrieve Liáng, I ask, "What were you two looking at when I came in?"

Puo says dryly over his shoulder, "More good news."

Great.

The basement is chilly. The cold air pools down at the bottom of the house. The watery hole down to the subway tube is dark, its surface flat. The hole feels sinister, like it's sucking up all the light in the room and something is about to crawl out of it.

Puo leads a frustrated-looking Liáng back down into the basement.

Seeing Liáng's frustrated face riles me right back up. "When were you going to tell us?" I demand of Liáng before he's halfway down the steps.

"Tell you what?" he snarks, gearing up for a fight.

"You know damn well what," I say. "I followed Shĭ—"

"Followed nem where?" Liáng shoots right back.

I can tell by the set of his jaws, and the growing fire in his eyes that he's not going to give anything away. The time we left him to stew let him collect himself.

Damn it.

I may not be able to get who Shĭ and Liáng are really working for, but I need to get something for tipping my hand that I followed Shĭ. "On nir date in Northampton."

"Date? What date?" Liáng asks, his tone way too interested.

Well, that's one mystery solved. Liáng likes Shĭ. Not a fair exchange for exposing my surveillance of Shĭ. But something.

Except seeing Liáng try to control his disappointment and his over-interest in the fictitious date makes me feel bad for lying—*Why in the world do I feel bad?*

And why am I disappointed? The flirting was fun the other night, but nothing more than that. *Was it?*

I can't back off the lie now, but suddenly neither do I want to pile it on. So instead, I sidestep the question and tell Liáng, "Ne was being followed by two British agents on the train from Hampstead to Northampton."

"Who did they work for?" Liáng asks, followed quickly by, "Was that what you meant by date?"

"That," I say, referring to the first question and ignoring the second, "was something I thought you might know."

"No," Liáng says. "I know nothing of who might be following nem."

We all stare at each other as we try and figure out a way forward. The computer system hums in the background. The single white fluorescent bulb lighting the basement paints everything in a bright garish light. The dirt pile from excavating the hole to the flooded underground tube squats silently in the corner.

Finally Liáng says, "I need to talk to nem."

"No!" Puo and I say at the same time.

I pick up the explanation, "If Shǐ is under surveillance, nir comm-links and other electronic communications are likely bugged."

"You'll risk exposing us," Puo says.

"If you haven't already," I add.

Liáng gives Puo a concerned look. Then Puo looks at me and says, "There's something you should know."

Puo brings up an email attached to our post office box. We have a package waiting for us to be picked up—a package we didn't order.

"Wait," Liáng says. "If you're concerned about Shǐ being tracked—"

Puo shakes his head no. "This is Jay Brewer's original email account. I'm signing in, just like he would. I even spoofed our IP-address to be exactly his. Digitally, I am Jay Chadwick Brewer."

"Look at the sender," Puo points out to me.

"Shit," I mutter under my breath. The address is the same one that delivered the SFID chip for our rogue squiddie.

The authorities are onto us. *But which ones? The Muppies? The cops on the train? Were the cops on the train Muppies? And do they have the rogue squiddie's SFID now?*

Damn it. This is Puo's fault. If I had made that lift, we would know who we were dealing with.

Chapter Seventeen

*W*HO WERE THE *cops on the train?*

That's the question that needs to be answered before we do something like stroll into the Muppies' headquarters and upload Cleaners' code into their central hub. I'm sure if the Muppies are tailing us, they'd love for us to bebop into a tightly controlled government building—it'd be like checking ourselves into prison.

Puo spent the last twelve hours scouring his system and the internet for signs we're under surveillance. He didn't find anything, but he was quick to say all that could mean is that they were very, very good.

Whoever *they* are, they obviously got to the SFID chipmaker. From which it isn't too far a leap to guess they know about the rogue squiddie, and may have even connected it to the one that went missing, and then the one that showed up at the British Museum. And then there's the whole dropping the stone through the Great Court ceiling. Which in retrospect, may not have been such a hot idea—*but I am not reckless.*

They know we're coming.

But do they know who we are? Do they know our plan to upload code? Do they know our objective? Are they searching the underwater tubes for a hole punched up to a creepy, old basement?

We need answers to these questions before we can safely proceed.

And since we can't contact Shĭ electronically, and Liáng might have already exposed himself at the Heath, that leaves me to drop in unannounced on Shĭ to figure out what ne knows and alert nem.

Which is why the next afternoon I'm getting ready for a night out at the opera in my upstairs master bathroom.

I shimmy into my tight, skinny jeans, made tighter by the black yoga pants I have on underneath. I slip a loose, white undershirt over my matching black body suit and a marigold sweater that hangs loose around my neck, with some holes, over that.

Liáng wasn't sure where Shĭ was set up, but reluctantly shared how he got in touch with nem. Puo then was able to anonymously arrange for two tickets to be sent to nem to the exclusive Nomad Opera House performance in Birmingham tonight—an opera house that sets up for only one performance in abandoned buildings and factories and doesn't advertise.

I look at myself in the mirror and pull my straight black shoulder-length hair into a ponytail. The ushers would probably have a fit if I tried to walk into their ultra-exclusive, super fancy-schmancy opera night like this in jeans and a marigold knit sweater—so it's a good thing I'm not actually planning on being seen.

With all the layers, it's starting to get warm in the bathroom. I've started applying some light makeup when there's a knock at the door.

"Come in," I call out, not taking my eyes off my puckered lips as I apply some plain lip balm—it's cold out there.

Puo steps into the bathroom and closes the door behind him. His face is a mask of no-nonsense seriousness. "Liáng's downstairs waiting for me to go out and get dinner—"

We still haven't moved past being able to get food alone.

Puo continues in the same breath, "—so this needs to be quick. I think they're working for—"

"Puo!" Liáng calls out from the hallway upstairs. He must have followed Puo up. "You ready?"

Puo grimaces and calls out over his shoulder, "Yeah." Puo gives me a pointed look and then turns around leaves.

I follow quickly into the hallway. "Puo," I say, "maintain comms tonight on the ingress and egress."

"You got it," Puo says.

"I thought we needed radio silence," Liáng asks Puo as they head back downstairs.

Puo explains it's a safety measure on the way to the job and the way back to make sure things are go smoothly.

The real reason is so Puo and I can continue this conversation before I talk with Shǐ.

Who does Puo think are they working for? And why did he look so worried?

* * *

I managed to snag a seat on the 16:50 bullet train north to Birmingham, full of commuters, most of whom are distracted on their pocket tablets or staring out the window after a long day of work.

I amuse myself on the ride by planning out how many lifts I could do before we arrive, and what kind of profit that would produce. But ultimately I restrain myself, as that would prove a needless risk—I'll have to make sure I mention my restraint to Puo, particularly when there are so many people who are just asking for it by not paying attention and leaving their stuff in open view.

I often wonder if some people really do want their stuff to get stolen so they can replace it with new merchandise or have insurance cash them out or just to have a story to tell. People are funny creatures. I swear there was one woman once—

"Majestic Lion here," Puo says over my comm-link, inventing his own code name. "Mule, you receive?"

"Nice try, Toad," I say to Puo for calling me Mule—softly, to avoid attracting attention from the other passengers. Toad has been the code name we've used for Puo in the past that he hates.

"Majestic Lion—"

"Toady—"

"Majestic Lion—!"

"How about we split the difference," I say, "Majestic Toady."

"Only," Puo says, "if you go by Malignant Mule."

"Try again," I tell him.

"Malevolent Marsupial? Megalomaniacal Meerkat? Meddling Moose—?"

"You're going by Annoying Ant," I say.

"Oh yeah, Annoying Ant, that's real clever," Puo says. "You know, you got to put some thought into these things."

I grind my teeth at Puo. "Can we can get back to more important things?"

"Mmm," Puo says, "How about this. You're still Queen Bee, and I'm Chameleon? Still a reptile, but one of my choosing."

"Fine." Queen Bee is what I've gone by in the past.

"Okay, good. Chameleons eat bees, ya know. So I win—"

Freaking Puo!

Puo continues, "—Plump Panda is here with me—"

I hear Liáng object to this moniker, probably the plump part. There isn't an ounce of fat on the well-defined muscles of Plump Panda.

"—And now children," Puo says, "it's time for a story."

I snort. Puo's stories are always ... interesting. Always inventive, never true, and rarely on point. I think they only ever make sense to him. "Oh, good," I say. "I didn't think I was going to get to hear one this trip."

I hear Puo explaining to Liáng that the point of the story is to spend the time in conversation to know that both parties are safe and to *shush* during story time.

Puo turns his attention back to me. "In sixth century south China, pangolins were domesticated and prized for their delicious flesh that tasted like deep-fried butter—"

"What's a pangolin?" I interrupt to ask.

Puo answers, "A cross between an anteater and an armadillo roughly the size of a foot. Now—"

"Plump Panda," I ask, "is any of this true?"

"Of course it's true!" Puo roars. "I'm no liar. And Plump Panda can't hear you."

I can hear Liáng in the background who heard me perfectly well, "Pangolins are in south China, but do not taste like deep-fried butter—"

"Mutiny!" Puo mocks, "Treachery! Lying thieves! *I* am telling this story. So quiet now, close thy mouths and open thy ears. For what you may hear may change the course of history."

"Well, that's not grandiose at all," I say.

"Shush!" Puo says.

I keep quiet for a second, but when Puo doesn't say anything I add, "All right."

"Shush!" Puo admonishes again. When it's quiet for another second, Puo continues, "Now back to sixth century south China. The pangolin was prized for its delicious, buttery meat, and so an enterprising farmer decided to round them up for domestication, forming the first-ever pangolin farm. At first everything went well, but less than a year in, the farmer noticed that the pangolins weren't breeding."

The scenery outside rushes by in a near blur as the train reaches maximum speed.

"Suddenly," Puo continues, "the farmer's burgeoning business wasn't going to make it more than a year or two. Now he tried many things. Dim lighting with soft music—didn't work. He even tried giving them alcohol through fermented berries— didn't work, although that is how the popular pangolin alcohol shooter out of the snout was invented. Strangely enough, what did work was using charcoal to draw enlarged genitals on the pangolins themselves—"

"Eww," I can't stop myself from saying. "Gross."

"It's true," Puo swears. "You can't make this stuff up—"

Pretty sure you can.

Puo continues, clearly enjoying himself. "—But that's not even the strangest part—"

This should be good.

"—The wife of the farmer thought it was disgusting too. So she sewed little outfits for them to cover up the fake genitals. And damned if the little buggers didn't breed even better. They liked their little outfits and role playing—"

"Role playing?" I can't help myself.

"Oh, yeah," Puo says. "Kinky little creatures. Apparently, the hard-working baker was the biggest hit. They loved the little chef hat—"

Freaking Puo.

"—Anyway, a local government official got wind of this and came to visit one of the breeding sessions."

I hear Liáng in the background make a rookie mistake and ask about 'breeding sessions.'

"Oh, yeah," Puo says. "The breeding sessions were the best Friday night activity around. People came from miles around for the Randy Rodeos—"

I have to cover my mouth with my hand to keep from laughing out loud and drawing attention to myself, as well as not to encourage Puo.

"Well," Puo continues, "the government official witnessed this grand event. And by that time, there were vendors hawking hot food, and the precursors of rock music would play in the smoky arena—"

"Camille—" I say, riffing off Puo's code word of Chameleon. "—stay on point."

"Chameleon! It's Chameleon—"

"Stay. On. Point."

Puo grumbles, and picks up his narrative, "So when the government official visited the smoky arena with the smell of fire and sizzling meat, they say that he bought a stuffed animal souvenir, and a candle off in his brain. And thus, entertainment taxes were born."

The pleasant female train voice announces that we're three minutes from our destination.

"What's your point, Camille?" I ask.

"It's Chameleon, and my point is that whenever the government gets involved, it all goes to poo."

That isn't so much a message but a given fact.

And shit.

Message received loud and clear. Puo thinks Shǐ works for the Chinese Government. But what about Liáng? *Agent or blackmailed pawn?*

Chapter Eighteen

G ETTING MIXED UP with an official government on a job is a supremely dumbass, dangerous thing to do. It's almost a guarantee they're going to try to screw you.

They say there's no honor among thieves, but if that's true then governments are lying, scheming, backstabbing assholes that make thieves look good by comparison. They either try to blackmail you on the back end with exposure and jail time (which is usually done to try and get out of having to pay you, and what they may be doing with Liáng) or they set you up as the fall guy, so another government can have someone to publicly arrest and blame.

Either scenario would be ideal from Shǐ's point of view in our current situation. Which brings me back to my original assessment: shit.

My impending meeting with Shǐ just took on a whole new dimension.

The Nomad Opera House is setting up in an abandoned old textile factory, a few blocks south of the main train station in downtown Birmingham—close enough that I choose to walk, enjoying the cool night.

The nighttime city smells of the street, and an agglomeration of the various restaurant foods I pass. The sidewalk tables are stored for the season, and the patrons look snug and warm through the glowing windows. The cold nighttime breeze brushes past my bare cheeks, causing me to pull my arms tighter to my body in my navy-blue trench coat, despite the multiple layers I'm wearing.

Cigarette smoke swirls in front of me from two smokers standing on a break. The burnt smell mixes together grossly with the restaurant scents. Crushed tan butts litter the cobblestone street.

The abandoned textile factory takes up half the block and is made of weathered brown bricks that seems to sag on top of each other, that lamely climb up three stories to a slanted black-painted metal roof. It's still an hour and half early for the opera, so I don't see many signs that they're setting up in the abandoned factory.

I stroll by quickly, like I'm on my way to something else, and mark where I think the main entrance will be—down off an alley. The door is propped open, and I hear a box of glass *clink* as someone sets it down—either glassware or a box of booze.

I walk past the alleyway and then slow down to take my time circling back to the factory to come in from another direction. The factory is large, taking up half a block in each dimension— the opera won't be using all that space. It'll be easy to slip in and get into position.

The waiting around part—not so much.

* * *

It took me all of ten minutes to climb into the ratty old building and locate where the opera was setting up the bathrooms for my planned run-in with Shï. These old buildings are hardly a challenge; there's no tech on them, and teenager delinquents routinely find their way in to have parties.

If drunk, moron teenagers can manage it, it's not a challenge to a professional.

The real challenge was sitting still for the next sixty minutes waiting for everyone to show up—*booor-ing*.

The biggest unknown in the whole thing (after whether Shï would even show up) was how to get the vial of ipecac, a clear chemical solution that causes vomiting, into Shï's drink.

Fortunately, the opera organizers know how to move alcohol, and Shï, wearing a purple, shimmery gown with calf-high slits, queued up for a drink almost immediately after arriving.

The pre-curtain call was an organized mess, and it was simple to slip in behind the bar with my head down, like I was supposed to be there delivering another box of booze, and slip the sugary ipecac solution into Shï's Manhattan cocktail.

After that, I ditched my outer clothes for the tighter black yoga pants and body suit, and now I just shimmied into the industrial sized vent that passes over the woman's bathroom for the inevitable aftermath. If Shï was being followed on the train, then ne's likely being followed now. So it's important that we can talk without me being seen.

I don't have to wait long. Ipecac is some quick-acting nasty stuff.

Shï rushes into the three-stall bathroom and promptly runs to the nearest stall, drops to nir knees and starts vomiting violently.

The two women applying makeup in the small mirrors above the sinks give each other disgusted looks as chunks hit the toilet water with heavy plops.

Shĭ moans between heaves, then starts another round.

The two women leave in a hurry, and I make my entrance, opening the vent with a metal screech.

Shĭ looks up at me, nir eyes watering, nir face pale. Ne flushes the toilet, and the sound of whooshing water fills the bathroom.

I grin and wave hi at nem, dropping down into the far stall. I step out of the stall and lock the outer bathroom door so we can be alone.

"Hi, Shĭ," I say cheerily. "How are ya?"

"You," Shĭ manages to say, breathing shallowly. "You did this."

"Yeah," I admit. I hold my hands behind my back, and twist my body away from nir like I'm a school child being caught for being naughty. "But we needed to talk."

"And this—" Shĭ stops to collect nemself. "And this was your solution?"

"Well," I say, "it could've been shooting out the other end, but I thought you would prefer this."

Shĭ is just able to shake nir head no before launching into another round of decorating the inside of the toilet. Mostly dry heaves this time.

While ne's collecting nemself, I grab a clear plastic cup from the stack on the vanity and fill it up with water for nem.

"All right," I say, "your preference is duly noted. Next time we need to talk, I'll have it shoot out the backside."

Shĭ doesn't turn around, but rests nir head on the tips of nir fingers. "What do we need to talk about?"

"You're being followed," I tell nem.

"I am aware of that." Shĭ continues to cradle nemself on the bathroom floor.

I think over this response and decide to play a hunch that isn't exactly related. "Liáng contacted you," I say. "After we told him not to." I'm betting Shĭ already knew ne was being followed before that day on the train.

"He is not without his own resources," Shĭ says, nir voice pale and shallow. "It's one of the reasons I recruited him."

Recruited? "He likes you, you know," I blurt out of nowhere to give me time to think. *If nem is Chinese Government, then what is Liáng? Agent or blackmailed pawn?*

"Yes," ne says. "I am aware." Ne pauses to retch more. Ipecac is some powerful stuff.

When ne's done, I ask, "Do you like him?"

Ne leans back and exhales slowly, nir lips puckered in an "o" shape.

I hand nir the glass of water I've been holding.

Ne hesitates and looks questioningly at the glass.

"It's just water," I tell nem.

Ne takes a sip and spits it out. "What is it to you?" ne asks me about Liáng.

I shrug in response, still unsure how I feel about the other night. "He's part of my team. His personal life is part of my business. I can't have him distracted out there. So if you're going to ultimately turn him down, do it after the job, not before—"

Shĭ looks up at me, the uncertainty still plain in nir eyes. Ne still doesn't know about Liáng.

I'm tempted to ask what nir hesitation is, but we don't have time for girl talk at the moment. *At least I think it'd still be called girl talk, right?* Even though Shĭ is non-binary. *Non-binary-girl talk?*

"Excuse me, but was there a point to this meeting?" Shĭ asks, bringing the conversation back on point, but ne can't pull off the necessary self-righteousness to the statement while kneeling down by the toilet and trying not to retch.

"Who's following you?" I ask. Based on our interactions, I think I've got everything I'm going to get out of Shǐ in regards to Liáng.

"MI5," Shǐ answers.

British intelligence, in charge of domestic and counter-intelligence operations. Equivalent to the American FBI.

"You're MSS, aren't you?" I ask. Chinese intelligence.

Shǐ doesn't answer. But nir stare might as well be a dog slavishly nodding its head and barking, "Yes! Yes! Oh, yes!"

Great. Just. Freaking. Great.

"Standard or informed?" I ask Shǐ about MI5 following nem. *Was it standard surveillance or are they aware we're up to something?*

"It—" Ne stops to revisit nir oversized porcelain cup.

Jeez. How much did I give nem? "How much do you weigh?" I ask.

Ne spits several times and rinses out nir mouth. Ne sits back and says, "I hate you."

"Yeah," I say. "A lot of people do. Standard or informed?"

"It started standard," Shǐ says, and wipes nir mouth. "But ever since your stunt that's made the near constant news cycle—"

Dropping the stone through the roof of the Great Court. Yeah, that might have gotten their attention.

"—They've been more focused. So good job on that."

Oh, hey, look at that. It takes three hundred and forty one licks to get to the center of a lollipop, and it takes three minutes of intense vomiting to break through Shǐ's façade of serenity.

"We received an unscheduled package," I tell nem, "at our post box from the same place that we got the SFID chip—"

The bathroom door shunts inward against its lock. Someone immediately bangs on the door. "Excuse me, miss," an older male voice calls through the door, "Is everything all right in there?"

I quickly make a gagging motion at Shǐ, who promptly turns around and hurls more. Once ne finishes, ne flicks me off and calls out in a weak voice, "No. Your food has made me violently ill. I will find your manager—" Ne pauses to fill the porcelain bowl more. Although at this point, it's just dry heaves and poor Shǐ has tears running down the side of nir face.

It kinda makes me feel bad.

Shǐ continues once ne's able, "—I will find your manager when I am well enough to leave. I do not require medical assistance. Please have a sealed water bottle ready for me."

"Yes, ma'am," the male voice calls out uncertainly.

Shǐ and I stare at each other for a second in silence, continuing to give time for the voice to step away.

Ne asks in a quieter voice, "Did you pick up the package?"

"Of course not. The question is: who sent the package? The Muppies tracking the missing squiddie, or MI5 pulling at loose strings hanging off of you? And how about a courtesy flush?"

Shǐ takes another sip of water, spits it out and manages to pull nemself up to sit on the toilet and flushes it. Once the initial whirl of water drops an octave, ne says, "It would be prudent to assume they're connected."

If they're connected, then Shǐ was very likely followed here. And that older male voice likely had a much different motive for trying to barge in first rather than knocking.

Which means I have to get the hell out of here.

"If they are connected," I say, "then we need to go silent. No more contact, except at our choosing."

Shǐ gives me a dark, discerning look. It'd be more threatening if ne wasn't so pale from vomiting.

I save nem the trouble of having to threaten me and say, "We're still a go—"

Ne reaches into nir shimmery purple clutch purse and pulls out a folded manila envelope and hands it to me. "The Ministry information."

Whoops. I had forgotten about that part in the whole MI5-is-on-my-ass revelation.

"I thought," ne says, "that the manner of the random opera tickets arriving was Liáng asking me out. So I took the opportunity to take care of this."

"Oh ... ?" I raise my eyebrows knowingly at nem.

Ne heads me off icily, "That is why I agreed to come at all."

"All right, all right," I say and put my hand up holding the manila envelope defensively.

"Well," I say, "It's been nice. But I gotta run." I motion around the toilet area. "And sorry about all that." I do actually feel bad. I didn't think it would last that long. "I won't be in touch," I say to end the conversation and step back toward the other stall to climb up into the vent to make my getaway.

"Good," ne says. "If you need to, have Liáng do it. As much as I enjoy your company, I'd rather not have anything else shooting out of either side of me."

* * *

The evening has settled into a cold night as I make my way back toward the Birmingham train station. I'm back in my everyday clothes of tight skinny jeans and marigold sweater under my navy-blue trench coat, hurrying along with my head down—presumably against the cold. But really it's an excuse to keep checking behind me to see if I'm being followed.

Which is how I pick up the short portly man who's keeping pace with me about thirty feet back. His natural gate is much shorter than the quick steps he's taking to keep up with my longer strides.

I already signaled Puo that I had an admirer and would check back with him once I dealt with it.

I keep an eye on the short portly man as I switch back away from the train station, and continue to think.

MI5. Freaking. Great.

I'm not sure if that's better or worse than if it were the Muppies. Probably worse. MI5 is probably informing the Muppies.

The short portly man follows me dutifully. The sound of his steps are lost in the sounds of the street full of people out on a Friday night—although Birmingham's streets are always full, as it's the most populous city in the British Isles.

It's overcast tonight, threatening to rain. I can smell the brewing mist over the layer of street grime and the cold.

I turn down a less populous side street, increasing my pace as soon as I'm out of sight. There's a side entrance to an old Victorian pub and I duck into it, past the propped open dark-green door.

The pub is separated by dark wooden booths around the central bar that fit five to eight people. I quickly make my way over the black-and-white tiled floor and mingle into the dense crowd, keeping an eye on the side entrance.

I pretend to look over the beer menu and can't help but smile at the sign screwed into the wall that reads, "Caution. Pickpockets are known to operate in this area." *Why yes, yes they do.* Caution. One just walked into the bar. Caution. She's standing right next to you.

The stocky man walks past the side entrance, his round head swiveling back and forth as he tries to locate me. Whoever this guy is, government intelligence agent he is not—they tend to be much more competent.

But there's something familiar about—

It's Ham the Cleaner.

Son of a bitch. As soon as I realize it, he turns and looks straight at me.

What horrible voodoo was that—that as soon as I identify the piggish dick, he can magically locate me in a crowd?

Ham makes a beeline straight for me.

I'm going to need a drink for this. What the hell is he doing all the way here overseas? I'm not seeing things again, am I? Although Ham would be the last person I desired to see.

Back when Winn was with us, we skimmed the Cleaners' code off of Ham. We created a situation that scared the shit out of him and caused him to panic, which enabled us to copy the code without his knowledge and made him happy to just not be in jail.

I move out of the packed booth I'm in (picking up some drink money out of the burnt-orange safari purse hanging ignored on the back of the stool as I set the menu back down) to find a quieter spot to brush off Ham.

Deeper in the pub, the wooden booths around the bar give way to normal standing room. I step up to the bar and order an amber ale.

A clammy hand grabs me around the upper arm. "We need to talk," Ham says.

I hate this asshole. I turn toward him and with my free hand flick him hard on his Adam's apple.

He sputters, and removes his hand from me to cup his throat.

"Don't *ever* touch me again—" I move into his personal space. "Next time I'm going to break bones, scream, and have you arrested for assault."

Ham gives me an equally dangerous look. "You'd have to file a complaint to do that."

He means deal with the cops.

I really hate this small, soft little man. "Try me." My I-don't-give-a-shit meter just went up a tick.

Ham continues to massage his throat and casts his gaze furtively around the pub. He whispers, but no more civilly, "We need to talk."

The bartender drops off a rich, deep-amber ale in a pint glass in front of me. There's not much foam, and the small bubbles swirl from the bottom of the glass in what looks like a choreographed dance.

I drop money from the ignored safari purse on the bar and grab the pint glass to find somewhere more private to deal with Ham.

We find a table secluded enough in the back corner and sit down. I choose the stiff wooden chair facing the wall, rather than the built-in padded bench—easier to get away. And given Ham's personality, easier to use the chair as weapon to smash over the bastard's face if my I-don't-give-a-shit-meter spikes to new levels.

"What are you doing here?" I ask him. "You have some sort of exchange program set up?" I leave off: *for assholes.*

"I know what you did," Ham hisses at me.

"Did what?" I ask, annoyed. If Ham could prove anything, a friendly meeting in a pub tipping me off is not how the Cleaners Guild would move.

"You know what."

Fuck! All my frustration at Winn, at Puo, at Liáng, at possible MI5 involvement suddenly has a target. A small, soft, piggish asshole who I thoroughly detest. "No," I say. "I don't."

I roll my eyes to emphasize his stupidity and take a sip of the amber ale. It's a tasty beer, light like a pale ale, with tones of caramel offset by a minor bitter finish.

"Yes. You do," Ham insists. He then continues in the same dumbass conspiratorial tone, "You have no idea what you've started—"

Started? But Ham talks over me before I can retort.

"—It's going to be bad for both sides. You need to tell them what you did."

"Ham," I say leaning forward, "I don't know what the *fuck* you're talking about. Tell who? About what?"

Ham actually looks scared for the briefest of seconds as he stares at me. "You never could just listen."

Yup, there it is. My I-don't-give-a-shit-a-meter just went up several ticks. I've had enough of this meatbag who's filled way more with cockiness than confidence.

"What the fuck are you doing here?" I ask as a last ditch effort before I do something stupid.

"Hiding."

What? That was unexpected. I can only stare at him as I process that.

He's not lying. I can tell by the manner he said it. And he immediately looks like he regrets it.

The simple truth saps my frustration. "Ham," I say much more seriously, "What is going on?"

Chapter Nineteen

I T's ONE-THIRTY in the morning, three hours after my unexpected run-in with Ham, and I'm sneaking into Puo's room back at the house in Hampstead. The two of us need to talk without Liáng listening in.

The three bedrooms upstairs are all off a narrow, carpeted hallway. The carpet has short fibers but is surprisingly springy, feels soft against my bare feet.

The night and house are quiet. Everyone is supposed to be sleeping. The only steady sound is the wind brushing up against the house. Trees rustle at frequent intervals. Even less random is the sound of a hovercar driving overhead.

Puo's white generic bedroom door is cracked open—that's Puo and me. We operate on the same wavelength. He knew I would come visit to talk over everything that had happened and left the door open for me.

I creep into the room, silently closing the door behind me.

Puo hasn't stirred—he needs to work on his reflexes.

I ghost over to the near side of the bed and try to rouse him— *Where the hell is he?*

I can't find him. All I can feel is his balled up sheets.

I turn on the table lamp next to the bed.

Freaking Puo.

The punk made a Puo-shaped figure in his bed with his clothes and covered it with the blanket.

Well, if he's not in his room, then he's in the basement.

I turn off the light and silently retreat, returning the bedroom and door to its previous state.

Sure enough, a sliver of bluish computer monitor light under the back kitchen door leads down to the basement. I open the door and walk down the stairs.

Puo sticks his head around the monitors to watch me close the door.

"Good morning," Puo says as I walk up. He hands me a hot cup of tea in a thermos—it's still really hot.

Show off.

"What are you doing?" I ask.

Puo gestures toward the screen. "Looking over the sequence of how the Muppies hijacked our squiddie. You look for me in my room first?" Puo clearly can't wait to ask.

Bastard. He purposefully baited me. "No. Why?"

"No reason," he says innocently in a tone that makes it clear he doesn't believe me for a second. "But look what I found with an image search." Puo gestures at his computer screen.

I walk around the other side of the desk and look. It's a badly translated Chinese newspaper story about a string of high profile arrests of Chang'an members. And there's Liáng's picture front and center, except the name reads Wei Jing; arrested for gang related activities and sentenced to thirty years of hard labor in West China.

"So he's a pawn," I say.

Puo nods and brings up a different news story from a French

news outlet. Same picture. Same crime. "Looks like it. And Shĭ is his handler."

Great. Just. Great.

"We have other problems," I say to pile on the bad news.

"Yeah, so about your meeting with Shĭ ...." he mistakenly leads me.

Oh, right. Shĭ. All three of us, including Liáng, covered my meeting with nem last evening when I got home. Puo thinks there is more to discuss without Liáng present.

"I ran into Ham."

"Ham? The Cleaner Ham?" Puo asks in disbelief, sitting up.

"That Ham," I confirm.

"What is he doing here?"

"He said he was hiding—and I believe him."

Puo wipes his large hands over his face. "What is he hiding from?"

I go over our conversation in the pub and my inability to get anything concrete out of him. But there are certain things it points to. He thinks we stole his code (which we did, but he can't prove). And the "both sides" verbiage points toward—

"Colvin and Christina," Puo whispers.

I nod. James Colvin is the Boss of the Seattle Isles, the guy in charge of brutally enforcing order on the criminal world there. And Christina was the head of the Cleaners Guild there until she tried to overthrow Colvin. Now she's dead. And we kinda played a small, teeny-weeny role.

It's why Winn left. All that death.

When I recruited Winn, I told him we never hurt anyone, which was true. But since he joined, we've left a wake of dead bodies behind us.

Shit.

It all comes suddenly slamming back. Waking up that morning to an empty bed. Winn had told me he loved me only hours before it all went to hell. And then the next morning he was just gone, his silver caduceus necklace curled up on the plastic-storage nightstand. It had been my gift to him.

I even said I loved him back later that evening after remotely watching Colvin execute one of the traitors. *If I had told Winn I loved him when he had said it originally, would he have stayed?* Never had my bare feet that morning sounded so loud moving across the wood floors of the empty bedroom.

Puo shoots out of his chair and helps support me as I collapse into his chair, suddenly weak.

This is not what I need right now. I take deep breaths and exhale slowly, filling my lungs, deep down to the bottom, expanding my ribcage in a dull pain that's somehow comforting.

Puo hands me the thermos of tea I had hastily set down on the table.

The metal thermos is hot in my hands, bringing into sharp relief how freaking cold it is down here. I sip the hot tea: chamomile. I can tell only by the floral scent—the water is too hot and burns my tongue to keep me from tasting it.

After a minute or two, I say, "Sorry."

Puo chews on his lower lip, worried, staring at me. He starts to say something, then stops. Eventually he just reaches out and rubs my shoulder in a comforting and fortifying way.

"You believe Ham?" Puo asks quietly.

"Yeah, why?"

"If he's hiding, why reveal himself?" Puo asks the obvious question that I completely missed.

I'm getting sloppy to have missed that. This shit with Winn needs to get resolved so I can get back to being myself.

But why indeed?

Puo continues his train of thought, "It's not like anyone familiar with you would fail to notice your touch of smashing rocks through the glass roof of the Museum."

I cock an eyebrow at him.

"It was all over the news," Puo says.

"Mmm ..." *right.* That did have a certain kind of ballsy panache. Big-ass rocks smashing through their precious underwater museum that no one can visit—I imagine that did piss off quite a few people.

Heh. Well that's somewhat comforting. Winn hasn't completely made me a duffer.

But with Ham in the area accusing us of stealing his Cleaners' code, we can't sneak into the Muppies' headquarters anymore and upload the Cleaners' code. That will only convince Ham more. Another idea starts to form.

"What are you thinking?" Puo asks quickly.

"What?"

"You got that look on your face."

"What look?"

"That look that we're about to do something stupid."

"I was just thinking—"

"Isa," Puo says, his voice rising in worry, "We got MI5 on our butts, the Muppies are sniffing around, and now potentially the Cleaners for some reason. All of them know, or likely know, that we're here operating. And all the signs point to the British Museum—"

"You're absolutely right," I say, and throw up my hands in mock surrender. The Chinese Government isn't going to come after us for the lost capital, making the job easier to split from. But this job was going to *finally* pay off the Citizen Maker once and for all.

Puo looks at me, clearly not believing my agreeing with him.

I pause to draw it out—let Puo know he doesn't know everything.

He continues to stare at me, waiting on what I'm about to say.

Finally I say, "We'll have to do a smash and grab."

"What!" Puo says. "Isa, no. We need to get outta of here. It's time to cut our losses—"

"Yeah," I mutter to myself. *A smash and grab.* "I like that." It's what's left to us, and not what they should be expecting.

And if smashing rocks through the Great Court's glass roof is recognizable as one of our jobs, then I'm going to leave the British Isles behind with one hell of a signature.

Chapter Twenty

IN THE END, I love this shit.

All the hassle, all the near-death experiences, the broken heart, the dead bodies, constantly looking over your shoulder—at the end of the day, I *love* being an underwater reclamation specialist.

I feel like I did back in the rental air-delivery vehicle over the North Sea before I dropped on Amsterdam. Full of energy and an I-don't-give-a-shit attitude. *Let's do this thing.*

Puo on the other hand, balances me on the cosmic scale and looks positively wretched.

Puo and I stand alone in the front entrance of the house in Hampstead just after midnight waiting for Liáng taking his sweet-ass time. Once pretty-tattoo man shows up, then we're off, while Puo stays behind to get things ready here and work his digital magic.

"Everything in place?" I ask Puo again to try and help smooth out the awkwardness of us standing there and Puo looking like he's going to grab me in a big hug and start bawling.

"Yeah," Puo mumbles.

Rain patters against the front door from the leading edge

of a storm. We've been waiting for an optimally timed storm to come through to help provide cover. Fortunately, we didn't have to wait long in England in late November.

"C'mon, Puo," I say cheerily, "we're going to make *history* here today." I grin at him. "One way or the other."

"It's the other that has me worried," Puo says.

"Bah," I say. "We'll be fine."

Liáng finally crests the top of the stairs and heads down. He's dressed similarly to me, in black tight pants and a black polyester-sporting shirt. In my mood I can't help me but grin at the unusual sight. I look good in tight clothes, thank you very much. So does Liáng for that matter, but it's just weird to see a man in them.

"Are you wearing a cup?" I ask.

Liáng blushes, and switches his equipment bag from one shoulder to the other. "Can never be too careful," he says without making eye contact. He joins us at the front entrance.

"Well?" I say to Puo.

"Well what?"

"It's time for your blessing," I say. "Here's the part where you tell me that this is stupid and reckless and is never going to work. C'mon, it's tradition." Once Liáng and I leave, we'll be out of comms for our dramatic entrance.

Puo doesn't look like he's going to oblige but then says seriously, "This is a whole new level of stupid and well beyond reckless." He looks like he's about to say more, but closes his mouth slowly to stare at us.

"Well, all right then," I say. A sudden urge to hug Puo hits me, but I resist. It'd be bad luck to be melodramatic. "See you in a few hours wearing a pair of hand-made jade earrings."

Puo just shakes his head as we leave.

* * *

The Elgin marbles, originally from the Acropolis in Athens, are something of a sore point between the British and Greek governments. Lord Elgin (an Englishman) in 1801 allegedly bought them from the Sultan of the Ottoman Empire and had them transported to London, where they've been ever since. I say "allegedly" because the original document permitting Lord Elgin to move the marbles is lost, while an Italian translation of the original is the subject of much interpretation and legal wrangling.

Personally, I wouldn't care, and might even side with the Brits on the grounds that thieves should stick together, but I thoroughly detest official governments acting like they're holier-than-thou when they're nothing but a bunch of thugs with legal backing.

So there's all this consternation between the British and Greek governments on the Elgin marbles about what the document actually said, and then floofy British arguments about housing the marbles properly in an "international context" and whatnot. I'd respect the Brits a whole lot more if they just said, "It's ours, you can't have it, nana-nana boo-boo."

But either way, the Elgin marbles remain controversial and are, therefore, an absolutely marvelous way to make a splash of an entrance.

There are fifteen panels, twenty-one figures and two-hundred-odd feet of a frieze in all that Lord Elgin removed. But mostly when people think of the Elgin marbles they think of the fifteen panels that were on the Parthenon, so that's what we're going with.

Fifteen heavy-lifting drones are now in flight toward the Sea of London carrying fifteen fake-Elgin panels. Each panel is roughly four feet square and two feet deep and weighs over one thousand pounds. The perfect size to hide all kinds of goodies inside of, including two humans, as the panels smash down into their targets.

Liáng and I are in separate, but specially modified panels (well, more modified than the other fake ones—the real Elgin panels are not two feet thick) in closed scuba suits. Based on the digital time floating out in front of me, we should be flying over the north coast of the Sea of London.

I'm smushed flat, like I was lying face down on a small bed, in a near pitch-black tight space with a very full equipment bag filling up the rest of the space, waiting to smash through glass, stone, and concrete—I'm not normally claustrophobic but at the moment, I'm a little antsy to get this part over. And since we're dark on comms because of the overtness of what we're doing and the interference caused by the fake-Elgin panel surrounding me, I can't pass the time bantering with Puo or Liáng.

The heavy *thump-thump-thump* of the drone's copters create a kind of white noise mixed in with fat rain drops pelting against the panel. Occasional gusts of wind buffet against and sway my panel. I exhale heavily. There's a slight tremor in my hands. It's pitch black in here except for the digital readouts floating out in the rendered void around me.

This is going to be one hell of a ride.

Fortunately, our panels, along with two others, all have drogues attached to help slow our descent. Once we touch down, the panels will split open and hatch two humans along with a number of other goodies.

The rest of the panels don't have drogues. Quite the opposite. The other panels have bubble jets attached to increase their speed of descent. Thousand-pound panels dropping at near terminal velocity in air is going to make a statement.

My stomach jumps. The drone carrying my panel just dropped in altitude, preparing to deliver its payload.

If that's true, the first group of panels should already be in the water, zooming downward in a bubbly froth.

Sweat slicks the back of my neck.

Fifteen panels are about to drop over three different sites: three on Buckingham Palace, three on Big Ben and the Houses of Parliament, and nine for the British Museum. Iconic sites deliberately chosen to make a statement to the British government over the controversial Elgin marbles.

We're about to announce our presence in very dramatic terms. The authorities might be able to contain the chaos we're about to unleash at one site. Maybe even two. But not three.

By the time the authorities have a handle on what's going on, we'll be long gone.

I feel the teeniest bit squeamish crammed inside the panel, which is mostly because I'm about to free-fall in a thousand-pound hollow stone, but partially because we *are* making history here.

The Brits are going to be pissed. *Royally pissed.*

Like, drop everything, it's-now-a-national-freaking-imperative-to-figure-out-what-happened pissed. But, hey, Puo wanted to drop on way more sites than we are, underwater carpet-bomb the Sea of London. But I argued for a more focused approach and won out. Now the authorities will think it was Greek activists or a Greek crew that was involved.

So, if you think about it, I single-handedly saved countless iconic English sites from being destroyed from Puo's underwater carpet-bombing. I'm practically a patron of English culture. Maybe I should join their preservation society.

The panel drops into free-fall.

My breath catches in my throat.

I squeeze myself tighter as the panel hits the water.

I jerk forward in the panel. I can hear water spray up into the air over the storm. The heavy *thump-thump-thump* of the drone fades away.

The panel shifts in the water as it sinks—*I'm upside down.*

Cold water seeps into the panel. I feel the water drip down onto the back of my thighs; feel it creep up past my helmet in a tilted line. The heater in my dry suit quickly adjusts, but not quickly enough for me not to feel the icy cold as it envelopes me.

The panel picks up speed. I'm rapidly submerged within the panel.

There's a slight *pop* as the drogue deploys at thirty feet underwater.

The panel jerks a hundred and eighty degrees as it rights itself and the downward motion arrests slightly.

My breath is hot and moist in my helmet. At least I'm facing the right way. The backs of human necks were not designed to be landed on.

BOOM! reverberates up from below me. There's no mistaking the sounds of the first panels with bubble jets plowing through the British Museum below. *BOOM! BOOM! BOOM!*

Within another few seconds the next and final round of bubble-jet panels strike. *BOOM! BOOM! BOOM!*

The second round is a precision round, dropped after Liáng and I; it's designed to strike where the first panels had already hit, plowing deeper into the vault tunnels below the museum.

The alarms of ploppers in the museum pierce the water, muffled by my stone sarcophagus. *NEE-eu! NEE-eu! NEE-eu!*

The panel jerks suddenly, throwing me to the side. A

horrible scraping sound drags past on my right. The sound cuts off suddenly and I start free falling again, until I smack suddenly to a stop, knocking out my breath. The panel feels like it's lying flat on its back.

I'm not moving. The *NEE-eu!* is louder here. I must be in the museum. Time to hatch this egg.

I retrieve the carefully placed trigger from a hard pocket on my calf and press the button. There are several small *pops* and a grinding sound as the stone splits lengthwise in the middle. Pneumatic chugs take over as the top of the stone is slowly lifted up.

NEE-eu! NEE-eu! NEE-eu!

Damn that's loud. As soon as there's enough of a crack, I turn on my nightvision and look out. Yup. A plopper stands about fifteen feet away. At least the plopper is helpfully lighting up the area for me to see in.

I'm about to turn on my comms to Puo when I notice the blue pixels becoming very well defined in a path carving its way straight for me: a squiddie.

Shit.

All I can do is watch as it zooms over. The crack in the panel isn't big enough for me to squeeze out of yet. And I can't stop the panel from opening or retract it. So I just sit there, like a delicious trapped piece of meat in a stone shell slowly and loudly shucking itself.

The squiddie stops at the entrance to whatever room I'm in, lingering over the plopper.

My heart thuds in my chest. I keep my hands below what I hope is the sight line into the panel from the squiddie and search the equipment bag between my legs for a stunner.

It wasn't possible to stick the stunner on a pole this time—it wouldn't fit inside the panel. If we're going to use the stunner on this job, the squiddie is going to have to be close enough for us to see its dull, dead eyes.

It's as if the evil, gangly creature can read minds. The rounded front of the squiddie swivels suddenly toward me. It stares for one heartbeat. Two heartbeats—

It shoots over toward me, traveling so fast its eight appendages stream out behind in a near straight line.

I play dead, my helmet turned to where I can keep it in view.

The squiddie stops an arm-and-half-length away. Just out of reach of my stunner.

It's eight appendages articulate so that all of them and their sensors are pointed at me.

The ploppers alarm keeps blaring. The squiddie is making small motions this way and that as it examines me.

Fuck! It's not going to try and drag me out through a crack too small for me to fit, is it?

Not while I have the stunner it's not. Come here you stupid mechanical bastard. Just another few feet.

The whole point of dropping so many of these damn panels was to confuse the shit out of everything. And now I'm not even out and they've found me already. But they sure as hell haven't gotten me yet. Except now they know where to dedicate their resources—

The squiddie suddenly reverses course and shoots off.

What?

It settles over the plopper again.

Calling for reinforcements? Reporting what it—?

All eight of the squiddies appendages shoot down onto the plopper and start dismantling it.

The alarm cuts off. The squiddie is still going to town on the plopper.

More distant alarms are still sounding in the museum.

The squiddie stops and turns back toward me. Waiting expectantly.

I use the unexpected opportunity to calm my breathing enough to go through the retina displays and turn on comms to call for help.

"Chameleon," I whisper. "Queen Bee here. Do you—?"

"Oh, thank God," Puo breaks in over the line. "I thought you were dead. Why the heck weren't you answering me?"

"There's a squiddie—" I try and stay calm.

"Yeah, that's me." One of the squiddie's appendages waves at me. "Duh."

Oh, thank God. I exhale once again through pursed lips. "How the hell did you get here so fast?" The crack from the panel is almost large enough for me to fit through finally.

"I tracked your descent. You're dropping in the middle of a thousand-pound panel, smashing through buildings. You didn't think I was going to keep an eye on you?"

He asks that last question like it was the most obvious thing in the world. I have no idea how he managed to do it. And right now, I don't care.

"Thanks, Chameleon," I say, using his preferred moniker twice in a row now. Very unlike me—*I must be grateful.*

The crack is finally large enough. I start to squeeze through.

"Aw, shucks," Puo says.

Once I'm free, I turn my helmet lights to low power and keep my nightvision on. "Let's go get Plump Panda."

Chapter Twenty-One

Now that I'm free I can see that my panel landed on the ground floor in the middle of the western portion of the museum, just off the original west wing and very close to the Parthenon gallery.

"Do you know where Plump Panda is?" I ask Puo, pulling my DPV out of the equipment bag. The vehicle looks like a thick pair of motorcycle handlebars but with enclosed propellers underneath.

"Somewhere in the northern section," Puo answers.

"You didn't track him as tightly?" I seal up the equipment bag, and slip it on my back, getting ready to jet off.

Puo lowers the power on the squiddie flashlights for my nightvision to pick up. "No," Puo answers simply. "Once you two hit, I could only track one of you in any detail."

I'm about to say thanks again, when Puo says with the regular swagger we use to banter with, "I know where my meal-ticket is."

"And don't you forget it," I say. At least we're settling in.

"I would ... *never!*" Puo mocks.

I grip the DPV's handles and start it up with a *whir*. It gently accelerates to pull me prostrate behind it. The water flows over my form as I exit out of the room down a short stairway into a square room. I can see the Great Court to my left and where they housed the Rosetta Stone (long since recovered). There's a distant roar, underneath the piercing sound of the alarms, of heavy rain steadily pelting the undulating sea surface and the sound of waves breaking.

Several rooms o my right should be the Parthenon gallery. But that direction is visually impenetrable in a silt cloud of blue pixels that I can't see beyond. I'm tempted to go into the gallery and survey the damage. Two of the bubble-jet panels were targeted there to underscore the Greek connection. But all the damn alarms sounding are crawling under my skin.

I try to contact Liáng on the comm-link. When Liáng doesn't answer, I ask Puo, "What's the best route to Plump Panda?"

Puo's quiet on the other end for a few seconds and says. "It'd probably be best to pass through the interior rooms, go through the Egyptian Sculpture room, and swing through the back rooms that connect the west and north wing. The interior rooms aren't as heavily guarded."

"Roger, that," I say. I swing the DPV to the left toward where the Rosetta Stone used to be. There's a plopper sitting right at the entrance to the Egyptian Sculpture room from the Great Court. The trashcan-sized plopper looks small compared to the soaring ceiling of the Sculpture room. This room must have once been impressive, now it's a decaying mess.

The plopper's alarm is damn near earsplitting. "Chameleon," I say, "there's another plopper."

"I'm on it." Puo's squiddie launches out ahead of me to dismantle the plopper.

I direct the DPV deeper into the room and turn north.

"Are our goodies deploying?" I ask. All of the fake-Elgin

panels that didn't house humans had several runners inside programmed to take off as soon as the panel split open— including at Big Ben and Buckingham Palace. About two-thirds of the runners also had stunners attached and were programmed to take out ploppers as they encountered them.

"They're deploying," Puo confirms.

Puo's squiddie stays ahead of me, providing enough light for my nightvision as we travel down the long room and then turn right through a stairwell.

It's an odd feeling to be comforted by a squiddie swimming along ahead of me. They've been our nemeses for so long, it's practically ingrained to run or freeze on sight of them. Perhaps we should use this trick again in the future. Isa Schmidt— mistress of the squiddies.

Thinking of the squiddies. *Where are they?*

"Yeah," Puo says, not realizing I hadn't meant to voice that out loud, "damn good question. I had been hoping to run into a few."

Better to avoid them for the moment. "What are the Muppies up to?" I ask as we glide through a set of smallish rooms. The sounds of the storm diminish. The ceilings here are only nine or ten feet tall, and plain. They're nowhere near the majestic scale of the other rooms we just came from. "Are they responding?"

"Oh, yeah," Puo says. "Yeah, they're responding all right. HiDARs are en route—"

Which should be mostly pointless. All the action is within the buildings, where the HiDARs won't be able to see us.

Puo continues, "—Cruisers have been alerted and are beginning to mobilize—"

"How many?"

"At least three—"

Fuck! "That's why there aren't any squiddies!"

"Why—? Oh," Puo says dumbly as he realizes it.

Wet teams. The authorities are sending in highly trained, actual people down after us.

* * *

Wet teams are made up of two frogmen and are rare. Very rare. There's just too much underwater real estate to protect to make them economically feasible for governments—which is why governments rely on squiddies as the backbone of their defense strategy.

We know the British Royal Navy has an agreement with the Muppies, but even then the British Government doesn't have the manpower to deploy wet teams to three sites like this.

I check my timer that's snapped to the passing museum wall. It's only been four minutes and change since it should've become apparent to the Muppies that buildings weren't randomly imploding.

It's close to three in the morning. We specifically chose this time to be three-fifths of the way through the Muppies' night shift, when the night is longest and heads are prone to nodding.

"Keep an eye on them," I say. I guess we're going to find out how fast the Muppies can mobilize. "Let me know when they dispatch."

"Roger, that," Puo says and then adds diplomatically, "Duh."

Puo's squiddie swims out ahead of me and takes out another plopper.

I emerge into a much larger room with shattered glass cases at the four corners and several empty stands where sculptures would go. It's the room directly north of the Great

Court. There're three other doors besides the one I came in. The door opposite me looks cloudy and disturbed, which is promising.

I direct Puo to have his squiddie take the lead. A shiver of cold water traces its way down the middle of my back as the DPV pulls me across the room—a weak spot in the suit. The rest of my suit is nice and toasty, a little warm in the chest actually.

I try, and fail again, to link up comms with Liáng.

We have a small time-window before the Muppies get here. The authorities holding back the squiddies is a mistake. Yes, squiddies are just as likely to drag the good guys to the surface as the bad guys. But if I were the Muppies, I'd be using the squiddies to do reconnaissance, and then pull them back. Sure, that'd announce the wet team's presence, but hey, we've already figured that out.

But something still just doesn't feel right. The wet teams can't cover all three sites. *Is that why they're hanging back? Waiting to figure which site to deploy at?*

Wet teams are bad news. They're highly trained, difficult to fool, and approved for lethal force.

Wet teams' rules of engagement are made widely public. The governments want to deter and stop crime before it even happens. All underwater reclamation specialists have them memorized:

Protect undersea heritage sites from unlawful looting and vandalism. This includes:

1. The disruption of any and all unlawful activities, while protecting and preserving our cultural heritage.

2. Capture trespassers alive *if possible*. (Emphasis theirs.)

3. Use of lethal force is authorized.

I have no idea why they emphasize number two but not three. The inconsistency and redundancy has always irritated me. But they even have a little saying: "Stay alive. Don't dive."

There's also some interesting wiggle room in there if you know where to look. But mostly, the government wants you to know they're willing to kill you over this. There're no police body cams down here. No third party cameras. No crowd with personal recording devices. It's strictly a he said/she said situation where dead, bloated bodies can't talk.

The screeching alarm from inside the room Puo's squiddie just disappeared into abruptly shuts off. The distant patter of the rain rushes in to fill the sound void.

"Queen Bee," Puo says. "You're free to flutter in."

"Roger—"

The shifting of heavy rubble shudders deep within the museum.

"You hear that?" I ask Puo as I enter the cloudy room.

"Yeah, the infra-sound sensors just lit off. Better find Plump Panda and hurry up."

"Any visual of the Panda?" I ask. I can't see anything in any detail except an arm's length in front of me. I try to contact Liáng on the comm-link again but to no avail.

"The panel is split open about fifteen feet in front of you to the left of your current position. It's too cloudy for me to tell if there's anything in it."

We treated the dry closed scuba suits with the same infrared protection the anti-gravity suits have (but not telling Liáng about the source) so squiddies (including Puo's) shouldn't be able to detect our heat signatures. Light, sound, and movement though—all still very detectable.

I'm about to tell Puo to keep his distance from the panel thinking of what I was going to do with the stunner, when Puo screams, "WHOA! It's me! It's me, Plump Panda! Stand down! Stand down!"

Puo's squiddie backs up rapidly, whooshing through a cloud of blue pixels.

I hurry my DPV forward, trying to take the most direct route to Liáng while avoiding the squiddie's flailing appendages. Through the murky cloud of blue pixels I come upon the fake-Elgin panel split in half with Liáng pushing the stunner out of the side. I manage to stop just several inches short.

If I can see him, he can see me. I tap my helmet over the ear.

A second later Liáng's heavy breathing comes in over the comm. "Hello? Queen Bee? Uh ... Lizard ... Thing?"

"Chameleon," Puo corrects helpfully.

"We read you, Plump Panda," I tell Liáng.

"I'm trapped," Liáng rushes, "I'm trapped. My helmet doesn't fit through the crack."

"Okay," Puo says. "Just take it easy. We'll get you out."

I open a separate comm channel to just Puo where Liáng can't hear us. "Chameleon, it's just Queen Bee. Do you have something clever in mind, or just brute force?"

"Brute force," Puo answers.

Yeah, I was afraid of that.

Back on the party channel, Puo directs Liáng to slide as much of his body that will fit outside the panel.

Liáng does as told and it looks comically like he's eight years old and got his head stuck in a fence looking for a four-leaf clover.

"Gee whiz, wiseguy," I say to Liáng's prostrated form. "Got any Vaseline?"

"What?" Liáng asks, still a little panicked.

"Don't worry," I say, "We won't call the fire or police department."

"Uh, thanks," Liáng says.

"Yeah, Queen Bee," Puo says, "you're losing me—"

Oh, yeah—I definitely know what we're binge watching when we get back to the Seattle Isles.

Puo continues, "—Get on the other side of him."

Puo's squiddie and I take positions on each side of his stuck helmet. I'm able to stick my fins within the crack to get leverage and bend down to get a grip on the upper slab.

"On my count," Puo says. "One, two, three—!"

I don't even have time to strain before Liáng's head pops free.

"Whoa," Puo says, "these things are strong."

"Thanks," Liáng says at the same time I say, "Glad I could help."

"Grab your equipment bag," I tell Liáng. To Puo I ask, "How are the Muppies doing up there?"

Puo's silent for a second and then makes a "mmmm" sound over the comm. I can imagine his face, his lips pressed together, his eyes narrowed as he stares at the screen, his face serious.

"That's not a good noise, Chameleon," I say. "What's going on? Have they dispatched the wet teams?"

"Not yet," Puo answers. "But they've cleared the air space."

Chapter Twenty-Two

CLEARED THE air space.

It's a pretty standard response, and one we were expecting them to take. But taken along with the squiddies holding back and the impending deployment of the wet teams, it just feels off. Like that feeling you get on the back of your neck when someone is watching you without your knowledge.

Liáng asks what's going on with the wet teams as he gets his own DPV ready, and I bring him up to speed on our situation.

"Chameleon," I say, "lead the way."

Two of the bubble-jet panels were targeted to go through the Great Court's glass roof in exactly the same place separated by a few seconds. There should be a large, gaping hole down into the bowels of the museum through the Great Court.

"Roger, that," Puo says. "Follow me." Puo's squiddie moves off the way we came and I reconnect with my DPV and follow at full speed with Liáng's DPV *whirring* behind me.

"Point of order," Liáng says—the panic and heavy breathing are gone from his voice. "But if Chameleon, is in fact, Chameleon, as you're referring to him, and not Toad or Camille, as you have in the past, then may I request that 'Plump Panda' be retired in favor of Dragon?"

"Negatory," I say. "You'll always be Plump Panda to me."

"But I am not, in fact, plump," Liáng says.

We enter back into the large, north room off the Great Court with the four shattered glass cases in the corners. The steady drumming of the storm becomes louder through the door connecting out to the Great Court.

"Neither are you droopy," I answer back to Liáng.

"Droopy?" Liáng asks, exasperation creeping into his prim voice.

"Droopy Dragon," I explain.

Puo barks a laugh. "I don't know, Queen Bee," Puo says. "How about Dainty Dragon, Dowdy Dragon; or Distraught Dragon, Doddering Dragon—"

"Neither of you," Liáng says, abandoning his calm voice, "have adjectives attached to your name."

"Whoa," I mock, pretending to keep the peace, "take it easy with the grammar there fella. We're all friends here—" Well, two friends, and one pawn who I'm pretty sure his handler is going to try and screw us with later. "—Believe me, I know there's nothing 'plump' about you."

Liáng goes awkwardly silent.

Puo doesn't pile on, no doubt enjoying the unexpected awkwardness.

I feel my cheeks burn inside my helmet. "I mean—we know you're lean. It's just—with your muscles—that's why it's funny ..."

Puo snorts. "Are you explaining why something's funny? It's not funny if you have to explain why it's funny—"

"Shut up, Chameleon!" I warn.

Why did it have to get so awkward?

"Shutting up, boss," Puo says.

I can hear the damn, smug smile on his round Samoan face.

Puo announces, "FYI: HiDARs are in the water. Hold up here, while I go scout ahead."

Good to know. But unless they're in the museum itself, we should be fine.

Liáng and I stop at the door to the Great Court. Puo's squiddie swims out in the great open space and quickly disappears around the circular edge of the Reading Room that takes up a large portion in the middle of the Great Court.

And now Liáng and I are alone together. Quietly. In silence. Where normal people would say something.

My mind is suddenly and stupidly blank. Asking Liáng how he's doing seems ... lame. *So lame.*

So I say nothing. *Annnd* it gets more awkward.

What? Is it something about the water pressure that does this to me? This happened with Winn too on our first time out over the sunken state of Florida.

Puo starts humming "The K-i-s-s-i-n-g Song."

"Okay, Toady, that's it!" I snap.

"Hey—!" Puo starts, but I barrel on.

"No! If you can't play nice, then you're demoted back to Toady."

Puo's silent on the other end for a second before saying, "*Ribbet.*" He then adds, "It was totally worth it."

Freaking Puo. And toads don't say ribbet.

"I will never understand you two," Liáng finally says.

"Well," Puo says, "it's good to keep a little bit of mystery in ... in a ..."

My building frustration at where Puo was headed switches gears quickly to curiosity. "You find the hole?"

"Yeah," but his voice is heavy, no excitement. "The cruisers are dispatching."

Shit. "How many?"

"All of them."

* * *

All of them?

How the hell are they mobilizing so quickly? It's storming to high hell out there. *Damn it, we're not even in the vault yet.*

"We need to move," I helpfully tell Liáng. To Puo I ask, "Toady, where are you?"

"Turn left out of the door," Puo says, "can't miss it."

My DPV *whirs* to life and pulls me along, gently accelerating out into the Great Court. Riders—the devices I used back in Amsterdam—these gentle sea cows are not. They really lack the pep that the urgency of the situation demands.

I lead Liáng left out the door. There's a light layer of blue pixels floating all over the place—a cloud of silt from several thousand-pound panels smashing into the Great Court. The rain pelting the stormy surface is louder in the Great Court, but still distant.

We specifically targeted three panels to land in the Great Court. Two right in the same path. The third to throw the authorities off from what we were doing.

So, why isn't the silt cloud as bad? I can see the rising, circular walls of the Reading Room to my right. The once-external, Greco-Revivalist façade of the East Wing is just visible to my left. Distant alarms continue their *nee-eu! nee-eu!* The thin water washes over me as the DPV drags me toward the gaping hole in the floor, my internal suit-heater keeps me mostly immune from the cold—best invention *evah.*

The hole is jagged. Huge chunks of concrete and rebar are twisted downward around the edge. The thin veneer of marble hangs off in slabs, waiting to break free.

I ride straight up to the edge.

What lies in the hole itself is much more opaque. Silt clouds billow and move down below. There's no telling how deep it is.

Puo's squiddie shoots down ahead of me to make sure Liáng and I don't dive headfirst into brick or concrete.

"Down the rabbit hole we go," I say and direct my DPV down into the hole. "ETA on the cruisers?" I ask Puo.

Puo's quick with the answer, "Two to three minutes. All three are headed straight for us."

Fuck. They know we're here. "Did the HiDARs see us?"

"I don't know," Puo answers.

And why the hell aren't they sending in the squiddies? The British Museum is a large place that they have to first find us in—*do they know where to look?*

"Toady," I say, "I am becoming very concerned with the lack of company."

"Company?" Liáng asks.

"Squiddies," I say. "Where the hell are they? Why aren't they being used as scouts, and pulled out after the wet team hits the water?"

Puo mumbles back his concern as well, but doesn't actually say anything useful.

The obfuscation from the silt continues as we descend through the jagged hole. There's little to see except random glimpses of the caved-in bricked edges. The water "feels" colder as we get deeper—not sure I can actually feel it, but my internal thermometer power consumption readout indicates it's self-adjusting. The sound of rain is louder in the hole, probably from the direct path to the surface.

"Well, where are they?" Liáng asks.

"That's the question," I answer.

"No," Liáng says. "I mean—before, you could track them. So if you can't detect them now, then where could they be physically in the water to accomplish that?"

My mouth drops open in my helmet from a range of horrible thoughts. The worst being they figured out how to cloak the bastards from us.

"Toady?" I ask.

"I'm not reading any right now," Puo says. "*Any*."

Shit. I force myself to take a deep breath and think. "We haven't seen any squiddies," I start thinking out loud. "But the three cruisers are making a bee line for us." *Where the hell are the squiddies?*

I keep pace with the four mechanical tips of Puo's squiddie's appendages visible in the silt cloud ahead of me.

"But," I keep thinking out loud. "They have to be somewhere as Plump Panda so helpfully pointed out. So what situations would arise to hide the whole damn squiddie navy? They're not cloaked are they?"

I follow the tips of the squiddie appendages that curve down and to the left, exiting the hole that continues down deeper.

Puo says, "Leveling out in the vault floor." He then continues about the missing squiddies, "It's unlikely they're cloaked. I'm not sure how they would physically pull that off. And why sandbag with them?"

"So what does that leave?" Liáng asks.

"That they're hiding," I blurt out. If they're not showing up on our scanners, and they haven't developed cloaking technology, then they're physically hidden. "But where?" I ask in a low voice.

I keep the tips of the squiddie's appendages in front of me and level out. It's so freaking murky down here I can't see jack shit. *Hunh.*

"What, hunh?" Puo suddenly asks.

I hadn't realized I'd said anything, but I take the opportunity to work some moisture back in my mouth. Apparently I've been thinking with my mouth hanging open too much in the dry air environment of the closed scuba suit.

"I was just thinking—" I start.

"You know where the squiddies are?" Puo asks.

"What? No." *That is what we were talking about wasn't it?* "The silt clouds. I can't see anything. How far can you see?" I ask Puo.

"Uh ... eight, maybe twelve feet," Puo answers.

So the squiddie sonar can't see very far either.

Liáng asks, "You think the squiddies are hiding in the silt clouds?"

I consider that for a moment, but then answer, "No. But it is one hell of a confuser to hide within."

Puo's silent at first and then says slowly, "Yeah—" I can imagine his head bobbing up and down. "—I see where you're going, but we can't do anything about that right now."

"Well you asked about my *hunh*," I say with a little bit of snap. I wasn't going to share, because Puo's right. If I had thought of this before we got started on the job we might have been able to exploit it more. "And why do I have to think of everything?"

"It's clearing up ahead," is Puo's response.

The thought that the squiddies are hiding, coupled with three cruisers heading straight for us, sparks another disturbing thought. I switch the comm-link to just Puo. "Toady, this place could be a sty." Code talk for an inside job. Shĭ might have sold us out, trying to do the same thing they did to Liáng.

Puo exhales slowly over the comm-link. "If it is a sty, there's little we can do to clean it at the moment."

"Once we get to the vault, I'll order you to go greet our guests. Once that's done, quietly scout ahead to our exit route and look for any surprises."

"Roger, that," Puo says.

The silt cloud thins some, and the brick-walled edges of the rounded tunnel start to emerge.

"Switching over to the party line," I say. I switch over so that Liáng is back on the line.

"Increase power on helmet lights," I order.

Six beams of white light lance out through the water column ahead of us, two per person/squiddie. The water is undisturbed, almost crystal clear ahead of us. Brown and gray silt coats the floor. Little strings of algae covered in silt hang off the brick.

Silt billows up below and behind us as we pass down the hallway.

The rectangular vault doors are set into their arched brick entryways. Ocean crud and little strings of algae hang off the once gleaming silver-metal doors. The crud-covered black oval sign announces the vault's designation. Alarm sounds pierce the otherwise silent hallway.

"Damn," I say, once I see two vaults' designations in a row.

"What?" both Puo and Liáng ask at the same time.

"We're moving in the wrong direction."

"Ah, poo," Puo says. "You're right. We need to turn around."

"Where are those cruisers?" I ask annoyed at the delay.

"One to one-and-a-half minutes away," Puo says.

As I pass the last vault door before heading back into the

silt cloud, I see the black, starfish-shaped air-gap sensor sitting above the vault door in a silvery, shimmery pool of collected air. *Sweet.*

"Looks like the runners have been through," I say to Puo.

"Yeah," Puo says, "I saw that too."

"But I said it first," I say. "So no credit for you." I try to say it lightly, but fail.

Several of the runners have been outfitted with bubble jets. Running through the halls streaming air bubbles to set off the air-gap sensors. The idea was to set off as many alarms as possible. But if Shǐ tipped the Brits off, they'll know right where to go.

"Uh, guys—" Liáng says.

"I am not a guy!" I snap, both at the verbiage and at the thought that Liáng may be in on it. I hate that phrase. Not a guy. No penis here. And I'm the *boss.* Only slightly worse is when some stoner moron refers to me as "Dude."

"Ohhh," Puo says. "Faux pax, Plump Panda. No good, no good." Puo does a better job at keeping the tension out of his voice.

"Squiddies!" Liáng shouts back. "What about the squiddies? Did you two forget about them? We were discussing—"

"I didn't forget about the squiddies," I say, still annoyed. "Did you forget about the squiddies, Toady?"

"No," Puo says. "I didn't forget about the squiddies. Did you forget about the squiddies, Queen Bee?"

"No," I say. "I didn't forget about the squiddies. Did you forget about the squiddies, Plump Panda?"

Pretty sure if it were possible to hear Liáng giving us a dirty look over the comm-link we would. Instead there's a loaded silence.

We're back in the center of the hole the panels carved through. The silt is heavy, swallowing our headlights. I can barely see the trailing appendage tips of Puo's squiddie.

"Uh-oh," Puo says. His squiddie stops in its tracks.

"What?" Liáng and I ask.

"Uh ... I think we're in the vault," Puo says.

"What?" Liáng and I repeat again. I'm randomly tempted to yell "jinx" at Liáng and tell him he owes me a Coke, but I'm still irritated at him and I'm not sure he'd get it.

The panels were supposed to hit near the vault to provide an easy entry point. Once we arrived the plan was to drill some holes around the vault door and fill them with explosives and detonate. Then stand back and let the pressure difference take care of the rest—no need to be subtle on this one.

"The panel smashed through the vault?" I say just to be absolutely clear.

"Yeah," Puo says.

Whoops.

Chapter Twenty-Three

DROPPING THE PANELS was never supposed to be super-accurate. The most smarts we put into them was for precision, to follow one another for a repeated pounding in some cases.

We talked about trying to drop a panel directly through the vault, but Liáng understandably didn't like that idea, and we weren't sure we could do it on purpose. *On accident (in hindsight), no problem.*

"Direct hit?" I ask Puo, "Or ... what?"

"Checking—" Puo starts, but suddenly cuts off. "The wet teams are in the water."

"Teams?" A spike of adrenaline hits me. I almost twist my head up with my helmet lights to look up near the surface.

"Yeah," Puo says. "Two."

"Vault," I say to Puo. "Talk to me about the vault. Then go greet them. Make a fucking mess, Toady. Sprint around and kick up as much silt all over the damn place as you can."

"Right," Puo says. "The vault. It looks like the panel sheared off the northwest corner, taking the door with it." Puo's squiddie emerges from the swirling silt cloud very close to me. "It's to your left. Head straight. Can't miss it."

"Good," I say. "Go," I order him.

Puo's squiddie shoots upward. "Gone."

I direct my DPV to the left and accelerate slowly to make sure I don't smash into anything. Out of the drifting silt cloud I see the edges of the vault. Smashed and broken brick hang off the edges like dry flaking pieces of skin.

"Panda, you with me?" I ask.

"Yes," Liáng says tightly.

Liáng vehemently spoke against the smash-a-panel-through-the-vault-as-a-way-to-open-it idea. Somehow, destroying some jade to recover the rest of it was a big no-no. *Oh, well.* Foolish nationalistic sensibilities.

Past the jagged, rendered edges of the vault lies the interior. It's cloudy and murky; visibility is two, maybe three feet. I see the top edge of a toppled wood and glass case. The glass is shattered, broken. The wood looks fresh, like it hasn't been sitting in water at all—which, of course, up until the last hour, it hasn't.

And there, inside the top shelf: jade. *Hello, my lovelies.*

This shelf is full of bracelets. Wrist-sized solid rings of jade from a deep green to a pale almost white stone. Some are plain, but most are carved on the outside in intricate patterns with dragons, Chinese lions and fish.

I whip the equipment bag off my back and dig out the first of several balloon bags—they're a riff off the leech bags. The balloon bags are designed to hold a bunch of stuff and then inflate/deflate to maintain neutral buoyancy, which makes moving them around in the water like pushing puffs of air.

"Found the goods," I tell Puo and Liáng. "I'm starting to pack it up now. Panda, look down at your feet."

Something heavy somewhere up in the museum goes *ka-thunk!*

"Roger, that," Puo says. "I'm working on the party decorations."

"Don't pull the place down on us," Liáng says. "We still need to get out of here."

"Agreed," I say. "Did you hear that Toady?"

"Loud and clear," Puo answers. Our escape route is down, not up. But Liáng doesn't know that yet. It was strategically safer to assume Shǐ was going to try and screw us over and not let Liáng in on everything—which, given how the night is going so far, was the prudent choice.

"Keep an eye on the wet teams," I tell Puo. "We'll need to know when to bolt."

"Roger, that," Puo responds in a tone that screams *duh! Freaking Puo.*

"Panda," I say. "Pack up as much as you quickly can."

I've already shoved a handful of pieces in the balloon bag and I'm working my way down the toppled wooden and glass case (more bracelets and now some pedants). "Don't bother wrapping individual pieces. There isn't time."

"They could be damaged," Liáng says defensively.

"Yes, they could," I conceded. "Blame it on the Brits. But it's your choice," I say. "Either go for a few, preciously wrapped pieces. Or go for a lot. Once we leave, the Brits are going to come back and pick up the rest."

Me? I'm going for a lot. A lot of slightly (if at all) damaged jade is going to be bring in more cash than a few pristine pieces.

"The agreement—" Liáng starts.

"The agreement didn't specify the quality of the delivered jade!" I snap at him. "Only the contents of the vault. Which I am currently bagging up and you are not."

"Our patron is not going to like this," Liáng says.

"Our patron can shove it," I snarl. "Now shut up and bag it."

The more I think about it, the more certain I am that our patron, Shĭ, screwed us over. So ne's going to take what I deliver in whatever state I deliver it in, and ne's going to better damn well pay us and give us a clean break. *One way or the other.*

It's clear Liáng is brooding in the silence. *Does he not want to upset his crush, Shĭ? Or is it that nationalistic sensibility rearing its ugly head again?* I get that jade is a Chinese national symbol. But I never understood the whole national furor thing.

I mean, I'm American. America's great—*fuck, yeah!* But we don't have anything so symbolic to get worked up over. I don't know—maybe bald eagles? Turkey and stuffing? Asking strangers for candy in the middle of the night? Canada?

I've filled one balloon bag, inflated it to neutral buoyancy and I'm attaching it to my DPV when Puo pipes in. He whispers, "The two wet teams have entered the museum, four frogmen total."

Chapter Twenty-Four

*S*HIT.

I start stuffing the second balloon bag faster. "Where are they?" I ask Puo.

Puo's silent long enough for me to almost ask again when he says, "You need to go mute with me. I think they can detect our transmissions."

I feel sick to my stomach, but keep my mouth shut. If that's true, they can zero in on us pretty damn fast.

Puo continues, "You can still talk to each other, just not me. Switch your comm-links to another channel *and* turn your transmission power in your settings to ultra-low—" Puo cuts off for a second and then says, "Yeah. Yeah, they're definitely tracking me. Hang on."

If they're tracking Puo's transmissions, then they're not likely tracking Liáng and me yet. I take the opportunity to do as Puo suggests and open a channel to Liáng on ultra-low while keeping a receiving channel open to Puo.

You track active sources, the sources that are putting energy into the water. It's how we track the squiddies in the first place. But it's not possible to track passive receivers. So it's possible for the authorities to track Puo's squiddie as he talks to us, but not track Liáng and I as we listen in. Puo's squiddie is essentially acting like a blow horn.

"Panda," I whisper. "Bag as quickly as you can. So long as they're chasing Puo, we have some extra time." Whispering, of course, is completely unnecessary, but it's hard to overcome the instinct of trying to remain hidden.

"Roger, that," Liáng says quickly.

Is that the first time Liáng's said that exact phrase to me? It sounds weird coming from him. Sounds like Puo. Not sure I like that. But at least he's not bitching about damaging the jade anymore.

I'm now tossing bowls into the second balloon bag. Some of the bowls are heavy, solid pieces, while others are small and delicate. They *clink* together as they shift to the bottom. I consciously switch to picking up the heavier pieces that aren't likely to break, but don't mention this to Liáng.

Puo comes back on the line. "They're using encrypted comms—"

No surprise there. So are we.

"—They came in through the holes the panels made and are attempting to herd me. I think I can buy you two, maybe three minutes as we play hide-and-seek up here. Wrap it up down there, and I'll follow you to the exit point."

"You hear that, Panda?" I ask Liáng on our separate line. My second balloon bag is nearly full. I set a two-minute timer in my helmet—there's nothing in the silt cloud for the digital clock to snap to so it floats in the lower right of my vision. "Set your timer for two minutes."

"I heard that," Liáng says. "How are we going to exit with the wet teams up there?"

Liáng was told was that we'd exit above and swim to the nearest underground station (with many distractions and feints along the way). "One thing at a time," I say.

Liáng is quiet for a bit. The only sounds in the vault are the *clinking* of jade pieces landing on top of each other in our bags and the distant alarms and drabble of rain on the sea surface. Eventually he says, "And what about the squiddies?"

"What about them?" I ask. Their absence has been niggling at the back of my mind, but there's little I can do about it at the moment.

"Where are they hiding?" Liáng asks. "You never finished that thought."

"They could be hiding anywhere," I say. One minute, thirty seconds left on the timer. "There's plenty of nearby buildings for them to hide in—"

"Or perhaps," Liáng says dramatically, "inside of underground stations."

"Bump-bum-bum," I snark back in a deep voice. "How long you been sitting on that? Couldn't just share? Had to go for the dramatic reveal?" I ask annoyed. *Is there something you know, Liáng, that you aren't sharing with Puo and I? That perhaps Shǐ told you?*

Then in my best announcer voice, because I'm feeling like a smartass, I say, "Will our heroines survive the dastardly evils of the villain? Will they escape alive? Tune in tomorrow. Same bat-time. Same bat-channel."

"What?" Liáng asks, annoyed.

I can't quite work up a laugh, but I do smirk at him (which he can't see). I make the 1960's Batman transition scene noise and continue to pack in the jade as quickly as I can.

"Why do I get the feeling you're not telling me everything?" Liáng says.

"Holy dramatic plot twist, Batman!" I say.

Liáng *grrs* over the comm-link.

"Relax, Plump Panda," I say, "You're coming with us. But like I said, one thing at a time."

The floating timer in my lower right shows twenty-seven seconds.

"Wrap it up," I tell Liáng, "We need to move—"

Puo breaks in breathless, "I lost one. Dang they're good—"

"One what?" I can't help myself from asking, even though Puo can't hear me. *One frogman? One team?*

Puo continues in the same breath, "—I think they know I'm playing the rabbit. One team kept snipping at my heels, and I lost the other one. Now I think the team keeping on my butt is trying to keep me occupied to prevent me from doing anything else—"

"Panda," I rush on our separate line, "we're outta here. Zip 'em up and attach 'em." I seal off the balloon bag I'm stuffing and hit the auto-buoyancy controls.

Puo continues, "I plan on giving them the slip and circling back to meet at the prescribed exit point."

Prescribed exit point. I moderate my exhale as I hurry. We need to get there first.

I attach the second balloon bag to my DPV. "Panda, how we doin'?"

"I'm almost ready," Liáng says. After a few seconds he says, "Done."

I know a harried voice when I hear one—a lot of games/cons rely on that moment when the mark's voice turns, which I don't know how to interpret here. Liáng's legitimately worried about running into the wet team. *But what does that mean? He's not working with Shǐ? Working with Shǐ, but the betrayal comes later away from the wet teams?*

These thoughts do me no good in the present moment. We still need to get our sweet asses outta here without running into a suddenly missing wet team.

The vault is a mess of silt that won't settle. Even with my bright helmet lights (that I'm suddenly paranoid about), I can't see more than a few feet or Liáng. "I'm just inside behind the vault door. On me," I command Liáng.

"Understood," Liáng responds. I hear the *whir* of his DPV, but only see a light haze of his helmet lights. After six more seconds his muted helmet lights come into better focus and Liáng says, "I'm behind you."

Winn's voice suddenly flashes through my mind, *I normally like being behind you* .... He said that to me once. Back in the Seattle Isles Sewers sneaking into what we thought was Valle's underwater vault. We had an unscheduled tryst on that job, couldn't keep our hands off each other. *He smelled of rubber from the dry scuba suits mixed with sweat. His skin was cold. That was the point, to warm up.*

"Queen Bee," Liáng says, "what's the hold up?"

"What?" I ask stupidly. I look back and see the orange tip of Liáng's DPV. Liáng is a dark cloudy mess behind his helmet lights. Two black balloon bags float above him.

Right. *Damn it.* I banish Winn's memory with a slight shake of my head.

"Let's go," I say and kick my DPV into gear. "Stay tight to me. We're heading down," I tell him. At this point, there's nothing to lie about. "The British Museum is secretly connected to the London underground tubes." It's how they moved the most valuable artifacts in and out. The closest station for people was Tottenham Court, which is where we sent our rogue squiddie through on the scouting mission. "That's where we're headed."

Liáng doesn't say anything to that. Nothing.

"Already knew that?" I ask. *Perhaps there had been reason to lie.* I maneuver the DPV out of the vault into the jagged hole left by the smashing panel.

Liáng answers, "It's been rumored for hundreds of years. I was trying to think through if you actually knew it for a fact or were gambling and we're about to get pinned."

"Thanks for the vote of confidence," I say.

"Any time," Liáng says.

I direct the DPV downward at a slow speed. The slow speed of descent has nothing to do with pressure equalization or nitrogen absorption (we're in closed-circuit scuba suits that protect us), but everything to do with the fact that I can't see more than two freaking feet at a time.

And the balloon bags? Great idea in theory. They do work—makes it stupid easy to move the jade—but, attached to the DPV: they float. Like in my face when I'm pointed downward. Making seeing ahead, an already difficult task, even worse. I should've had Liáng take point.

The jagged edges of brick pass by in the silt cloud, signifying we're dropping another level. We must have hit a thermal pocket. The water is noticeably colder along the middle of my back and the internal heater starts pulling more power. The water feels thinner too.

"Stay tight to me," I say to Liáng. "We should level out after one more floor."

Liáng doesn't respond verbally, but I hear his DPV following.

Through the heavy silt cloud the carved-stone façade of the fake-Elgin panel emerges. The panel is split open and empty, the runners having emerged to do their job.

The panel, however, is resting one level above where we

need to be. "Panda," I say, "Follow me. We need to find a way down."

I wonder what Puo's up to, but I don't want to try and contact him, potentially giving us away.

I direct the DPV out into the tunnel; the fake-Elgin panel slides away to get lost behind in the silt cloud. The timer floating in my lower right vision blinks zero at me—I turn it off.

Our progress is still maddeningly slow. Our helmet lights reflect the brown and sand-colored swirling silt. It's hard to gauge visibility other than: it sucks. The tunnel we're in mirrors the one above it, another brick vault tunnel. I can just make out the recesses of the vault doors as we swim by, but not the vault designations.

I shove off the thoughts of what might've been if we could've hit this place covertly. All kinds of unopened vaults are down here. And I'm pretty sure coming back isn't going to be an option.

The tunnel dead-ends unexpectedly. I look for some signs but don't see any. "Right or left?" I ask Liáng, intending to go the opposite way of whatever he suggested.

But Liáng doesn't take the bait, instead opting for a brooding silence.

Well, fine then. I go left for no other reason than gut instinct. Which seems to pan out about fifty percent of the time in situations like this.

We need to find a way down to the next level—or make one. But setting off the explosives we meant for the vault door would likely bring a whole lot of unwanted company.

The silt cloud is dissipating after we turned left, growing thinner. Our helmet lights increase their range.

Movement up ahead!

My heart lurches in my throat.

It's a runner.

I exhale heavily and tell Liáng it's only a runner, running around doing its job.

Damn. *Where is that unaccounted for wet team? And where is Puo? Why hasn't he checked in yet?*

I check the one-way comm-link to Puo—still open.

In my panicked thinking from the runner's movement the only weapons I have that I can think of are the stunner and the commando knife with the saw-tooth back attached to the DPV. The knife is about the only traditional real weapon useful in an underwater environment. Underwater guns are impractical for us and serve no real purpose other than to provide an excuse to the wet teams to fire at us in self-defense (the wet teams will definitely have underwater guns).

Oy vey—the whole point of being smarter and cleverer than the authorities is to avoid run-ins with wet teams, a point we've been successful with in the past. This is the closest we've ever been to a wet team.

I take a deep inhaling breath, feeling it expand out in my chest comfortingly. The Muppies had to have been ready, waiting to get here this quick. *Did Shǐ tip them off in a bid to blackmail us?*

The water is progressively becoming clearer. The runner we briefly saw has long since gone, off on its mission of spreading its air-bubble love.

Finally, I see a sign on the wall of a little green man going up stairs with an arrow. We're nearing a stairwell of some kind. I point it out to Liáng, who again doesn't respond.

What is with him? Still being pissy about offending his national sensibilities?

The vaults are smaller in this tunnel, but packed closer together. Now that the water is clearer I can see the inscription in the black oval sign, SABZ-3. Brazilian artifacts, maybe? There's got to be some good stuff coming out of the Amazon.

The brown metal stairwell door looms ahead at the end of the tunnel. The door looks to be melting into its frame surrounded in brick, the silt and ocean crud reclaiming it to its own purposes.

The only sounds in the tunnel are the *whirs* of our DPV, and the small sounds of the thin water rushing over my helmet and the two balloon bags strumming against the progress of the DPV.

I look back and see Liáng following closely behind. His closed-circuit scuba suit matches mine and is a patchy, almost pixelated, dark-blue and black—which is the best underwater camouflage (and also on wet asphalt for some reason). His helmet is a shiny black, reflecting a curved image of me looking back at him. I can't see his face, but I imagine it's the bored, pouty look he carries around so much.

I slow my DPV to a stop next to the stairwell door. The balloon bags slowly straighten themselves out, drifting forward from the momentum a moment ago. The brown metal door has a long silver metal bar across the middle that I push down to open it.

Something's wrong. It's obvious as soon as I can see into the stairwell.

The silt in the stairwell is stirred up. There are shadows cast on the wall to the right of me at an impossible angle to be from my helmet lights.

Someone's in the stairwell!

I smash the door open as hard as I can. It smacks against something solid before it's fully open.

"Panda! Help!" Adrenaline crashes over me. My forearms strain against the door. Pneumatic tension swells in my elbows.

A hand in a black, pixelated camouflage glove whips around from the door and tries to grab me.

"Shit!" I scream and back off. Then I immediately push forward and slam the door back in place.

How many are in the stairwell?

"Panda, where the fuck are you!"

The door pushes back on me. I have no leverage. It's easily pushing me back.

I scramble my legs behind me to try and get some kind of purchase.

A blacked-out helmet carefully emerges from behind the door to get a look at me.

My heart is pounding so hard, I almost think the frogman can see it jumping in my chest. Aside from my female form, all he should be able to see is the big middle finger in the center of my helmet.

The door keeps gaining ground against me. *Where the fuck is Liáng—?*

The door suddenly shoves forward and the owner of the blacked-out helmet pushes out from behind the door. Silt billows out from behind him.

He twists and pivots lightning fast and launches himself at me, arms outstretched.

I have a split second to register that his hands are empty: no knife. I use the door I was trying to crush him with as a shield and deflect his oncoming hands.

It half-works. It stops his momentum, but his hands in black gloves wrap around the edge of the door. He pulls himself around head first.

I use my adrenaline-filled panic to elbow him in the helmet away from me. *Ow!*

It doesn't look like his helmet broke. As he recovers, twisting away, I gather my legs to prepare to double thrust kick him away.

I don't want to kill him. But there ain't a whole lotta room in underwater fights. Almost everything that would be disabling in air ends up being a death sentence underwater. *How the hell am I going to get out of this?*

I unleash two very muscled legs at full force to try and connect, and hopefully knock him out.

He catches my leading leg above the ankle and pushes it downward while rolling over my other leg. Like a rabid monkey he expertly claws his way up onto my chest.

He's going for my rebreather tubes! *Bastard!*

He's in close. Right on top of me. Minimizing my ability to do anything.

I try to punch, grab, pinch anything, everything.

It's the frogman's standard dirty tactic. Disable the suspect's ability to breathe and then back off offering them a secondary breather off their tanks. Either tether yourself, essentially handcuff yourself, to the frogman or die. And the underwater gun pointed at you while you accept their lifeline will dissuade any ideas of funny business.

He continues to ignore my frantic attacks and fumbles at my rebreather tubes coming out of the back of my helmet.

It's not working! I can't get him off of me.

Damn it. I am *not* going to die down here.

I exhale out through my nose and force myself to think. *Think!*

I switch from trying to stop the frogman to trying to delay him. Mostly by shoving his head up and away to keep him from seeing.

He's going for my oxygen. We all need to breathe. But he's a frogman on a wet team. His oxygen system and components are probably safely tucked away for hand-to-hand combat.

I manage to get his head turned up away from me. His hands continue to probe and grasp at the back of my helmet. The area over his neck is soft compared to the hard plastic of the helmet. I squeeze with both hands.

His hands loosen. He shifts upward away from my grip.

Buoyancy! The turd may have his oxygen safely tucked away, but what about his mechanical fail-safe buoyancy valve?

I drop my left hand from his neck and fumble around at his waist. If we weren't fighting for our lives, he'd probably think I was trying to cop a feel.

He jerks away from me. Guess he really doesn't like a girl feeling around near his junk.

There! Got it you smarmy bastard! But before I can twist that little valve for all its worth, he jerks upward.

It's then I notice another pair of helmet lights in the stairwell. *Liáng!*

About fucking time!

There's also a familiar black band tied around the frogman's waist: a balloon bag inflated to full positive buoyancy.

The frogman shoots upward, until the balloon bag hits the underside of the stairs.

"Panda!" I call out. "Where you been?"

Liáng's response is to tap his helmet over the ear.

Damn. Either our comms are down, or they're jamming us.

And if they're jamming us, the source is likely the frogman floating ten feet above us pinned against the underside of the stairs.

I give Liáng the "okay" hand-sign and motion up toward the frogman, who is rapidly working on freeing himself.

Liáng nods and pulls out a knife and swims up to meet him.

I have a half-second hesitation before I grab Liáng's leg and motion "no" to him carrying the knife. All I can think about is what Winn would think.

Liáng nods his understanding.

It is not okay for Liáng to kill the frogman. It was never okay to take a life. That's always been true, even way before I ever met Winn. It's not who we are. Not who Puo and I are. We're smarter, faster, better. We don't need to take life in order to get the job done.

But all I can think is that if Winn hears about this, he's going to hear about a zero body count. I am not going to fuck this up again.

Confident Liáng got the message, I head back to my DPV to grab my own knife. While I feel strongly about not taking human life—robot life, not so much.

I keep an eye on Liáng and the frogman as I swim back from my DPV into the stairwell, my elbow still throbbing from where I smashed it into the frogman's helmet. It looks like Liáng has a handle on the situation by coming in from above between the balloon bag and the frogman.

Where are the frogman's friends? I wonder. *Where is the other member of his wet team?* There's no other sign in the stairwell of anybody else. *Was he out scouting on his own?*

Sure enough, the frogman's DPV is behind the door that I tried to crush him with. I use the commando knife and stab the DPV through the engine. *Thunk.* Well, I tried to stab it through the engine anyway. Turns out, fiberglass: not so easily stabbed.

Freaking military DPV.

I sort it out soon enough and find the latch to open the panel to the engine. Guess the military engineers chose to defend against a long-range attack, rather than a close-in attack by a sexy underwater reclamation specialist.

Stabby! Stabby! Stabby!

Yeah, that DPV ain't going anywhere any time soon. Now that that's taken care of, let's see what he's got in the carrying compartment: *Oh-ho-ho!* A handheld mapping sonar device. *Sweet.*

"Queen Bee," Liáng says, "You hear me?"

"Loud and clear, Plump Panda," I respond. I grab the handheld sonar and look up toward Liáng. "Good to hear your voice again."

"Agreed." Liáng is descending from the frogman.

The frogman's hands are bound by zip ties behind him. We packed them with the balloon bags—damn useful things and you never know when you're going to need them

"Nice," I say. "How'd you get him to cooperate so nicely?"

Liáng answers, "I wedged the knife between one of his breathing tubes and his back. He complied quickly enough. If he moved suddenly while I was tying up his hands, he'd of cut off his own air supply."

I grumble in response. It's right there on the moral boundary. But I'm not sure what else Liáng could've done to tie him up.

The frogman's hands are not only zip tied together, they're not moving at all. Nothing on him is.

"Panda," I say, my internal alarm growing, "Why isn't the frogman moving?" *Did he accidentally cut the breathing tube?*

"I suspect," Liáng answers in his dry voice, "that he's conserving heat until his cronies can come bail him out. The only way I could kill his jamming while keeping him alive was to kill his power."

It's a death sentence. A slow one, but a death sentence all the same. Without power driving the internal heater of the dry scuba suit the cold of the water will seep through and he'll freeze to death eventually.

Damn it.

The frogman must've called for help when we first engaged. His compatriots are almost certainly going to save him. But if they take too long, or can't find him, he'll die.

Winn's paling face from back in Colvin's library is vivid in my mind. *I can smell his sweaty, black curly hair matted on the back from blood. I can see his disturbed face backing up from the tablet on Colvin's fancy wooden desk. The profound silence from that library overwhelms me all over again. The haunting look in Winn's clear blue eyes are forever seared in my memory.*

"Panda," I say. My voice sounds disembodied to me. "We can't leave him like this."

"What?"

"We can't leave him like this," I repeat more vehemently. "We can't leave him in a state where he'll die. Zero body count."

"He won't! His friends are coming for him."

"Restore his power, keep him tied up." There is no doubt that his friends are coming. But I don't know how long they're going to take.

"He'll restore the jamming," Liáng argues.

"Agreed," I answer. "But zero, fucking, body count." Then I turn around at Liáng and gesture with my hands.

Liáng pulls his head back a bit at my gestures then gives me the "okay" sign. The he mutters, "I don't know why I listen to you."

Because Shĭ told you to, and you have an unhealthy crush on your captor.

Liáng understands my hand gestures. Or at least, he's doing as he's told.

Quite a lot can be communicated nonverbally—especially when both parties know that verbal communication isn't possible.

Liáng carefully ascends to the frogman and restores his power, then drops back down quickly.

The frogman moves his helmet around. Kicks his legs a bit. Then he looks right at me and gives me the slightest little head nod.

I tap my helmet over the ear in response. *Save your damn little head nod and restore my communications.*

The frogman shakes his head "no" and shrugs at me.

Gah. Bastard. And my elbow still freaking hurts.

Liáng and I swim back to our DPVs and maneuver them into the stairwell heading downward, passing under the trussed up, jamming frogman.

Still no word from Puo. And now we know there won't be.

Chapter Twenty-Five

T HE STAIRWELL BOTTOMS out after one flight of stairs to another brown metal door. I have a second's hesitation before pushing the door open. *Was the frogman coming down the stairs? Or going up? Where is the other member of his team?*

Unfortunately, the handheld sonar I reappropriated can't see through doors.

The door opens to a horrible *screeching* as the rusty metal hinges rub against themselves. Lovely. I'd like to believe that's a good sign. That we would've heard that awful noise if the frogman was coming up from down here. But then where are his compatriots?

The tunnel is clear. Both from hounding wet teams and silt. Our helmet lights penetrate out beyond fifty feet down here.

The tunnel is one long brick tunnel that looks to be gently sloping downward, no vault doors.

I use the frogman's handheld sonar and look down at the four-inch-square display. The tunnel is mapped out in surprising detail and cycles through a short, few-seconds movie of moving through the tunnel. It even mapped out behind us some and a little bit down the "T" ahead of us that our helmet lights can't yet see—*freaking cool.*

This is going to be a sweet little bonus toy. Puo's going to love pulling this thing apart.

The thought of Puo makes me a little queasy that we haven't talked to him since we were in the vault. He's unaware of our run-in with the frogman. Unaware of the jamming.

Puo should be physically safe if they capture our squiddie. *But how long will it take them to extract incriminating evidence from it?*

Liáng and I swim up to the "T" in the tunnel. The cross-tunnel is much wider and taller than the tunnel we just came from. There's a narrow railway built into the floor of the tunnel—it's clear this tunnel was used to move some big deliveries around— like off of secret trains.

I use the handheld sonar in both directions.

Water turbules wash over my right shoulder from Liáng maneuvering to look at the sonar screen. My dry scuba suit continues to keep me nice and cozy warm, while the throbbing in my elbow has subsided to a dull ache that can be mostly ignored.

No frogman. The tunnel to the right continues to slope downward, while the tunnel to the left slopes upward and gently curves away.

We take the tunnel to the right, and stop every twenty to thirty feet to use the handheld sonar to make sure there are no surprises up ahead.

After the third such stop it's clear we're on the right track. The sonar screen shows this tunnel emptying out onto a train platform and a cavernous space beyond.

As we descend farther down the tunnel, the cackle on the comm-link increases. "Panda?" I try again. "Can you—?"

"I hear you," Liáng says through a high amount of cackle.

It's low signal-to-noise ratio. But at least we can talk again. We must have traveled far enough away from the jammer, which must rely on line-of-sight, or at least not heavy amounts of brick between the jammer and jammed. This actually sparks a disturbing thought of: *how long had we been jammed before? And how physically close were they to jam us?*

The handheld sonar is painting a more complete picture of the underground tube station as we approach. There are two train tracks and a wide platform. The sonar even looks like it picked up some kind of loading device down a bit on the platform, though it's still fuzzy at this point.

Liáng says through the cackle, "Since we can talk at the moment, would you like tell me the rest of the plan?"

That's a perfectly reasonable request in light of the jamming. "No."

In between the straps holding the two balloon bags rising up from the DPV, I can visually start to see the underground station. The platform is concrete that's painted brown, or at least I think that's brown under the cream to sand-colored silt. There's also a yellow strip indicating the edge.

The station tunnel ceiling is curved with square, coffered tiles. The curved portion of the walls is covered in classic white subway tile.

We emerge out of the tunnel into the station. No sign of Puo. *Damn.*

I use the handheld device to paint each direction in the station in more detail.

Would you like to tell me the rest of the plan? Nope.

"Hey, Panda," I say, "You hear me?" There's no cackle on the line, and it's unlike Liáng not to respond in some fashion to the denial for information—likely some prim, holier-than-thou response.

Liáng doesn't answer.

I look back at Liáng and tap my helmet over the ear.

Liáng shakes his head no.

If we're being jammed again, then something is close, or closing. I motion to Liáng to look around, while taking another reading with the handheld sonar.

It's a squiddie. Down the tube tunnel. Closing fast and jamming us.

Without taking my eyes off the screen I try to motion to get Liáng's attention. *Is it Puo's squiddie?* He's supposed to meet us down here.

I ping the sonar again.

Definitely not Puo's! A dozen more squiddies just materialized behind it. *Shit!* Looks like we just found where the squiddies were hiding.

I scramble to my DPV to swing back the way we came, keeping the handheld sonar out.

Our only chance is to get out of the open tunnels and into somewhere more confined where the squiddies can't move as well and, therefore, might not be able to detect us.

Liáng may not know about the small armada of squiddies, but he recognizes my oh-shit-gotta-get-out-of-here motions and hurries up to follow me.

Our DPVs *whir* as we rush out of there and back up the tunnel.

The handheld sonar picks up another squiddie heading down the main tunnel toward us. *Fuck! They're closing us in.*

I estimate some quick distances. I think we can get to the side tunnel that leads back toward the stairwell before the squiddie reaches us. Except it's the stairwell that holds the frogman who's called his buddies—

That must be why the squiddies are here. Held in reserve for the wet teams to deploy. *Wonderful.*

The high whine of our DPVs fills the tunnel. If the squiddie ahead of us couldn't plain see us with its active sonar, the stupid whine of these vehicles would be a beacon for its passive sonar.

I wonder if the military DPVs make this much noise. Or go this slow at top speed? *Should've swapped mine out.*

The thin water glides over my form as we sprint up the tunnels. The water isn't as pure as when we originally passed— flecks of silt filter through the water from before.

I keep my helmet lights on. There's no point now in killing them. All it'll do is blind us without providing any kind of cover.

The squiddie coming down the tunnel at us is coming too fast. *We're not going to make it.*

And I can't coordinate with Liáng.

Blood pounds through my neck. *Can the squiddie even drag us to the surface from down here?*

The lights of the squiddie down the tunnel blare into focus. Two pinpoint lights growing rapidly in the tunnel as it barrels down on us.

I drop the handheld sonar in exchange for my knife and cradle it close to my body, trying to hide it. It's the only weapon close at hand—the stunner is an eternity away safely packed tight in the equipment bag on my back.

We're screwed.

I ignore the avalanche of panic rising up, particularly about what to do with the balloon bags.

The best play is to let the squiddie think it has us, and then at the opportune time: *Stabby! Stabby! Stabby!*

The squiddie is close enough for me to make out the center black teardrop shape rushing toward us. The circular window in the center feels oddly alive. Its appendages are flared out behind it.

I take a deep breath, preparing myself.

Will Winn know if I die down here? Will he know if I get arrested? Will my image flood the news feeds?

Will my father know?

I bring the DPV to a stop and distance myself from it, trying to make myself an easy target. Nothing for the squiddie to get overexcited about.

The knife blade is pressed flat against my forearm as I cup the handle. The saw-toothed edges dig in, beg for a better purchase.

Here it comes. All eight appendages snap forward, ready to pounce.

I try to force myself to be limp to better handle the shock of the initial grab.

I twist away and slam my eyes closed, bracing myself.

Turbulent water whooshes over my head, bringing with it a wave of gritty silt. But there's no sudden, violent grabbing.

I open my eyes and jerk around to follow the squiddie.

The squiddie screams over Liáng, toward the small armada of squiddie lights heading up the tunnel from the underground station.

Puo? Or better to arrive en masse then go one on two?

I briefly think of taking advantage of our momentary reprieve, but there's no way we're going to outrun them. Better to stick to the—

The lone squiddie bowls through the group of squiddies. *Clank! Ca-clank, clank!* Right down the center.

Puo!

In the process one squiddie grabs another squiddie and holds it still, staring from teardrop center to teardrop center before releasing it. As soon as that squiddie is released it turns toward one of its companions and does the same thing.

Oh, thank God.

Pretty quickly all of the squiddies have been greeted thusly.

The original lone squiddie (I think—hard to tell them apart) swims up toward us. The rest of the squiddie pack stays back, hovering in place as if confused.

"Hey-ya, Queen Bee," Puo's voice breaks in over the comm-link. "What ya doin' cowering down there?"

Chapter Twenty-Six

"I AM NOT COWERING," I say to Puo, "Thank you very much."

"Nah," Puo says, "You were definitely cowering."

Freaking Puo. How can he go from saving my ass and being the best, most awesome person in the world to needling me so effectively so quickly?

"Where you been?" I ask Puo. "You know what? Never mind. Panda, you on the line?"

Liáng answers, "Yes. I'm here—"

"Great," I say. "Let's get out of here. Head back down to the underground station."

"Uh, okay," Liáng says. "What is going on with the squiddies?"

"Ah, yes," Puo says smugly, "very mysterious indeed is the arcane practice of the digital magician. But fear not my analog muggle—"

"He hacked the Muppies code," I say to short-circuit Puo's smugness—*I was not cowering.* "The code they used to hijack our squiddie."

Puo's squiddie hijacking trick was too risky to incorporate into our main plans. We weren't a hundred percent sure it would work, or how the authorities would respond once they figured it out (like pulling all the remaining squiddies away for example). That, and Puo took his sweet time figuring out how to do it.

"Whoa," Liáng says, and then adds, "Good job."

"Why, thank you good, sir," Puo says. "At least someone among us knows how to express gratitude." He pauses expectantly.

I grit my teeth. My jaw muscles burn from clenching. *Freaking Puo*. Finally, I manage to say, "Toady—" About thirty inappropriate things run through my mind, but I settle on, "—I say thank you all the damn time. Most recently when we were upstairs. And now if you think I'm going to—"

"All right, all right—" Puo starts.

"Don't all right me," I say. I can too express gratitude. I just don't like doing it when it's an expectation. I philosophically believe that true gratitude can't exist when the other person is demanding it. So Puo can take his "thank you" and—

Puo interrupts my thoughts, "You were so cowering."

"I was not! For your information, I was preparing to defend myself." I brandish my knife at him. "You're lucky you didn't come any closer."

"Ohhh, a knife," Puo mocks. "Scary. Don't believe in stunners?"

I ignore him and start up my DPV, turning it around to go back down to the station. The cadre of squiddie lights all blare at me, mostly motionless.

"I'm still logging this one," Puo says.

"Logging?" Liáng asks over the low whine of his DPV starting up to follow me.

"Aggh!" I clench my teeth. "Why, Plumpy Panda? Why did you—?"

Puo talks over me, all too happily by the sound of it, "I'm glad you asked, my perplexed Panda. Every time I save Queen

Bee's butt, it goes in the log for prosperity. Last I checked it was one hundred and fourteen times to twelve."

I cut in, "There's no log. And if there were, you're not counting all the times I chose not to strangle you in your sleep. How many days have we known each other?"

The wall of squiddie lights continue to stare at me, unmoving, as I approach.

"Toady," I say, "Move your ... your ... whatever the hell a group of toads is called."

"What is a group of toads called?" Puo wonders out loud.

The squiddies turn around as a group and head back down to the underground station.

Puo and I are silent, waiting for Liáng to answer.

Finally Liáng says, "Well, I don't know. How about we talk about the muppie back in the stairwell? Or how about where Toady-Chameleon was? Or how we're getting out of here?"

Puo asks, "Muppie?"

I fill Puo in on our encounter with the frogman. "That's probably why the squiddies showed up," I finish with.

Puo's silent while he mulls this over. Eventually he says, "I don't think so. The squiddies can't move *that* fast. They must have already been in the tunnels to get here that quickly."

Well that's not good. I drive the DPV down to hover over the tracks and disengage, pulling the equipment bag off my back.

Puo continues, "You let the frogman intentionally jam you?"

Before I can answer, Liáng says, "She insisted. Said zero body count."

"Interesting," Puo muses, drawing the word out.

I grind my teeth. I don't need Puo's insinuations or corner-store psychology right now.

Puo's squiddie comes to hover over Liáng and me to provide some extra light to our work.

"So you think," I ask, trying to bring us back on point, "that's where the squiddies are hiding? In the tunnels?" I fish out a rider and clip it to the railway.

"Makes sense," Liáng says, at the same time Puo says in that same annoying musing voice, "Yeah."

I think that over as I untie the two balloon bags from the DPV and attach them to my waist.

"And they deployed," Puo says, switching back to a normal tone, "very quickly."

I chew the bottom of my lip as I power down the DPV and shove it back into the equipment bag. "They knew we were coming," I conclude.

"Yup," Puo says.

This isn't actually a horrifying realization. The missing squiddies, the original stones we dropped through the Great Court almost three weeks ago, MI5 following Shǐ, they'd have to be daft not to think something was in the works.

No. The scary part is the squiddies in the tunnels. To Puo and Liáng I say, "Deploying all of the squiddies in the tunnels shows anticipation. But what were they anticipating, our ingress or egress?"

"Both," Puo says. "They probably figured—"

"Egress," Liáng says. "If they arrested us on the approach, we'd just be trespassers. If they catch us with stolen goods, then we're grave robbers." Grave Robbers: all governments' favorite term for underwater reclamation specialists. Plays well with the public. Horrible, deranged criminals disturbing the dead to steal things—which, of course, is total bullshit. We don't mess with graves, and Puo's only slightly deranged. But the legal penalties for stealing from protected sunken city zones is much steeper than simply trespassing.

"If that's true," I say, slipping the equipment bag on my back, "then they have yet to make their main play."

I reach down and get a good grip on the rider—now *these* things can move.

"Toady," I say, "lead us out of here."

The two balloon bags tug lightly at my waist as I situate myself, getting ready for Puo's squiddie to move off down the tunnel.

Puo's squiddie doesn't move. It continues to float there dumbly.

"Toady," I say, "let's move!"

No response. *Shit.*

I jerk around toward Liáng. He's already tapping his helmet over the ear.

Jammed. *Again.*

But from what direction?

I gesture frantically toward Puo's squiddie to lead the way.

Puo gets it and takes off.

The rider whips off, nearly taking my arm out of its socket. We never did slow down the acceleration on these puppies, which I'm thankful for at the moment.

My glance backward reveals more than just how Liáng is faring: three frogmen. They're heading straight out of the tunnel and down into the station, staring right at us.

But not chasing.

I'd like to think that the frogmen see a group of squiddies chasing after us and are waiting it out. But I doubt it. The riders may be able to outrun the military DPVs, but they can't outrun comm-links.

Chapter Twenty-Seven

IT DOESN'T TAKE LONG for the fact that we can't outrun the comm-links to become readily apparent. At the first underground station we approach, a brand new group of squiddies are waiting for us.

Six shiny new squiddies all with their appendages out and pointed down the tunnel at us.

Puo's pack of squiddies convert them to our cause fast enough. But it's the squiddies' presence that's worrisome. The Muppies must have identified this as a potential escape route and are now converging on it.

"Toady," I say—we've traveled far enough away from the wet team jamming us to be able to talk again. "Send several squiddies to scout ahead."

"Roger, that," Puo says.

To Liáng I say, "Let's slow down a fraction."

I ease back on the riders controls and slow down ten percent or so. Just enough to give the squiddies time to swim ahead and convert any unfriendlies and report back what they find.

The two balloon bags lessen their pull on my waist. My arm muscles are starting to burn from the strain of holding onto the rider.

"How are you doin'?" I ask Liáng.

"I'm hanging on," he replies dryly.

"Ooh," Puo says, "weak pun. Weak pun, Plump Panda. You got to dig a little deeper if you want to have witty dialog. You can't be spurting out the first thing that comes to mind."

Liáng audibly exhales over the comm-link. "What is the plan? How much farther?"

The tunnel curves to the left, as we zip along the graceful train track. There's a layer of silt (of course) over the track, but otherwise we've been fortunate—no stopped trains on the tracks to cause delays.

I haven't answered Liáng yet, still ruminating on the best time to inform him, when he adds, "And what am I to do if they jam us again?"

A real possibility, and a good point. It's already caused headaches.

"Toady," I say, ignoring Liáng's point for the moment, "Can you pipe in music—?"

Puo doesn't even wait for me to finish the question. "Yeah, I'm on it." We had pulled this trick back in the Seattle Isles to know when our communication had been shut off.

Low, classical music filters in through the comm-link. It's a brooding, low-tempo piano piece with some strings accompanying. I inform Liáng that now when the music randomly cuts off, we'll know we've been jammed.

This really should become standard for when we're on jobs. To Puo I say, "About their jammers—the Muppies still have to communicate, right?"

Puo answers, "Yeah, likely in a different band."

"Can we use that band?" I ask. *Or jam it?*

"Maybe," Puo says, "depends on the band and if our

receivers/transmitters can operate there. But I don't know what band that is, and the next time we run into them they'll be jamming us so I won't be able to tell you what band to switch comms to."

"Can you jam them?" Liáng asks.

Damn it, that was my *idea.* This punk is always stealing my lines.

"Yeah," Puo says, "That's a good idea." Then in a knowing smartass tone Puo asks, "What'd you think of that idea, Queen Bee? I think it's pretty good."

Freaking Puo.

But before I can respond, Puo rushes on, "Squiddies are waiting at the next station for us. Twice as many as last time. Initiating conversion."

Puo falls silent as his pack of squiddies tries to recruit more members—they're like a spreading infection through the underground tunnels.

I instinctively slow my rider before rushing headlong into a squiddie fight, waiting for the outcome. I glance behind me to be sure nothing's following us, but all I see is Liáng and a cloud of silt kicked up from our passing.

Puo says, "It looks like the Muppies kept one squiddie back near the stairwell. It bolted before I could convert it."

"A scout," I say. "The Muppies are getting wise."

"Yeah," Puo confirms.

"Is the next station a changeover?" I ask. "We need to get off this track." And start introducing permutations as soon as possible.

Puo's quiet for a few seconds, while he presumably checks some things and then says, "Yeah. We can changeover at the next station and still get to the next waypoint. But it'll take longer."

"Understood," I say. "Plan on the changeover." The Muppies are closing in. The sooner we're not where they expect us to be, the better off we are.

"Where is the next waypoint exactly?" Liáng asks.

Chapter Twenty-Eight

ST. PANCRAS International Station was once a major train station in north London built in the beautiful Victorian style. Now it's a decaying mess like most of the buildings tucked in under the Sea of London's frothy blanket.

But decaying mess or not, there are a number of tracks that pull into and out of and diverge off the main tracks into St. Pancras. It's an ideal waypoint to inject some confusion, particularly since we've had some time to set up some surprises in the two weeks leading up to this. Fortunately, those two weeks were a lot of Puo's practice with the rogue squiddie.

That's the problem with a smash and grab; it *always* leads to a chase. And if the chase isn't immediate, then the authorities are quickly hunting you down as the trail hasn't had time to cool off while you make your getaway. This is why most of our jobs are the subtle kind—by the time the authorities learn of the theft, we've already split town and moved the goods through a fence. So with a smash and grab you *have* to have a strategy in place to give yourself more time to escape. And while we planned for a chase, we didn't plan for it to be happening so quickly.

Puo, Liáng and I approach St. Pancras from the southeast—a different (and longer) direction than we originally intended. We switched tracks at the first underground station after the one where the lone squiddie got away to report to its masters. And then switched again for good measure at another station.

The three of us (and the group of slaved squiddies) travel into the underground station of St. Pancras. The tight curved tunnel opens up to an underground platform with higher curved ceilings. Square signs and billboards dot the wall. Stairs in the center lead upward. A plopper sits still at the entrance to the stairwell—Puo's squiddie shoots ahead to dismantle it. Fortunately, outside the British Museum, ploppers aren't networked together, so the Muppies won't know for some time it's been dismantled.

"Toady," I say, unclipping from the rider, "head upstairs and sniff around." My shoulders ache in a good way now that the strain is gone from holding on to the rider.

"Roger, that," Puo says. Puo's squiddie swims off toward the stairwell. The converted squiddies stay behind, floating there dumbly, awaiting orders.

I wiggle a bit to get the equipment bag off my back with the two balloon bags tied to my waist.

"Plump Panda—" I start.

"I am not plump!" Liáng suddenly snaps.

"Take it easy—" I start to say.

"What is the plan?" Liáng demands to know, frustration boiling over. "You're not telling me anything."

"No, Wei Jing," I say, using his name from the newspaper article of his arrest, "I'm not. Toady and I have no desire to end up as someone's lackey. I'm sorry that happened to you, but it is not going to happen to us."

Liáng doesn't respond at first, but then says more quietly, "I am not plump."

"No. You're not." That plump thing really gets to him. I half wonder if he was fat as a kid—kids can be brutal. "I tell you what. When we get up into the station, you do what I tell you, when I tell you, and when we come out of this we can discuss a new moniker." *Look at me being diplomatic.*

I retrieve my DPV and tie my two balloon bags to it. A quick glance back at Liáng confirms he's following my lead.

"What's going to happen up there?" Liáng asks, a petulant undertone to the question.

"Distraction and diversion—" I start to answer.

"Oh, crap!" Puo yells on the line.

The converted squiddies suddenly launch themselves toward the stairwell after Puo.

"Toady—?" I start to ask.

Puo rushes, "There're squiddies waiting in the station! Not a lot, but they were right there waiting. They're running, not engaging."

Shit. The Muppies are going to know we're here much earlier than I hoped.

"Panda," I say, "Stay close to me, and do what I do. The key is, get as many set up as we can before they arrive en masse."

The DPV whirs as I accelerate it to full speed. After the slapdash of the riders, the DPV feels like driving with Grandma on her meds. *Gaa!*

"Get what set up?" Liáng asks. His DPV whirs up behind me.

"Balloon bags," I answer him, "on automatic riders. We'll also attach some to the converted squiddies if we can manage."

I angle the DPV up the narrow stairs. My dangling fins brush the top of the dead plopper as I hurry over.

Liáng asks, "Are the balloon bags the distraction, or the diversion?"

The stairwell turns ninety degrees upward. "Do you always take what I say literally?" I ask. Technically it's the distraction. But it's not what we should be focusing on. "There are automatic riders attached to all the railways, and two duffle bags of empty balloon bags should be waiting for us in the arcade. Grab one of the duffle bags and then proceed to the lower level railways and attach and inflate the empty balloon bags. Once done proceed upstairs and help with the upper-level tracks. Understood?"

"Do I activate the automatic riders?" Liáng asks. Then he adds, "And why say both distraction and diversion? They are different techniques you know."

"Yes, I know Bob. They're different techniques," I say and ignore the uncomfortable feeling in my stomach. Winn and I have had this conversation before. The distinction comes from the theory of stage magic, something Puo and I have been interested in for obvious reasons.

"But don't activate the riders," Puo breaks in on the line when I trail off in thought. "I'll take care of that."

"Understood," Liáng says.

There's another silence on the line before Puo says, "Queen Bee, how many of the converted squiddies do you want to attach balloon bags to?"

I can tell by Puo's tone that that isn't the question he really wants to ask me. He wants to ask me if I'm all right, if the déjà-vu-bait on the theory of stage magic rattled me at all. It didn't. It's just like pushing on an old scar, where you feel the edges of the scar but no pain. It's a perfectly natural response that's completely out of my control.

"Four," I answer confidently. "All to go separate ways when the times comes."

"Roger, that," Puo answers.

Liáng and I emerge out of the underground tunnel into a shopping center in the lower level of St. Pancras. White block tile with a low level of silt spreads across the floor left and right. Across from us is a row of abandoned stores. Their glass fronts are mostly intact, and several have their metal security gates down as if they one day expected to open back up for business.

We steer the DPVs to the right and glide past several of the empty stores: a perfume store, a woman's clothing store, a luggage store. It's eerie to think of this place once full of people.

Puo cuts in, "Cruisers are en route and have launched HiDARs."

"Damn," I swear. They know we're here—at least this shopping graveyard is about to have more company.

HiDARs are not a smart move—St. Pancras is under a roof. But it's their equipment they're wasting—probably launched by a government employee that's doing the minimum respectable amount of work to not get fired. '*Look Boss, the flow chart said to launch HiDARs so that's what I did.*' *Snort.*

"Panda," I say, "the duffle bags are up ahead, grab one and proceed to the lower-level tracks. Toady will help guide you. Skip every other rider, and attach an empty balloon bag to two converted squiddies. Understood?"

"Understood," Liáng says.

I exhale and drive toward the two black duffle bags on the floor up ahead that Puo deposited for us earlier last week. If smashing rocks through iconic British sites is our signature, then we're about to dot the "i" in a spectacular finale.

* * *

Tying the balloon bags is simple enough, but it's a numbers game. The more we get in place before the Muppies arrive, the better our distraction and diversion will be.

I'm quasi-alone on the upper-level tracks, while Puo's squiddie is down below riding herd on Liáng. I say quasi-alone because two of the converted squiddies hover dumbly behind me on the train platform, and Puo's near constant chatter to Liáng is hogging up all the bandwidth on the comm-link.

The converted squiddies are just maintaining buoyancy back on the platform, their appendages hanging limply. They each have an inflated balloon bag tied to them. Their visage makes me think of evil zombie minions sadly watching their evil master overlord leaving on a rainy, nighttime train. The evil master even bought them balloons, but the minions are still heartbroken. The low classical music piping into my helmet even takes on a mournful note. How sad.

Inflating the balloon bags to positive buoyancy is the fun part. Once they're attached to the automatic rider, you push the button on the outside of the bag, and they self-inflate, rising up in the water. Pretty neat.

Unfortunately, I don't have time to watch each one. As soon as one is tied off and inflating, I'm off to the next. Only the low, continued sound of hissing behind me informs me the bag is still inflating.

I'm about halfway done hurrying across the upper-level tracks when Puo announces to both Liáng and I, "HiDARs are in the water."

I keep working, not bothering to reply. Good luck with that. The handy-dandy glass and iron roof sixty feet above me takes care of those buggers for the most part. *Yay for the Muppies being predictable.*

"What's your status, Plump Panda?" I ask.

"About halfway done," Liáng answers.

To Liáng I say, "Skip down to the last two tracks, then let's rendezvous at the security office—Toady will lead you there." We're running out of time. If the HiDARs are in the water, other things should be nearby as well.

"Roger, that," Liáng says.

To Puo I ask, "Any sign of our friends?"

"No," Puo answers. The rest of the converted squiddies not waving goodbye to their evil overlords are patrolling the perimeter of St. Pancras, keeping watch for any sign of the Muppies. "But it's a big place."

"Thanks for the boost in confidence," I say.

"It's what I'm here for." I can hear the smile on Puo's face. At least he's in high spirits—probably riding the high of converting the squiddies. We weren't sure that was going to work, so our plans didn't count on it.

I maneuver the DPV to the end of the tracks to follow my own advice. The goal is to overload the Muppies, give them so many targets, spread out so far, that they don't know what to track.

"Queen Bee," Puo says, his voice now full of concern.

I finish tying the first of the last two bags at the end of the tracks. "What?"

"There's something coming in under the roof near you."

I stupidly look in that direction, flashing my helmet lights. I'm sure that was a nice sign to whatever's coming that something interesting is here, while in turn I see absolutely nothing. "What is it?" I left the handheld sonar device back on my DPV.

"I don't know," Puo answers. "I don't recognize it. Both of your converted squiddies picked it up."

The St. Pancras roof travels out quite a ways. There's the original glass and iron arched roof that I'm currently under, but also a flatter more modern section that extends out. Whatever is coming will be here soon.

"I'm getting outta here," I say. I push off the metal railway toward my DPV. "Keep the converted squiddies on me."

"Roger, that," Puo says.

"Panda," I say, "Meet me at the security office."

Liáng gives his affirmative.

The security office is our ticket out of here. There's a little known private entrance to the underground from there for VIPs, mostly government officials important enough to have their own security detail, that we plan to exploit.

The DPV whirs to life and pulls me along toward the platform and my two evil minions.

"Queen Bee," Puo says, his concern growing, "hurry."

"I am hurrying. Why?" Stupid DPVs with their stupid weak whirring motors.

I glide past the two converted squiddies who don't move to follow, and head straight for the stairs that lead down.

Puo doesn't answer.

"Toady—!"

"Oh, crap!" Puo screams. "Forget the DPV. Grab the squiddie!"

One of the converted squiddies springs to life audibly whooshing water behind me as it sprints forward. It slows next to me waiting for me to grab on.

I do exactly as Puo tells me, releasing the DPV in mid-motion and grab onto one of the squiddie's metal articulating appendages for dear life.

The squiddie launches itself forward as soon as I'm on, nearly ripping the appendage out of my grip, and jerking my breath out of my chest.

"Toady—!" I croak. I try and look back but see nothing as the squiddie rushes me toward the stairs.

"It's a HiDAR," Puo rushes, "being carried *by* squiddies!"

Oh, crap is right. Clever bastards. So much for minimum-work-government-employee manning the station.

Now they're going to have a damn accurate view of what's going on in here. Including a nice image of a sexy underwater reclamation specialist in a full dry suit trying to flee the platform. I kill my helmet lights—no point making it easier for them. Now only the squiddie lights the way.

The squiddie dives down the stairs with me in tow.

"Toady," I rush, "keep an eye on it. Prepare to light the candles."

The metal appendage is cold seeping through my death grip. The water pressure builds up on my helmet and chest, breaking down my back to roll off my fins.

"Roger, that," Puo says in a clipped perfunctory manner as he focuses on the new threat.

I can taste the salty sweat dripping into my mouth as we sprint by the ghosts left of once-thriving storefronts. The suit feels too warm.

"Panda," I say, "You know where you're—"

Liáng answers, "I know where I'm going."

"Good." At least I think good. A sudden spike of worry hits that left unsupervised, Liáng, if a turncoat, could present a problem.

Puo says, "I got a squiddie with him if he needs help." Translation: *I'm keeping an eye on him.*

The middle of my back aches from holding on. The stupid balloon bag tied to the squiddie keeps thumping down onto my left shoulder every so often, while the two balloon bags tied to my waist keep tugging at me. Shouldn't be much farther.

"Holy crap," Puo whispers, and then says much more loudly, "It's a whole freaking squiddie navy."

"Wha—?" I start.

"Squiddies!" Puo yells. "Hundreds of them swimming through the open wall of the train tracks!"

"Start converting them," I damn near shout.

"There're too many," Puo says. "Get in position so we can blow this candle."

"Roger, that," I say. "Panda, you copy?"

"Copy, that," Panda says. "I'm almost there."

Lights from a group of squiddies flash as they barrel up a set of escalators to the upper floor. "Uh, Toady?"

"They're ours," Puo confirms.

Almost there. My squiddie turns the corner off the main arcade to a smaller arcade where the main entrance and ticket counters are, as well as the security office.

Helmet lights! Four sets of them at the main entrance.

"Stop!" I scream at Puo. "The wet teams are in the building!"

Then too many things happen at once.

The squiddie I'm holding onto pivots so fast the appendage rips out of my hands and I get tangled up with one of my balloon bags before starting to drift down toward the bottom.

Horribly screeching, loud metal-on-metal sounds crash down from the platform above announcing the squiddie battle has started and is raging in the upper levels.

All four helmet lights zero in on me. A soft *pop* of pressurized air comes from the wet team's direction, followed immediately by *zoof*, a wicked fast air bubble shooting by three feet to my right—a super-cavitating fléchette.

They're not fucking around.

Hopefully, that was a warning shot. I don't move.

"Toady!" I yell. "Toady!"

No response. Only then do I notice the silence. No low classical background music playing.

Jammed.

Chapter Twenty-Nine

THE BALLOON BAG I tumbled into when I fell off Puo's squiddie is now overinflated. It now buoys up my midsection as I drift downward, making me a nice, dumb, fat target for the frogmen.

But no additional shots come, as the helmet lights steadily approach.

The sounds of the squiddie battle raging up above filter down the open stairways. Clanking and metal crashing together abound. It's eerie not to hear Puo's brand of not-swearing and not-cursing as they go to war.

My knife and the handheld sonar were on the DPV I dumped. And the stunner is in my equipment bag on my back. Not that the knife or stunner would help me—I'm pretty sure any sudden movement will bring increasingly closer fléchettes.

I take a deep breath as I watch the frogmen approach. I haven't absolutely lost until the prison bars slam closed on me. They still have to get me to the surface. And they still have to get me to a secure facility.

I'm suddenly aware of the small silver chain of Winn's necklace pressed against my skin, a slight pinching sensation. I activated the pearl pendant digi-scrambler when putting on the dry scuba suit—the necklace really was the perfect gift for me. It should buy me a few extra moments to do something stupid to try and escape before they get an image of me once they drag me to the surface.

The bastards are probably going to take the necklace away. And then all I can think is: *Damn, that's not fair.*

The helmet lights are close enough I can make out four black helmets behind three black DPVs—two of them are sharing one DPV. At least my stabby efforts back in the stairwell weren't completely in vain.

The lead frogman has an underwater rifle propped up on the DPV pointed at me. Silt dusts up behind them.

Liáng emerges on his DPV behind the frogmen from the narrow corridor the security office is down. His two balloon bags are missing. *Where did he dump them?*

Liáng eases out into the corridor, hiding in the silt cloud from the frogmen's passing, and heads straight for them. The whine of his DPV is lost amid the other four frogmen, a perk of sound traveling too fast in water for our ears to locate sound underwater.

Oh, good—I won't have to wait to get to the surface to try something stupid.

Liáng's helmet lights are off—I wouldn't have seen him through the silt if it weren't for his motion.

He's going to try and sneak up on them? And then what?

I don't know what he's thinking, but I do my part and not focus on him. Instead I slowly move my arms to give the oncoming frogmen the one finger salute with both hands.

Whatever Liáng's going to do, he needs to do when the frogmen are close to me if he wants me to help—because floating here like a dumbass with a balloon bag buoying up my midsection does not lend itself to quick movement.

Liáng is creeping up on them; he's closed half the distance.

One of the two frogman sharing the DPV farthest from me starts to turn around.

Whooshing sounds suddenly fill the smaller arcade: squiddies.

Squiddies come barreling down the stairs, tumbling from around the corner, heading straight for the frogmen—*Puo!*

Great silt clouds billow up from the squiddies' mad dash.

The frogman with the gun starts *popping* off shots at the squiddies.

A metal *ka-thunk* sounds off as one the fléchettes hits it mark. One of the squiddies goes limp in its forward progress and drifts to the silt-covered tile floor.

The other frogmen cease their forward progress and reach for their handheld guns.

Squiddies zoom between me and the frogmen, kicking up a silt storm to hide me.

One of the squiddies slows as it approaches me, clearly wanting me to grab on—*don't mind if I do.*

Pop, pop, pop. The super-cavitating rounds bubble in the water around me. The bastards are firing indiscriminately.

Ka-chunk. Another one of the squiddies is hit.

The squiddie I'm hanging onto drags me back the way I came, away from the trigger-happy frogmen, ducking around the corner. I use the opportunity (and leverage) to return the overinflated balloon bag around my waist back to the proper level.

The sounds in the small arcade change. A scuffle. *Liáng.*

I let go of the squiddie as it rushes ahead.

Puo must be paying attention because it stops immediately and turns back to me.

I motion back toward Liáng and the frogmen.

The squiddie uses an appendage to shake "no."

Liáng came to help when he didn't have to. If he were working with Shǐ to screw us, he could've just let the frogmen do their job.

I motion back toward Liáng and the frogmen.

I can't hear Puo, but I can imagine his growl of begrudging acquiescence. The squiddie moves slowly at first to pick me up and then picks up steam as we head back into the fray.

The small arcade is a mess. Silt invades the space like a thick fog, swirling as looming, dark masses move within it.

Multiple sounds dominate the space from squiddies dragging their metal appendages across the tile, stirring up as much silt as possible to the *pop, pop, pop* and bubbling *zoofing* from super-cavitating fléchettes.

My helmet lights are still off; I try the nightvision. Nothing but silt clouds.

The squiddie carrying me skirts along the edge of the small arcade, zigging every few seconds.

Several sets of helmet lights up ahead are dancing around in quick furtive motions—like roving spotlights at the entrance of a club.

The dark, looming forms resolve themselves into five forms.

Liáng is struggling with one of the frogmen, embracing him—using him as shield from super-cavitating fléchettes.

Another frogman is lying at the bottom of the small arcade, motionless. A third frogman is trying to get to his fallen comrade and get a shot at Liáng with his underwater handgun.

The fourth frogman is above the fray keeping watch, aiming an underwater rifle—*at me!*

My squiddie shoots downward the same time I hear a *pop*, and a *zoof* whizzes by so close I can feel the water turbules between my neck and shoulder.

Another squiddie flies out of the silt toward the frogman with the underwater rifle.

My squiddie interjects itself into the mass, zooming between the third frogman with the handgun and Liáng. And leaving me staring directly at the frogman. Like, suddenly face-to-face with the frogman three feet away, who is holding a handgun.

Uh, Puo?

I lash out to kick away the frogman's gun that's swinging toward me—pushing my fins sideways through water takes a lot of the *oomph* out of it. But before I connect, my leverage against the squiddie's appendage shifts under me, jerking me around.

I whiff on my kick and am suddenly dumped into the struggle between Liáng and the frogman he's hugging.

I promptly start stomping the frogman below me using my heels, while still hanging onto my squiddie. I think the frogman's hard suit and piping and valves do more damage to the bottom of my feet than I do to him.

But it works. Liáng is able to separate a few inches. Then I see what's in his hands: a stunner.

I'm able to get my legs out of the way when Liáng tries to shove the stunner against the frogman's chest.

The frogman deflects it, and backs off quickly.

Liáng uses the free second to grab one of my squiddie's appendages and as soon as he's on, the squiddie takes off with both of us as if that's what it had been waiting for.

The squiddie drags the two of us down the way we came, away from the security office.

We turn the corner, out of the line of fire. But we need to go in the opposite direction to get to the security office to get out of here.

Low classical music comes back on the line.

"Toady!" I yell, "Do you—?"

"I hear you!" Puo yells back excitedly. "They dropped the jamming. I'm dropping their jamming as well."

"Why?" I ask.

"Quid pro quo," Puo says. "They probably think that their own jamming is cutting themselves off."

"But why now?" I ask. The squiddie is dragging us down the main arcade. The sounds of the squiddie war up above gain and fade as we pass between stairways. "And where are we going?"

"Anywhere but here," Puo answers. "And I don't know."

"I do," Liáng says. "I stunned one of them—" *The frogman motionless on the ground.* "—They probably need to call for help."

Damn it—zero body count.

"But stunning him shouldn't kill him," Puo says, too familiar with my thinking patterns.

"They need to evacuate him," I say. "Toady, keep a squiddie-eye on them. I want to know what they're doing."

Anxiousness piles up within my chest, great weights resting on my sternum. Winn's necklace is pressed awkwardly against my skin, pinching the edge of my left breast.

Zero. Fucking. Body count.

I breathe in deeply, pushing those weights off, and say, "We have a bigger problem. We can't blow the candle with them in the building."

Puo's quiet on the other end of line. He knows this. It's too risky—it could inadvertently kill them. But it's the blow-off; it's how we're getting outta here.

Puo says, "So what do you want to do? Sneak away?"

"No," I say. They could follow us, or at least find our escape route too soon before we've had sufficient time to clean shop. "We need to lure them out of the building."

The squiddie pulls Liáng and me into a departure lounge

and kills the squiddie's lights. "What's the bait?" Puo asks in a tone that suggests he knows the answer.

"Seeing as you're already trolling with two pieces of juicy bait—" I start to say.

"No way," Puo says, breathing through his nose. "Know when to cut losses and run. It's time to run. They have guns, Queen Bee, and they're firing them."

Liáng says, "I agree, with Mr. Toad. If we can slink away, let's do so. There's plenty of cover with the other squiddies, and you can still activate your distractions."

"Seconded," Puo immediately jumps in to agree.

"This is not a democracy," I say.

"Queen Bee," Puo pleads, "for the love of Neptune. We talked about this. We don't need supergirl here—the moment's passed. The Muppies are playing a good game. We just need a win. Not a shutout."

The soft piano notes have a meandering tempo. The two balloon bags tugging at my waist lessen as the squiddie slows down. *Winn isn't affecting me—he's not.* We *need* to give ourselves the proper amount of time to escape.

The sounds of the squiddies upstairs continue to dominate the aural landscape. "How many of the squiddies have you converted?" I ask. "And what's with the sports metaphor?"

"Zero," Puo answers seriously. "They must have figured out what was going on and shut off that feature."

Damn.

"Queen Bee," Puo starts again. "Restoring the frogman's power back in the stairwell was questionable—"

"What about the surface craft, Toady?" I cut him off.

"What about forcing me to drag you into the middle of a gun fight with no weapon!"

"What was I supposed to do—?" I start to ask exasperated.

"Nothing, Queen Bee! Nothing. I could've sent squiddies in without humans attached to them."

"Then why didn't you?"

"Because God only knows what stupid thing you would do if you didn't get your way and I left you behind." When I don't answer right away, Puo plows on, "It's time to cut our losses and go home—"

"Fine!" I say to shut him up. "Fine." I don't want to hear it, and I can't think of a great reason not to slink away. But fuck. If we were going to do that, we should've done that ages ago.

And Winn is not affecting me.

* * *

We waste more precious time waiting for two new converted squiddies to show up and escort us off. The squiddie we've been clinging to has an empty balloon bag attached to it for a decoy.

Now that we've decided to wave the white flag of lameness and slink away, waiting around for extra seconds is like hearing nails on a chalkboard.

"They almost here yet?" I ask Puo. One of the two of my balloon bags drifts forward from the inaction and bumps me in the back.

"Almost," Puo says, "I'm bringing a whole group of them by as a screen."

"Sure you can handle two of us on separate squiddies?" I dig at him. "As much as I appreciated being laid out front and center for the frogman back there to get shot, I'd rather not do that again."

"There was a lot going on!" Puo defends himself. "And I think I'm doing pretty darn good for only just learning these things a month ago."

Yeah, he is. "There's still a lot going on," I say, but without any real snap to it.

Puo *harrumphs.*

A group of converted squiddies pass by outside the departure lounge, two of which break off and make their way in, turning on their helmet lights as they approach. The squiddie that had escorted us swims off to join the pack that had passed.

"Plump Panda," I ask, "where are your balloon bags?"

Liáng answers, "I left them back in the security office."

"You left them back in the security office?" Puo clarifies. *Good—I was hoping he caught that.*

"Yeah," Liáng answers. "They seemed like they'd be a distraction trying to rescue Queen Bee."

"Assist me," I correct him. I grab onto the squiddie's outstretched appendage that stops near me. "I am not some helpless damsel in distress in need of rescuing."

"Looked like you needed rescuing to me," Liáng says.

"Then you need to get your eyes checked," I say. "I almost had them where I wanted them." I freaking hate the whole man-needs-to-save-helpless-woman bullshit. If the woman really was that helpless, then she had already outlived her life expectancy having survived that long as freaking helpless. "If anything, you nearly screwed everything up."

"I'll remember that next time," Liáng says dryly.

"Children," Puo says, "I hate to interrupt, but are you two ready to go?"

Liáng and I both say, "Yes," like two perfectly reasonable adults and not at all like petulant children.

The squiddies kill their helmet lights, plunging us back into darkness. Their active sonar should be enough to guide their way.

Puo says, "The frogmen are on the move. Two of them are forming a sling between them to move the motionless one. It looks like they're going to head to the nearest exit."

My squiddie starts to move forward; the metal appendage is cold again through my hands as I tighten my grip. "Where's the fourth?"

"Uh ..." Puo mumbles.

"Toady!" I snap.

"I don't know!" Puo says, and then preemptively cuts me off. "A lot's going on! All right?"

"No!" I say. "It's not all right."

"Then be quiet and let me concentrate," Puo snipes.

I raise my eyebrows at his tone, but don't prolong the argument. Hopefully, the frogman can't aim an underwater gun based on his handheld sonar alone.

We glide out into the main arcade and turn left, away from the security office and where the Muppies are evacuating their comrade. My two balloon bags strum out behind me.

Puo whispers, "I intend to bring you to the stairs near the south entrance, and sneak you up through the upper level to the stairs near the far platforms on the east side. That will dump us down right near the security office."

"What about the squiddie battle up there?" Liáng asks.

The sounds of which are getting louder as we turn the corner and see a set of stairs in the middle of the arcade leading up.

"About that—" Puo starts.

Oh, great—I know that tone.

"—I'm going to turn off the active sonar, and identification pinger. They're pretty busy to do a visual sweep. We'll sneak right through."

"So, we're flying blind?" I ask just to make sure I understand.

"Not blind," Puo says. "I have situational awareness from the other squiddies."

"Like you did when you deposited me in front of the frogman to get shot?" I ask. *And the missing cruisers? And the missing fourth frogman?*

"You're never going to let that go, are you?" Puo says. "You're fine now. No one shot you. And it'll be fine—"

"Activate the distractions," Liáng suggests.

Damn it. That's a good idea to activate the riders on the rails, and I was right about to say it. Instead I say, "Use the converted squiddies to escort the riders, protecting the cargo."

"There's a bit much going on for me to direct them as escorts," Puo complains. "I don't actually have six hands."

"Then use one of the hands you do have," I tell him. Then more helpfully I say, "We'll wait."

"Roger, that," Puo says. "Standby."

The squiddies dragging Liáng and I slow down to a stop near the stairs leading up. My balloon bags drift upward, bumping into the back of my helmet.

"What are we waiting for?" Liáng asks.

"Toady to grow six hands," I say.

"For me to get everything in place," Puo answers.

"How are the Muppies looking?" I ask. The two balloon bags tug at my waist.

It's dark in the hallway except for the flashes of light and the sounds of the squiddie battle traveling down through the stairwell. If a frogman were five feet away, I wouldn't know it.

"Good," Puo answers absent-mindedly. "The two of them are still transporting the third one out."

"But where's the fourth?" Liáng asks. "I can't see a damn thing."

"Neither can I," I say. "Toady, can these things detect the active pulse from the frogman's handheld sonar?" I had to abandon the one I had upstairs when the squiddie army with the HiDAR arrived. *The HiDAR!*

"Toady, what about the HiDAR?" I ask.

"It's destroyed," Puo says matter-of-factly. "And yes on the active pulse. Nothing in the arcade."

"When did the HiDAR—?" I start to ask.

"Earlier," Puo says shortly. "A lot's been happening."

I imagine I can hear Puo typing frantically over the classical music through the comm-link as we float there in the dark. The building piano notes are woven in with a woeful cello accompaniment.

"Okay," Puo says. "Here we go. Hold on."

"Holding on," Liáng and I repeat back to him.

My squiddie first articulates its appendages upward with small, crinkly sounds and then moves slowly around the other side of the stairwell; one of the appendages bumps one of my balloon bags, causing it to pull sharply on my waist. Liáng's squiddie is right behind me. The light from the squiddies fighting and chasing each other up above illuminates the stairs in blue pixelated detail.

"Activating distractions," Puo says.

The zipping sound of the rapid acceleration of the riders undercuts the squiddies' *clanking* and *whooshing* around.

Almost immediately there's a subtle shift in the squiddies' sounds as they give chase.

My squiddie eases me to the upper level and immediately skirts to the right, staying low, heading for the distant small sliver of a walkway between the farthest train track and east wall.

The squiddies in the distance to my left look like an old nighttime World War Two aerial battle. Flashes of light, like heat lightning on a summer day, dipping and weaving around each other in the expanse under the glass and iron roof. They look completely focused on themselves, oblivious to anything on the ground, fighting in a world all their own.

I can see a few of the balloon bags, highlighted in blue pixels, zooming down the tracks with squiddies following overhead illuminating them. The tangled mass of other fighting squiddies move in that general direction.

Sweat drips down the sides of my neck as I tightly clench the squiddie's appendage. I swivel my neck around, feeling the sweat grind in, and search for any sign of the missing fourth frogman.

The narrow walkway opens up to another set of platforms on the right and a set of stairs leading down to the lower level, which should be right across the hallway the security office is down—convenient, that.

"The Muppies cleared out?" I ask Puo.

"Yeah," Puo says. "Heading down now."

This is the last bit. Once we're in the security office, we'll use their private entrance into the underground tunnels to make our getaway. I can't help but shake my head though. We had the perfect setup. Now lost.

The security office is a steel cage, a bomb shelter designed to protect against enemy planes, bombs, and terrorists blasts. Once we lured all the Muppies' mechanical toys into the station and we were in the security office—*ka-blooey!* We were going to bring the whole thing down on top of them.

The Muppies would lose all their assets, and they'd probably think we were dead. By the time they dug everything out and figured out where we were and how we got away, we'd be long gone.

It was *perfect*.

Now all they need to do is complete a sweep of the building. That'll take some time, but not nearly as long as digging through a pile of rubble.

My squiddie swims down the stairs into a curved narrow hallway with a low ceiling—well, low compared to everywhere else in this place. The small arcade the ruckus was in is behind us, and still a big silt mess. I can't see very far at all with the nightvision in that direction, only a cloud of blue pixels without any structure to it behind Liáng clinging to his squiddie.

"You sure the Muppies are gone?" I ask Puo again.

"Yes," Puo says, but doesn't elaborate.

The small arcade feels quiet from the ruckus before. There are no flashes of lights. No panicked banging or dark shapes looming in the silt.

"Where are the other squiddies?" I ask.

"I moved them away so as not to draw attention to us," Puo answers.

Our squiddies swim down the center of the hallway as it slowly curves to the left. There's a slight kick up of silt lingering in the hallway, but it's nowhere near as bad as where the ruckus was.

We pass ghostly storefronts, abandoned and broken. An eatery takes up the back corner of the circle the curved hallway makes. Several tables and chairs once set up in the hallway are knocked over and pushed up against the half-wall of the eatery, covered in draping silt.

"Why's the silt kicked up?" Liáng asks.

"Because you were in the security office already," Puo says in a perfectly plausible voice.

Liáng doesn't respond to that as we travel down a hallway that splits off the curved loop to head straight back.

We pass by more broken glass from a large store on the right, while security gates lowered down onto countertops on the left give an basement-bowel kind of feel to this part of the building.

The security office is a nondescript door up ahead to the left. In fact, it stands out as not standing out. No sign on the door or near it. Whereas everything else in this station has multiple signs making their messages clear.

My squiddie swims right up to the door and an appendage curls out to push the handle down and pull it open.

"Nice trick—" I say.

Pop! Zoof!

Clank! My squiddie reels backward from the super-cavitating fléchette puncturing it through its tear-dropped body.

The fourth frogman is floating just on the other side of the door, helmet lights blaring and handgun pointed straight at us.

"Let go!" Puo screams.

Liáng obeys and his squiddie launches into the open door, it's appendages whipping out at the frogman.

Pop! Pop! Pop!

Clank! Clank! Liáng's squiddie is hit.

Liáng and I are pushing our way through the door toward the frogman. In a situation like this, you need to close the gap as quickly as possible to try and nullify the handgun.

Liáng's squiddie continues to thrash in front of the frogman providing cover for us as we slip in.

I push around to the right side, skirting around the flailing squiddie, while Liáng goes left. I bat my annoying-as-shit balloon bags away from my line of sight.

The frogman tracks me with his helmet, two beams of light swiveling onto me, while he struggles with the squiddie in front of him. *Pop! Pop! Pop!*

The squiddie jerks at the impacts. Its appendages go limp.

The frogman starts to turn the gun toward me.

I burst over to him as quickly as I can.

I brush up against him and bring my knee hard into his abdomen.

Pain explodes against my knee—it's like kneeing hard plastic.

Liáng comes up behind him—stunner in hand.

Shit! I push myself away from the frogman. Two balloon bags bouncing off the back of my head and shoulders.

Liáng stuns him from behind.

The frogman goes instantly limp, no jerking, no twitching. Alive and trying to kill me one second, completely still like a dead mule the next.

"Toady," I say, breathing heavily, "Get three squiddies here stat. Panda, good work. Grab your balloon bags and get ready to roll."

"Three? You can't be serious," Puo says.

"Yes, three," I say. "We have an extra guest for the party. And since the other guests have now left, we're going to light candles after all."

Chapter Thirty

PUO COULD ONLY scrounge up one converted squiddie on short notice like that—the one that was dedicated to making sure the other three frogmen were outside the building.

We've just squeezed down the narrow stairs from the security office to the private underground entrance. Liáng and I had to carry the frogman between us in the tight space after zip-tying his hands and feet (Puo retrieved Liáng's DPV). Puo also made sure the stunner scrambled the frogman's communications. But the asshat frogman still struggled to make things difficult. I still maintain zero body count, but that doesn't mean I'm a pacifist. And the quickest way to get your point across with a man is to kick him in the scrotum. This asshat took three to get the point across. Masochist.

Fortunately though, we tied all four of our balloon bags to the squiddie ahead of us so they wouldn't annoy the shit out of me anymore.

"Queen Bee—" Puo starts.

"I don't want to hear it, Toady," I say, climbing onto the same appendage that Liáng is holding onto. The other appendages are picking up and cradling the motionless frogman.

"Well you're going to, damn it!" Puo plows on anyway. "This is nuts! *Nuts!* You're going to bring one of them into the house? How long will it take them to track us down after that?"

"We can't leave him behind," I say. Besides, they were going to find the house in Hampstead eventually. "And lighting the candle will provide the best escape—"

"Falcon—! Falcon!" Puo sputters. Falcon is Winn's codename on the comm-links. "This is all about Falcon again!"

"No it's not!" I shout back.

"Then why restore the frogman's power back in the museum?" Puo brings up again. "His friends were coming! You gave our position away. And now, why not pull this frogman out of the building and alert his friends, and not blow up the building? There are alternatives, Queen Bee!"

"Blow the building, Toady!" I yell at him. The squiddie pulling all three of us moves into the curved underground tunnel.

"It's like you're incapable of compromising—!" Puo says.

"Blow the building!" both Liáng and I shout—well there's an unexpected ally.

"Arrggh!" Puo growls.

Booom! Booom! Booom! The successive sounds are deep seated and distant, but there's no mistaking them. For several seconds the *boooms!* carry through the underground tunnel.

By the time the initial explosions settle, a deep rumbling fills the tunnel, shaking its sides.

Silt shakes free from the roof overhead.

The low classical music (violin this time) cuts off suddenly.

"Toady—?" I ask.

"I'm here," Puo answers. "I just can't listen to that crap anymore." Puo falls into a silence on the comm-link that cackles with a pissy tension.

I start to say, "You need to turn—" *the music back on.*

"No," Puo says.

I can picture his arms across his body perfectly, not looking at me. I toss out my first two responses to this petulance. *Freaking Puo.* I swear I'm going to—

Liáng diplomatically interjects, "What's done is done. For better or worse, given Queen Bee's decisions, blowing the building was the only decision—"

"Funny," Puo bitches, "how she often only leaves us with an 'only' decision."

I bite off any response—I'm going to keep my mouth shut. Keep the peace.

"She only ever thinks about herself," Puo starts. "She doesn't compromise or think of others—"

Fucking Puo! "You know the rule!" I scream at him. *Asshole!* "You know it existed long before Falcon—"

"There are other options, Queen Bee!" Puo yells back.

"What other options!" I shout right back.

But Liáng cuts both off, "Enough! Toady, prepare for our arrival."

Puo waits a heartbeat before saying, "Roger, that." His tone says anything but.

This has nothing to do with Winn.

Nothing.

* * *

The journey through the flooded underground tunnels back to the hole in the basement in the house in Hampstead is uneventful, our route clear of ploppers—the fruit of Puo's prep work. No unexpected opposition.

Except Puo's moodiness.

The progress is slow with three of us weighing down the squiddie. And quiet.

Puo has petulantly kept the music off.

I unhook my balloon bags and push them up through the hole to the basement first, before pulling myself through. Water spills out along the sides of the hole, spreading out on the concrete floor of the basement.

Damn, it feels good to be out of the water, back into a more familiar arena. A floodlight set up in the corner lights up the basement. I slip my flippers off from my feet, not quite the same as slipping off a pair of heels, but close.

Liáng pushes his balloon bags up through the hole. I grab them and set them to the side.

"Double check that the frogman's power is off," I tell Liáng still in the water. We don't want to take the chance he has a homing beacon that will give us away when he gets out of the water.

Liáng does as told, and a minute later, out comes the frogman. I try to grab him under the arms to drag him out of the hole but the bastard starts twisting and turning like a sweaty child trying to avoid a bath.

I drop him back in the watery hole. As the dark water splashes over the sides of the hole, I say to Liáng, "Cut his air tubes. If the bastard wants to be difficult, he can suck water until he wishes to be compliant."

"As you wish." Liáng does as instructed.

I wait a slow count of fifteen. "Let's try this again."

It takes one more try before the frogman finally gets tired of cold water rushing into his suit and cutting off his airway supply.

I fireman-drag him out of the hole to rest on the floor. He lays there with his hands and legs zip-tied together.

I kneel down and unhook the frogman's helmet, slipping it off over his head. "Oww," he complains as it rubs against his thick forehead.

Liáng pulls himself out of the hole. He smartly keeps his helmet on to keep his face hidden from the frogman. "Where's Toady?" he asks me over the comm-link.

The basement's empty. No tables. No computers. No Puo. Just a pile of dirt in the corner. And Liáng hasn't even seen the rest of the house yet.

Where indeed?

I ignore Liáng's question for the moment.

The frogman is a middle-aged black British guy, with a huge head. The kind of head that looks like he took too many steroids for too long. And he's definitely British, judging by how he's shouting at us that we're "under arrest" and "cock-up," and "barmy" this and "bloody" that.

I tap my helmet over the ear and act like I can't hear him.

He starts barking even louder. If he were a dog, he'd be frothing at the mouth. And he really doesn't like it when I flick him off and point to the acoustic tiling on the wall we installed to dampen the sound of our drilling through the concrete floor almost nine weeks ago. Alpha-male pricks hate to be tied up and have someone get the better of them judging by how much he's yelling and struggling. Once Liáng and I clear out, we'll tip off his friends to come collect him.

"Where's Toady?" Liáng asks again over the comm-link, alarm growing in his voice.

"Somewhere safe," I say. I square off toward Liáng.

"What's going on?" Liáng asks.

"You tell me, Wei Jing," I answer back, and take a step to the side to get a better position on him.

Liáng keeps his helmet face toward me as he grabs one of the balloon bags and picks it up much too easily. Alarmed he drops to his knees and opens it. Empty.

He grasps for the next balloon bag. Empty. "What the fuck is going on!"

"You work for a snake," I say. "And we have no intention of being eaten." I switched my balloon bags with the forlorn minions watching me back when I was attaching distractions to auto-riders. And Puo switched Liáng's when Liáng so helpfully left his behind in the security office—it's nice when things unexpectedly fall your way.

"What!" Liáng jumps up, two hundred pounds of pure muscle suddenly looms toward me. "We need it! Where the fuck is it!"

It's in a coastal cottage, where Puo is holed up at the end of the line, with two of those "distraction" riders with escort squiddies.

Liáng doesn't make it even two steps before he convulses and falls to the ground.

"Good to know you're still on my side," I tell Puo.

"I am always on your side," Puo says over the comm-link still petulant. "*Always.*" Which is why Puo suggested adding that small detail of tasers to the inside of Liáng's dry suit.

"Need it?" I ask Liáng on the ground. *And why "we"?*

Liáng doesn't answer me, and we don't have time to dick around. "Fine. Here's the deal," I say to Liáng, "we have the jade. And we are willing to honor our original agreement with one small modification—"

"Modification?" Liáng says through clenched teeth.

296

"We control the jade at an undisclosed location. If you want it—as per our original agreement—Shǐ will meet us alone at a location and time specified by a third party."

"Third party?" Liáng asks.

"Yup," I answer. This isn't about avoiding a potential double cross. It's about avoiding what happened to Liáng and not becoming pawns to the Chinese government. And the best way to deal with that: inject a third player into the mix to change the dynamics.

Liáng pauses only for a second before biting off, "Where?"

Chapter Thirty-One

THE LIBRARY OF BIRMINGHAM really is a gold-plated rats' nest. I'm back in the library, sans Puo, two days after the lift.

It may have been a bit of an understatement to say the British would be royally fucking pissed. They immediately locked down *all* transportation around the Sea of London (which only opened up again this morning). Uniformed police officers are all over the damn place, and the cops are turning the screws on all the old felons to try to sniff out leads.

And that's just the stuff we can see. Puo insists on staying as quiet as we can digitally.

The Greek government has publicly denied any involvement and has offered to send help, while British public opinion on the matter is split. There's some real vitriol that makes me sick to my stomach coming out in some corners toward the Greeks—a number of Greek businesses have been vandalized, and there's been at least one publicized beating in relation to it. It's not quite what I had in my mind when I created my Elgin deceptions.

I take yet another uneasy deep breath as I walk through the rows of library books on the fourth floor off the rotunda toward my meeting.

There are always Neanderthals out there who only need an excuse to act out violently. Still, I provided them that excuse.

I try to shake off the feeling before my confrontation with Shǐ.

The British authorities haven't publicly stated what contents were stolen yet, but it's not lost on us that the Chinese government has come out quickly (for them) and condemned the acts of vandalism and offered whatever support the Brits needed. As in, 'give us the jade that we haven't already stolen.'

The library is too warm in November; blasts of warm, hot air fall down on me from the interspersed vents above. I keep my navy-blue, fur-lined trench coat on all the same.

I find the right library call number: the title of the fiction book is *Double Cross*. *Cute*.

Shǐ walks up purposefully, nir long black hair is down and swaying behind nem. Nir dark eyes are narrowed on me, while nir black knee-high boots over charcoal slacks thump on the carpeted floor.

Ne folds nir arms over nir chest, the fabric of nir thin black coat rustling—for some reason ne reminds me of a horse rider about to go out for a ride. "This was unnecessary," ne says.

"Not from our point of view," I say.

"Their fee comes from your cut," ne insists.

I shrug in response. If it keeps our asses out of jail or becoming pawns for the Chinese government to use whenever they want, then it's well worth it. It's still enough to pay off the Citizen Maker once and for all. There'll be hardly anything left over, but we'll *finally* be out of debt.

Buzzed chestnut hair moves between gaps in the library shelves announcing Kafarov's arrival. He steps around the corner and gives us both a smile. I had forgotten that he was shorter than me.

"Hello, Ladies—" he says in his accented English.

"Ne's not a lady," I say. And then freeze, my cheeks burning. Ne's not a lady, but how is ne supposed to be referenced here?

Shĭ seems to understand my predicament and says, "I identify as non-binary and prefer non-binary pronouns. However, I'd rather conclude our business quickly than educate you. So, if you please."

"All right," Kafarov says, eyeing me. "This is relatively easy. You—" He points to Shĭ. "—send the money to us, and we hold it. Once she—" He points at me. "—is safely out of the country, I tell you where to find your merchandise. The money is then wired to you—" He points to Shĭ again. "—minus a small fee, of course." He smiles.

Small, my ass. I need to get into his business. Easy money—so long as everyone plays by the rules.

"How do I know," Shĭ asks, "that my merchandise is all there? I've never seen it."

"Liáng," I say, "can verify it."

I feel a slight pang about Liáng. He was definitely a good asset to the team, despite his penchant for verbalizing my ideas a half step before me. I would've offered him a permanent spot if he weren't in Shĭ's pocket so much. As it was, we didn't leave on the best of terms with Puo and I hiding the jade on him and tasering him. But I left him a golden carrot as a thanks though—it'll be interesting to see if he takes it.

"Liáng," Shĭ says, "doesn't know the totality of the merchandise."

"No," I admit. He doesn't know what I shoved into my balloon bags. "But he does know his half. And these guys—" I gesture at Kafarov who is smiling like a high-school student who's suddenly found himself in a graduate-level physics class.

"—don't know whose is whose. Liáng will be able to tell you if anything is missing from his half. That should be good enough."

Shǐ considers this for several seconds and then says, "Very well." To Kafarov ne asks, "Where do I wire the money?"

Kafarov gives nir the necessary information.

"Are we finished?" Shǐ says, and then adds snidely, "Seems hardly worth dragging me out—"

"No," I say. "We are not finished." A flash of anger burns in me that this little non-binary bitch likely tried to sell us out to MI5 and the Muppies. And ne was definitely going to try and turn us into pawns. I take a step closer, "Our friends here are also holding a friendly recording of a conversation in a warehouse bathroom with some rather unfortunate retching sounds—"

Shǐ's dark eyes widen.

"—But that's not all they're holding," I say. "See, radio signals don't just magically leave communicators." I flutter my fingers in an imitation of Puo. "They have to pass through antennas and relays before they reach their destination. And every time they touch a new piece of hardware is an opportunity to record them for posterity's sake. So, say, when a person requests the funds to buy acoustic tiling for a basement in Hampstead, a record is made."

"Those messages are encrypted," Shǐ says.

"Yes, they are," I say. "But encryptions aren't difficult to recover when the pocket tablet with the encryption card is left lying unattended upstairs while the owner is trying to use a core drill in the basement." There was always a plan to mirror Liáng's encryption card, but when he presented us the opportunity when he first showed up, we took it immediately.

Shǐ's face drains in color. That's enough for me; ne was planning something.

"If you *ever* fuck with us," I say, "their instructions are not only to deliver this to every British agency in existence, but also the Americans, the Russians, the Japanese and every news agency in the world that might be remotely interested in it."

Shï just stares at me, nir lips clenched shut in tight red lines.

I make a gagging gesture at nem to say goodbye.

Nir eyes narrow into severe hatred.

Kafarov nods at me, and I walk away without looking back.

This is not our first fucking rodeo.

Chapter Thirty-Two

Think that's the last we heard of nem?" Puo asks me diplomatically.

"I hope so," I say quietly. If they do approach us again, it's going to be damn well polite and respectful, that's for sure.

Puo and I sit in a private cabin on one of the first air transports back to the States once the Brits opened up transportation out of the Sea of London again.

Things have been a bit tense between Puo and me since our screaming at each other over the comm-links about Winn and blowing St. Pancras. Puo's apologized, and so have I. But that doesn't mean Puo was necessarily wrong.

I stare out the window; the coast of Greenland is coming into view. It looks like a mountainous wasteland, pretty from forty thousand feet up.

Puo plays with the tan cotton fabric of his pants; the rustling carries over the hum of the transport's engines.

I save him the trouble and say, while still looking out the window, "We were lucky this time."

The reflection of Puo in the window runs his tongue over his teeth, before saying, "We get lucky a lot."

Heh. That's my line. "Well," I say, "if we're going to switch roles, then I suppose I should accuse you of mooning over Winn and making terrible decisions."

"Not terrible decisions," Puo says, "just not optimal ones."

I turn toward him and quirk an eyebrow. "The two words I've heard more than any others lately are 'reckless' and 'stupid.' "

"Yeah," Puo says, fighting a smile, "your decisions have been pretty stupid."

I give a weak smile back.

"Do you miss him?" Puo asks me point blank.

Winn was something different—right from the very beginning. He didn't have that cynical take on life that all criminals have. And he wasn't just interested in what I could do for him, or sex. He was normal. It's so very hard to find normal in my line of work.

Puo already knows the answer, but I confirm it for him anyway and nod.

Winn and I were having a lot of fun together. Even the stupid stuff was more fun with him around, like running errands or doing chores. It wasn't perfect, but at times it felt close. Then things went and got real.

And Winn bailed. No word. No warning. Just gone.

"Are you going to leave me too?" I ask quietly, not able to look directly at Puo.

Puo exhales and shakes his head. He picks himself up and comes to sit down next to me, wrapping me up in a warm embrace. "No way, kid. I ain't ever gonna leave you. But that's what's scaring the bejeezus out of me so much. That you're going to be the one that leaves me—in a body bag or handcuffs. You've got to find a healthy way to deal with this."

I lean into Puo's warm body, and mull over what Puo said. *A healthy way to deal with this.* There's only one way I can think to do that.

"Don't unpack when we get home," I tell Puo, making a decision.

"Yeah?" Puo asks. "Where we headed to next?"

We still have to figure out what my run-in with Ham the Cleaner was all about, but first: "Vancouver."

"Yes!" Puo suddenly shouts and fist pumps. "I *love* Canadians, eh! Score!"

I can't help but smile.

Puo continues his antics to make me laugh, but he knows full well that there's only one thing in Vancouver that remotely interests me: Winn.

End of Book 2

Read on for sneak peek of
Leverage: Sunken City Capers Book 3.

Sneak Peek of:

LEVERAGE

SUNKEN CITY CAPERS BOOK 3

BY

JEFFREY A. BALLARD

NEW ROCHESTER
PUSBLISHING

Chapter One

EXPLOSIONS ARE QUICK dirty things, over before you realize they're even happening.

I'm mid-air about to hit the frigid, churning water of the English Bay below me when I realize it was an explosion that threw me off the upper-deck of the sight-seeing boat Puo and I were on.

All I can think is: *it's December. In Vancouver.*

I hit the water and all I know is pain. Icy coldness stabs me, scorches my upper-right back.

Burning flecks of saltwater bite my throat. I can't stop gasping.

Saltwater attacks and stings my eyes as I flail around.

My soaked, heavy winter clothes pull me down. My heart thuds in my chest.

Puo! Where's Puo? I look around for his honey-colored down jacket on the waves. I can't see him. The sightseeing boat behind me is already half-way under, flames ripple out from the top. Thick, black smoke surges into the overcast afternoon sky.

A multitude of partially-submerged buildings rise up out of the English Bay around me, like a petrified forest of steel and concrete. I force my shaking limbs to start swimming toward the nearest one, fifty or so feet away.

I'm shivering uncontrollably. My fingertips ache. I don't know how long I have before hypothermia sets in. My feet already feel like leaden boots, like dead weight I'm forced to carry around with me.

Puo and I were on a scouting trip on the *Underwater Vancouver City Tour*. We were the only two goobs stupid enough to be standing outside on the upper deck in the near-freezing cold. Everyone else on the tour, all eighteen other souls, were down below in the heated underwater observation deck watching the ghostly visage of old Vancouver glide by below them.

Mostly families. *Now they're probably all dead.*

The sheer, steel wall of the nearest building rises up to tower over me. Several of the windows are thankfully broken at the sea surface level--I can get into the building and climb up to get out of the water

I glance back looking for Puo, the boat is three-quarters of the way under.

I finally gather enough breath, "Puo!" I have to pace myself before managing another, "Puo!"

He grunts somewhere to my left. It's not a healthy sound.

I work up to being able to shout, "Make for--" I have to catch my breath. "--building. Through the broken window!"

He weakly grunts back.

I can't feel my hands anymore. But my arms and legs continue to obey the will to survive and drunkenly paddle me through the nearest broken window. I barely register that I should be careful of broken glass, but it's all I can do to get through the window.

It's an office of some kind, with an open door. The desk and chairs are pushed up against the far wall. White ceiling tiles are missing. A fluorescent light box hangs down by its wires.

I'm able to stand, but the water comes up to my chest. I can't stop shaking. My back burns, stings to the point of tears in my eyes.

I turn around and see the honey-colored coat of Puo making its way toward me. He's pushing a piece of flaming wreckage in front of him. *Thank God!* At least one of us has their wits about them.

"Puo!" I call out, "through here!" I wave my hand out of the window and grimace at the pain it creates.

Puo's black Samoan eyes lock onto me through the waves. His face is grim.

Something's wrong. I can see it in his eyes. More wrong than just being blown up and thrown into near freezing water.

I wade over to the office door and pull it open. My right leg doesn't feel quite right, but it's hard to tell through the growing numbness. There's got to be stairs here somewhere that lead up and out of this water. It's dark in the wide office space populated by cubicles. I can only make out the details of the cubicle walls near where other office doors are open.

Hallways. The stairs have got to be near the end of the hallways.

"Isa," Puo says weakly from behind me in the office.

I turn around and rush in to help him.

Puo's pulling himself through the window. Puo's a three hundred pound, six-foot Samoan man, pulling himself safely through the window is way more of an issue than me at a lithe five foot nine inches.

I pass by the piece of flaming wreckage floating in the middle of the room, its heat alluring me to stop and try to warm up, but I press on.

I get to Puo and help him through, making sure there's no broken glass. As he stands up, I say, "C'mon, we need to get upstairs and start a fire."

Puo's unsteady on his feet, but slowly moving forward. "Go ahead," he says. "I'll catch up."

"What?" *What a dumbass thing to say.* "No, let's go together." I push the flaming wreckage toward the door. *Fire-- heat and light, what a wonderful invention.*

Puo gulps. His face is snow-white, which is quite a trick for his complexion. "Just go, Isa."

"What--?" I stop near the door.

"GO!" Puo manages to roar.

"What the fuck is going on, Puo!" I shout back. "We're wasting time!"

"There's nothing you can do. Just go."

"Puo! I swear to God--!"

Puo stares at me; his mouth is open, hot white breaths escape out into the room. "Heart attack," he says softly.

Oh, no.

"I'm having-- I'm having a heart attack."

"Okay," I say way more calmly than I feel. I wade back over to him and slide his heavy, sopping arm over my shoulder, supporting him the best I can. Cold water dumps down my neck stinging my back; I resist the urge to scream. "Let's go."

Our teeth chatter in concert together, and we exit out of the office. I push the flaming wreckage in front us.

"I never could get you to listen to reason," Puo says between shudders.

"If it's reason to leave you behind," I say through chattering teeth, "then why don't you let go?"

"I think I would, if I could feel my arms."

I laugh at the absurdness of it, the absurdness of our situation. *What the hell happened?* It's not a question my brain lets me dwell on as we both continue to shake.

At the end of the hallway is salvation: stairs. We push into the stairwell and climb our soaking bodies out of the water, shedding our wet, heavy outerwear. I think the air is colder than the water, but convection is a worse heat transfer method than conduction.

I lay Puo down on the closest stairwell landing and place the flaming wreckage near him before scrambling up the stairs like a numb, drunken, injured person to find a better area for us to set up a fire near a window to signal the first responders.

"Aspirin," Puo calls out after me.

I stop and stick my head out over the railing. "What?"

"Aspirin," Puo says, "I need aspirin." He has his pocket tablet out and unfolded, searching the internet.

"Your tablet works!" I shout in surprise. "Call for help!"

"So does yours," he says weakly. "And, I am."

"How does your tablet work?" I can't stop myself from asking, while shivering uncontrollably.

"Go," Puo says, his face gaunt. "Just go, I'll explain later."

This time, I decide to listen.

The adventure continues in
Leverage: Sunken City Capers Book 3!

Read the story of how Isa and the gang stole Ham's squeegee in *The Skim Job: A Sunken City Capers Short Story*. Exclusive only to newsletter receiptents—read how to sign up on the next page.

Ground Sensors. Chemically-laced air. Molecular-realigning windows.

How hard can hitting a smart house be?

Forced into the company of Ham, the friendly neighborhood Cleaner, Isa must balance her desire to complete the job and her desire to kick the obnoxious ass in the throat. But when things go from bad to worse, both are soon only hoping for escape.

Author's Note

Word-of-mouth and reviews are vital for any author to succeed. If you enjoyed reading this story, please consider leaving a review wherever you purchased it. Taking a moment to leave a few lines sharing your thoughts would be helpful for other readers and very much appreciated. Thank you for reading!

Jeffrey A. Ballard is hard at work a brand new series. If you want to be the first to know when the new series is going to become available (and receive free Sunken City content available to newsletter subscribers prior to the public, and occasional other goodies) you can sign up for his mailing list at: http://www.jaballard.com. Your email address will never be shared and you can unsubscribe at any time.

About the Author

Jeffrey A. Ballard writes and lives in the Texas Hill Country just outside of Austin. From a small child he has always been fascinated with the ocean, leading him to earn a B.S. in Ocean Engineering from FAU and a M.S. in Acoustics from Penn State.

His overactive imagination followed him into academia, where he is currently a researcher at the University of Texas. Eventually, he circled back to a boyhood ambition of writing down all his dreams/daydreams/fantasies, an active playground for that overactive imagination. He writes daily now and has found a wonderful second life for his college textbooks.

Learn more about Jeffrey at jaballard.com.